Butterflies in the System

D1528096

jane powell

Butterflies in the System
Copyright © 2020 by Jane Powell

Tellwell Talent
www.tellwell.ca

ISBN
978-0-2288-4017-6 (Paperback)
978-0-2288-4018-3 (eBook)

Table of Contents

Support for Butterflies in the System

"Great read! The first chapter alone brought me back 30 years. It's fiction, but it was still very close to home for me. I recommend this book to anyone who even spent 48 hours in the system." *–Lyne Meilleur, Alumna 1989-92, Shawbridge Youth Centres (Prévost Campus) and Youth Horizons in Montreal, QC*

"I loved *Butterflies in the System* for its raw and honest look at life in the DYP system as seen through the eyes of someone living it. As a Childcare worker and Special Care Counselor, I found the narrative accurately heartbreaking and inspirational. Sam's journey is poignant, funny, riveting and brutally honest. The story reflects what <u>still</u> does and doesn't work in our flawed social service network. A compelling read!" *–Janet Gallagher, Special Care Counsellor and Child Care Worker in Montreal, QC*

"As a retired Child Care worker, I was pleased to be included in Jane's proof-reading group. Jane's depiction(s) of life in the system as an 'end user' was enlightening and at times frightening—a really good read." *–Ross S. Hillenbrand, Front line worker for 32 years Summer Hill*

Group Homes, Youth Horizons, Batshaw Youth and Family Services in Montreal, QC

"*Butterflies in the System* is a gripping novel of trials and tribulations for teenagers. I recommend it also to all who have had a tough childhood, to parents whose kids are having it tough, and especially those who need to understand tough kids." *–Penny Powell, parent and teacher in Laval, QC*

"An excellent follow up to *Sky-bound Misfit*, *Butterflies in the System* showcases Sam's struggles when she finds herself within the youth protection system. I found the story fascinating and had a hard time putting it down. The characters were vividly real in the sense that they were easy to connect with and relate to when reaching into the past and recalling some of the "coming of age" experiences of our own younger years. I loved the connecting pieces that related to *Sky-bound Misfit*. Vincent's appearance, along with Frankie's, was stellar ... a great way to tie both novels together, which left me wanting to read *Sky-bound Misfit* all over again." *–Alicia Grills, mother of teenagers in Golden, BC*

Butterflies in the System can be read alone or as a sequel to *Sky-bound Misfit*. The lead character in this book, Sam, was featured in *Sky-bound Misfit* as Frankie's best friend during their early teen years.

This novel is a work of fiction. Although inspired by the author's life experience and interviews with youth protection alumni and workers, the story told within this book is a product of the author's imagination. Characters, places, and events are either fictitious or used fictitiously. Any resemblance of characters to actual people is a coincidence.

Trigger warning

This book contains episodes of physical and emotional violence, sexual violence, and substance use that may be disturbing or upsetting to some.

For all youth gone wild, past and present

CHAPTER ONE

The Morning After

July 31ˢᵗ

System rats. That's what they call us. Lost causes, fuckups, the *unwanted*. And they wonder why we run.

I took a long drag off my smoke and blew rings towards the sky. Swallows played in the morning mist that hovered over the river. The quiet was nice. I emptied the last few drops of my beer into the weeds and got up from the log I was sitting on. The place was littered with bottles and crap from the night before. I'd woken up on the beach by the river, under the train bridge. What a night.

Running my fingers through my hair, I shook my head to get the remaining sand out. The shaking made my face hurt. I stopped and held my head in my hands. I'd managed to get myself into two fights this time. Well, more like two chicks managed to get themselves into fights with me. I sure as hell wasn't looking to fight. Some crazy jealous bitch at the party knocked me flat on my ass, then I awoke this morning to Frankie shaking me, screaming like a disappointed banshee.

I touched my swollen eye and flinched. Time to ditch this place.

As I began to walk, I remembered my right shoe was still missing. I found it next to the fire pit, partly melted. My toes didn't quite fit in. I wore the shoe like a slipper, with my heel hanging over the back. It wasn't comfortable, but it worked. I put my earphones on and pressed play on my Walkman. Madonna's *Live to Tell* unwound, up along the wires into my mind, like a reflection with a secret.

My third day on the run. Freedom felt good, but mornings were damn lonely.

With no clear idea where to go from there, I stepped onto the tracks and headed south, Montreal-bound. The trains were real rattlers, and they'd be on Sunday schedule—if one somehow surprised me, I would sure be surprised.

My thoughts whirled around my fight with Frankie. What was her problem anyway? She'd turned into one of those annoying girls that had a perfect life but didn't realize it. I mean, seriously? She has one rough spot and her happiness implodes like a dying star with a burnt-out core. The definition of spoiled brat, plain and simple.

Yet, something inside me had crumbled as she'd yelled at me. Deep down, I knew the shit between me and Frankie was more about my crap than hers. But what to do? I didn't even know what to feel about it. "*Deep-down-Sam*" was a big ball of twisted up junk—like yarn the cat got into, all knotted and screwed up and unable to escape the fate prescribed by someone else's game.

Alone on the tracks in the boondocks, I held my emotions in check. Nope, not going to cry over someone else's bullshit. Fuck 'em. I am a survivor. I would survive this, show 'em all, and rub their prissy ass noses in it. I am fuckin' *strong*!

With my music turned up high, I stretched my arms to the sky and howled like a wolf signalling a successful hunt. I am the hunter, not the hunted. I laughed aloud, then shouted, "Fuck you, Frankie! Mom! Dad! It's my ball of messed up yarn, so screw off! Assholes!"

Startled, the doves on the power lines took flight. At least the boondocks are good for something—I could yell my guts out and only the birds took issue.

I searched my blouse pocket for the cigarette I'd bummed off some guy the night before. I'd bummed a few and this would be my last. Being broke sucked. Gripping the smoke between my lips, I felt my other pocket for my lighter, then realized I'd left it at the bridge. I stopped, cursed myself, and turned to go back for it.

That's when the train's horn hammered me for the first time.

Looking up, I saw the approaching train in disbelief and momentarily froze. The sound of its horn vibrated through me for the second time. I tried to jump right, off the tracks, but tripped on a rail nail, and then hit my head hard as I landed.

Dazed, I attempted to roll away from the track, but my body wouldn't respond. Adrenaline hit me hard. My mind became alert, but the rest of me was terrified. It was like trying to push myself through waist-deep mud. Everything but the train moved in slow motion. Its screeching brakes were deafening, the loudest nails-on-chalkboard ever. It occurred to me that this was it. This would be my ending. On the tracks, alone, after I'd told my whole world to fuck off.

People say that your life flashes in front of you when you are about to die. All that flashed within my head was complete and utter fear, no thoughts, just active unrelenting "get me out of here!" FEAR. I was about to be cut in half, and my body was stuck in 'park'.

The scream trapped deep inside my gut surfaced, shortly before my failed defence system shut me down completely and I passed out.

9 .

I opened my eyes to strange faces, floating above me in a universe of multi-lingual concern and surprise. My lower body was under the front of the train and its wheels almost touched me. Never before had I considered myself a lucky person, but I began to re-evaluate. *Holy shit, I'm alive! I think.* Or was this some weird kind of heaven? I studied the faces above me.

An old guy in uniform with a handlebar moustache looked down at me intently. The moustache tugged at my memory.

"Oh, Mon dieu! Fille chanceuse, qu'est-ce que tu fais là?! You are one lucky girl. What de 'ell were you tinking?"

Oh, yeah, the French conductor guy. The one that Frankie likes. What a relief! Not in heaven. I stared at him wide-eyed, amazed that I still lived.

A rumble of laughter gurgled up within me, slowly increasing in volume until it turned into a hysterical cackle. This wasn't the reaction people expected, and I couldn't explain it myself. Just happy to be alive, I guess? Concerned, the train conductor asked me questions, but I couldn't hear him through my hysteria, so he gave up and waited for the first aid crew.

The first responders concurred that I had likely sustained a head injury. They loaded me into the ambulance, and we headed for the hospital. Having trouble stringing words together to answer questions, no one could figure out what my native language was. This resulted in a jumble of French and English, often one sentence in the former followed by the exact same in the latter. Awfully amused, my laughter persisted, contributing I'm sure to the diagnosis of concussion.

I tried to tell them I was just thrilled to be living, but it came out: "*J'suis un loup!* A lucky wolf!" I howled laughing, "Happy to be *en vie! Oui, oui, joix de vivre!*" Maybe they had reason to worry.

A ridiculous thought occurred to me: perhaps my mother's wish had come true, and I'd finally got some sense knocked into me. I howled again as we sped away towards the hospital.

CHAPTER TWO

*J*udgement Day

Early August

(after 4 days in hospital,
due to concussion and a
suspected psychotic break)

The courtroom wasn't much different from any other dated room where the rule of law is intended to prevail. Everything you could touch without too much bending or stretching was made of wood, everything below, linoleum, and everything above, the colour of cream pie.

I sat on the long wooden pew at the back of the room, plugged into my Walkman, flanked by my parents' lawyer, social worker, and mother. We'd been here for over an hour, waiting our turn to be heard. Waiting *our* turn to be *heard*. That's the way the lawyer put it. I would describe it more like waiting *my* turn to be sentenced to silence. There was no 'our' in it, and 'being heard' I'd come to understand as an obvious triviality in the youth justice system. Personally, I'd never been permitted to speak in a courtroom. The lawyer did the talking, I did the listening, and my mother did the weeping. That was the process. That's the way it *always* went.

Pat Benatar's *Heartbreaker* thumped in my ears as I fiddled with the hole in my webbed tights, thinking. A few months ago, I became a ward of the court. I lived in a medium security group home not far from Montreal's *Centre Ville*. Not because I came from a typically defined broken family. Just because ... well ... just because. Maybe it was all *me*. I was the faulty part, I suppose. There had to be some reason for my brokenness, but I hadn't yet figured out what it was. What I did know was that I was glad I wouldn't be returning home. But that doesn't necessarily mean I was looking forward to going back to the group home. If I had a fairy godmother, I would've wished for complete independence.

The judge finally motioned for us to proceed to the front of the courtroom. On cue, my mother began to sniffle. It was strange to see her cry. Her normal stance towards me was one of anger and disappointment.

When I was born, my parents decided that I would be their only child. Rather than divide their attention between two or three children, they would put all their energy into creating one star child. Lucky me.

My mom's dreams for her only child to become successful had been shattered, and she would never get over it. Dad wasn't much different, but instead of blaming me for my failure at perfection, he blamed The Montreal School Board. He'd spent his childhood in a boarding school in England, where he'd been moulded into the proudest and most intelligent form of human being. My dad couldn't accept that his daughter, the fruit of his sublime British loins, could be cast in any other way. I was not *his* failure, but rather the school system's.

As a kid, I *had* been a star child. I was a real smarty, with top grades, falling in line with all my parent's expectations. I did everything with the intention of making them happy. As long as they were happy with me, I got everything I wanted. I played the flute like an angel and my parents like a fiddle. In their eyes, I could do no wrong, as long as I stayed *perfect.*

I tried excruciatingly hard to stay perfect. But perfection is a fragile standard that tends not to allow for limits, and something in me broke at the age of fourteen. I hit my limit and their world fell to pieces. The first-class bubble that had been *me* popped like a soap bubble does when it touches something hard and real. And now the system had been granted the responsibility of putting me back together again. Here's what my parents failed to realize: a reality once contained within a bubble cannot be reassembled into its original form. Like a popped soap bubble, I will never reform back into the rainbow-tinted spherical shape that my parents ordered up.

Yup, I was changing alright. But not as Mom and Dad requested. So, here I stood, in queue with society's broken youth, waiting for judgment.

I pulled my earphones down around my neck, followed my parents' lawyer to the front of the courtroom, and *the process* began.

Mother and Ms. Cohen (my social worker) sit down in the pew behind us.

Judge motions for the lawyer to approach the bench, and she does so.

Parents' Lawyer presents Judge with a folder, which presumably contains a list of my failures, and returns to stand beside me, and we stand there, stiffly, watching as Judge silently reads through the list.

Judge sighs and looks up at me. She takes her glasses off and stares at me. Her hair is short and dyed blond, her face bony and wrinkled, and her eyes tense and tired.

Judge smiles (or is it a frown?) and says, "Well, then. Sam, is it?" She checks my file and misses my nod. "I have here that you were about to be discharged into your parents care, after being in youth protection because of repetitive running away from home, an—albeit forgiven—theft charge, and a concern that you were a danger to yourself. Is this correct?" Judge glances down at my file, missing my nod again. She continues, "Yes. Yes. That is what your file says. It also says that you ran away shortly before your discharge date. Is there an explanation for this?" This time Judge looks at Parents' Lawyer.[1]

Parent's Lawyer responds, "There is no explanation, your Honour. We are recommending that Sam remain in the custody of the youth justice system, as she has proven to be a continuing threat to herself and others."

Judge sighs again. "Please go on."

Parents' Lawyer continues, "Sam was found drunk, face bruised, and stumbling along the train tracks in Pierrefonds. The train was forced to stop because she would not remove herself from the tracks. Frankly, she is lucky to be alive. The police delivered her to the hospital, where she tested positive for marijuana use and was treated for alcohol poisoning. Furthermore, as you can see," the lawyer looks me up and down, "she also has an eating disorder. For these reasons, we think she needs more supervision than her mother can provide and should therefor remain in youth protection until she has proven she is not a risk to herself or others."

Judge glances back down at the papers on her desk, then studies me through her strained over-worked eyes. "What a shame. Your whole life ahead of you and you start it like this. I do hope you learn something from this and straighten up. I don't want you back in here, do you understand? You're from a cultured family. You look like a bright kid. Now, smarten up! Youth protection it is. Ms. Cohen and, uh ..." She motions to my social worker and lawyer, "both of you, see me in my office to discuss sentencing."

Judge dismisses us all with an impatient wave of her hand.

Yeah ... the gist of it: apathetic, predetermined, and no room for *me*.

❦

I arrived back at Charles A. Group Home shortly before suppertime. My room was not as I'd left it. In fact, I'd never seen it so clean. I briefly wondered whether they'd ditched all my stuff, as I couldn't see any evidence of it. My breath caught at the thought. I quickly opened my closet door and breathed a long sigh of relief when I saw my clothes within it. If the staff had ditched my clothes, I would've been forced to depend on my mother to replace them. She would have surely turned me into the pretty n' pink prep she'd always wanted. I thanked the almighty fashion god for sparing me from that humiliation.

Instantly, a more concerning thought hit me. When I'd split, I had forgotten to bring my journals with me.

There were three of them and the options for hiding places in my room had not been good—under my mattress or jammed behind my chest-of-drawers. I'd remembered the journals shortly after taking off, and the choice was either to keep running or to turn myself in only an hour after my great escape. I'd chosen to risk the discovery of my journals.

Pulling my chest-of-drawers out from the wall, I searched behind it. Gone. I wasn't surprised. Any moron could figure out where secrets were hidden in these bare rooms. I squeezed my eyes shut, devastated. Someone was now in possession of my most private thoughts. I hoped it was a childcare worker. If another kid stole them, I was bound to be bullied or blackmailed ... most likely both.

I muttered "Fuck" as loud as I could without being heard, then fell backwards onto my bed and stared at the ceiling. The whole room had been painted eggshell white and the ceiling was no exception. Even the furniture was white. The bedrooms in this place lacked creativity like Madonna lacked virginity. There must've been some purpose to the sterile blandness, I thought. Were they trying to bore us into submission? Yup, probably it.

I lay on my bed contemplating the concept of boredom, worrying about my journals, wondering what tomorrow would bring.

Gabe bounded in through my open door, interrupting my thoughts, and jumped onto my bed. He stood over me, bouncing up and down, laughing and chanting, "The cat came back, the very next day, the cat came back, she just couldn't stay away away away AWAY! HA! SAM! I knew you'd be back! I knew it!! Sucker!!" He collapsed on the bed beside me, rolled over and wrapped his arms around me. He squeezed as if trying to do me in. "I missed your skinny Asian ass, girl!"

Gabe was referring to the quarter of me that is Taiwanese. I'm much more British than Asian, but my Asian roots show through my almond shaped eyes and straight black hair. Being *Taiwanese* was way more interesting than were my stale British roots. So, to my friends, I was Asian.

I pushed him off, "Gabe! Breathe! Gimme some space, dude! I was away, like, a whole three days ... I didn't come back the very next day. Dickweed." Sometimes Gabe behaved like a hyperactive three-year-old. But it did feel nice to be missed.

Gabe's huge smile revealed how much he'd missed me. He was my closest friend in the system, as I was his. I regretted not taking him with me on my AWOL[2] adventure. Things may have turned out differently if Gabe had been with me. Maybe I wouldn't have got beaten up by some dude's jealous girlfriend. Maybe I wouldn't have fucked up my friendship with Frankie. Maybe I wouldn't have flirted with death on the train tracks.

My memories of that second night on the run were blurry. I'd met up with Frankie, friend from my previous life (you know, the life where I was 'the good girl'), and we'd gone to a party at the train bridge near Roxboro. I spent most of that night getting drunk and high with some hot rocker guy, until his girlfriend showed up and lost her shit on me.

Next thing I remember was waking up on the river's edge in the morning, with Frankie freaking out at me. She said she'd thought I was dead. Man, what a drama queen. Then I freaked out. We fought. She left. I drank some more. Then there was the train incident ...

And here I was. Back in the fuckin' system after only three days on the run. I really should've brought Gabe with me.

We were both lying on the bed now, staring into the whitewashed abyss above us. Gabe turned his head towards me and observed me thoughtfully.

"Hey man, what *was* that anyway? You were supposed to get out next week. Why'd you run? You were almost free! Your parents serial killers or something?" He chortled, jokingly.

I smiled at the thought of my parents deviating so radically from the social norm. Mom and Dad, with blood up to their elbows and crazed smiles, plotting lustily over what they could do to their poor rebellious victim next. Ha! My parents, the epitome of human perfection, gone mad—what a sight that would be! The only thing they'd ever plotted to kill was my happiness.

I replied to Gabe, "Yup, something like that." My parents were serial killers of happiness.

Gabe laughed. Apparently, he thought I was joking. He replied, "So, what next then? You staying a while?"

"Seems so." I paused and sighed, not really knowing what to say. I didn't want to be in the system, but home was worse. Soon I'd be sixteen, which meant I could legally get a job and possibly live on my own. My present goal was just to survive the next few months.

9

"So, welcome back!" Dave smiled at me as he leaned back in his creaky wooden office chair.

I caught an inkling of sarcasm in Dave's tone, likely directed more at the situation than at me. For a childcare worker, Dave was OK. I couldn't help but smile back at him, slightly sheepishly.

"Yup, in the flesh. What's my punishment?" The others had just sat down for supper and I hadn't eaten since breakfast. My issues with food came and went. I knew we had to do this, but I hoped Dave would hurry up and get it over with.

Dave relaxed even further into his chair and put his hands behind his head, weaving his fingers together. His curly salt n' pepper hair sprung up wildly over his bald spot as he did this. Dave was Dave. And he had all the time in the world.

"Sam, Sam, Sam. What happened? You were scheduled for discharge. Worried that you'll miss us or something?"

I nodded. Advice from a growling stomach: best to keep conversation to a minimum.

"Well then. You'll need to fill out these intake forms. Your social worker will be here in the morning ... save your explanations for her." Dave paused, observing me thoughtfully. "You know ... I think the time added to your sentence is punishment enough. Unless your social worker has something to add, let's leave it at that. Sound good?"

I nodded again, "um, yeah ... thanks."

Rumour had it that Dave had been a system kid himself, way back in the 60s. He had this way of understanding us that was different from the others. Although I didn't share much, if I *was* going to share stuff, you know, about myself, it'd likely be with him.

I entered the dining room and half the table cheered, mocking me playfully. The others were newbies. Except for Gini, of course, who glared at me, but that was nothing personal. Some chicks were born bitchy, and they didn't discriminate with their targets ... so, as I said, nothing personal. I ignored her glare and sat in the seat Gabe had saved for me.

"Eh man, what the fuck, what'r ya back fer?" Jack asked, genuinely perplexed.

Jack had been group home surfing since he was nine, after people stopped wanting to foster him. He was cool, but he had a ... how to put this? *Emotional? Passionate?* Let's just say, a *feverish* streak that some thought worrying.

"Language." Dave glanced at Jack and continued eating.

Jack mouthed "Oops!" and rolled his eyes. "No effen way I'd AWOL a few days before my discharge. Yer batshit nuts. Barely a scratch to show for it. What, d'ya hide out in *Le Château*?"

Jack always said things exactly how he saw them. No filter. Ever. Strange that folks had stopped wanting to foster him.

Some of the others laughed, unable to contain themselves. Jack had this thing for teasing me about my upper-middle class status—he'd playfully nicknamed me "*The Shopper.*"

I glanced at Gabe for support, but he was too busy admiring Jack's wit. Gabe was enthralled by Jack, and lately it had got damn annoying.

Wil controlled his smile. He said, in his best parent voice, "Now, now children, give Sam some space. She's just come back from an arduous adventure in a *Le Château* changing room. She's absolutely exhausted. The clerk was such a bitch and slow as hell. Sam tried to set her straight, but as you can see, *that* backfired. I mean, look at the poor girl. Black eye with nothing to show for it. Didn't even come away with fake leather!"

The room burst with laughter.

Jen glared at Wil, but even she was having trouble controlling herself.

Gabe glanced at me. His smile faltered. He studied his food intently.

This had to stop. I stood up and addressed the table in a voice that I meant to be calm but ended up sounding more like a cat's hiss.

"Here, here, my mighty tiddly-winks. The next person who mentions my AWOL or asks me why I'm back or who says anything about my effed up release date, is going to have their tongue pulled out and sh ..." Dave shot me a hard look and I softened my threat, "... twisted in knots. Got it?"

Jack cracked up and Wil tried, with obvious intention, not to follow suit. The others cringed, then suddenly became very preoccupied with hydration. Newbie Kim picked up the water jug and disappeared into the kitchen to refill it.

I lost my appetite. I didn't know why I was back. Why had I AWOLed? Home sucked. The system sucked. My head hurt. My eyes hurt. And I hated cold mac n' cheese. I left the table to cry without witnesses.

Jack yelled after me, "Eh, Shopper! Can I have yer Mac n' Cheese?"

CHAPTER THREE

Bad Buzz

Early August

I sat on the fire escape outside my window and lit my second smoke. Technically, we weren't allowed to climb out our windows, let alone smoke out there, but what were they going to do, ground me? Living in this place was already a form of grounding. Our actions were constantly observed, dissected, and controlled. Sounds like a good grounding to me. I couldn't imagine what they could add to it that would make it worse. I suppose my mother's yelling—yup, that would be worse—but they weren't going to send me home.

I lay back against the steps, blew smoke rings, and watched as they grew bigger and bigger until they disappeared up into the city's smog-clogged muggy August air. Jack could actually blow rings through rings, which was pretty cool. I tried again and failed again. I'd been pissed at Jack when I'd left the dinner table, but it wasn't his fault. He was just being himself, good ol' Jack—'same same, but different' should be his motto. I wasn't sure why I'd left the table, why I'd felt all suddenly choked up. Life sucks, I guess. But ... I was really enjoying this smoke, alone, on the fire escape.

My thoughts skipped through the day's events. The most concerning part so far was my missing journals. Even my mother's tirade in the car on our way over wasn't as bad as losing my journals. She never said anything different anyway. Always the same crap about me being the cause of all her and dad's misery. Today, she'd dropped a gift into my lap before starting her journey down the *shit-on-Sam* path. I'd opened it quickly, while her mood was still semi-positive. It was a watch with a pink band and diamond-encrusted frame—the kind I liked before I'd become 'bad girl'. She took my smirk as her cue to speak.

Mom always started out positive and today was no different: "Sam, you know I love you, right?" Barely pausing, she went on, "We're just worried about you." And on, "Why do you want to worry us so much?" And when I didn't answer, "Do you think this is fair to us?" With the pretense of still waiting for me to reply, she kept going, "We have given our lives to you. We worked so hard to ensure you got into the best private school, with the best music teacher in the city. You *were* a musical prodigy! But all you do is mess it up, throw it in our faces, and waste your life away getting drunk and smoking that stuff, marijuana. What is wrong with you, Sam?"

Yup, that was the essence of almost every conversation we've had since I left home a year ago. Like I said, my journals were more of a concern to me.

I butted my cigarette out on the metal stair and let it fall to the ground beneath the winding staircase. I watched it as it bounced off each grated landing, falling between the cracks, to finally make it all the way to the grubby ground far below. I could easily follow it down and disappear into the night, never to be seen again. I considered it briefly, then crawled back through my window and collapsed on my bed. Where would I go? What would I do? My last AWOL turned out to be a lonely mission towards getting caught. That, with a side of vexed mother. It had been far from worth it ... then again, it had served a purpose.

9

"Sam? You in there? Can I ..." Gabe opened the door, poked his head in and smiled. He stepped into my room before waiting for my response.

I took the opportunity to ask him about my journals. If anyone knew anything in this place, it was Gabe. He had a nose for mischief and an ear for gossip.

"Eh, Gabe? I'm missing my journals. You heard anything?" I said casually, as if it was no big deal but I'd like them back at some point.

Although I trusted Gabe, if it got around that I was panicking about my journals, they'd surely be produced in the most embarrassing way thinkable. Besides, there was stuff written in them about Gabe—personal thoughts kind of stuff—and it wouldn't serve our friendship well for him to get too curious. That's the thing about journals— emotional cesspools of personified thoughts, an attempt to make sense out of the crap going on around us. I wrote the words in my journal for *me*, not for anyone else, not even Gabe.

"Oh. My. God. You lost your journals?!" Gabe said this with a look of pure astonishment, like it was the worst thing ever but also more than a little hilarious at the same time. "Jeee-zus ... what are you gonna do? What if whats-her-face has 'em?? Or Dave ... maybe he's read 'em all and has passed them onto your mom ..."

"Gabe! Shut it, OK?! Dave doesn't have them. He would've talked to me about it. And he's not a dick. He wouldn't give 'em to my mom. Shit, man. Can you help me out here?" I sounded exasperated because I was.

"Yeah, yeah, of course, sure thing. What d'ya want me to do though? I mean, I haven't heard anything. Maybe your SW found them?" Gabe was referring to my social worker. He shrugged, came over to my bed, and fell back onto it next to me.

I bit my lip, thinking. I'd be meeting with Ms. Cohen in the morning. Perhaps then I'd have my answer. Gabe and I lay side-by-side, staring mournfully at the sterile ceiling.

He broke the silence, "Think they'd notice if we stuck some glow-in-dark stars up there?"

I glanced at him and then back at the ceiling, "Nope. You have some?"

He nodded and smiled, "You can have half. I'll get 'em." Gabe jumped up and sped out of my room to fetch the stars.

❦

My SW arrived as planned right after breakfast. Ms. Cohen and I sat side by side in the 'office-living-room' that was reserved specifically for meetings with social workers.

Designed to make kids feel 'safe' and 'calm', with a sofa and one of those huge round bamboo futon chairs, this room always had the opposite effect on me. My animal instincts were alert and ready for danger in this falsely at-ease *Hansel and Gretel* situation. If I let my guard down, the evil witch would surely trick me into getting her way and I'd end up in a big boiling cauldron of naughty children and rats' tails.

I sat on the edge of the sofa, quietly waiting for her to tell me where my life was heading. Ms. Cohen looked up from the form she was reading and acknowledged me with her usual 'welcome' smile that relayed a sense of 'you're safe with me, you can tell me everything', but that made me feel even more wary.

"Sam, how are you?" Said Ms. Cohen, tweaking her tone with reassurance.

I nodded, "Um, fine." Best to keep conversation to a minimum with people who were taking notes.

She studied me, with a hint of regret in her eyes, and I braced myself for bad news. She put her hand on my arm, in a comforting gesture (which always signalled something foreboding).

"Sam, the court decided that, given your history of AWOLs and the situation with the train, you should be subjected to stronger consequences."

My breath caught and I stared at her, silently waiting for more.

Ms. Cohen took my hand in hers and continued, "You'll be transferring up to Manny Cottage Youth Detention Centre for a bit."

Manny Cottage? I thought about what I'd been told about the place: faraway fenced-in institution with bars on the windows and kids who eat other kids for breakfast, lunch, and supper. This wasn't happening. I couldn't go there. It was jail for kids and I'd only AWOLed a few times. Got shit-faced drunk and stoned while out, but who doesn't? And, OK, almost killed. But I'd never hurt anyone but myself.

I blurted, "What? Why? No, no, please! Manny Cottage?! Why?"

Ms. Cohen seemed sincerely touched by my emotion, "Oh Sam, I'm so sorry. It won't be for long though. You'll be back here in two months. It's really not a bad place. Everyone who works at Manny Cottage is there to help you. You'll even get one-on-one tutoring, so there'll be an opportunity for you to advance in your school subjects. Concentrate on school and time will fly by, I promise you."

I put my head in my hands, and she stroked my back. I bristled, "Stop. Just ... stop." She withdrew her hand from my back. "When do I go?"

She regarded me thoughtfully for a moment. "Friday. I'll pick you up after breakfast and drive you up myself."

Normally, kids were transported up in a 'jail bus'. I recognized Ms. Cohen's attempt at support and thanked her with a nod.

When I exited the meeting room, Gabe was leaning against the wall in the hallway, waiting for me. I could see from the expression on his face that he'd been eavesdropping.

"Shit ... wow ... What're you gonna do?" Gabe followed me up the stairs, back to my room.

I shrugged, "Go, I guess. What am I supposed to do? Not like I have a say in it."

Gabe shook his head. "Damn, girl. Argh! I hate this place without you! I'm gonna visit you, OK? We still have two days. Let's do something ... like a going away party!"

I stared at Gabe as if he was from a totally different universe, "Seriously? You wanna end up in there with me?"

Gabe thought for a moment ... "No man, we'll all take our outdoor hour together, y' know, and meet up at the canal. It'll be like a *see you later* picnic." Gabe smiled a little too mischievously.

I considered pushing him on his party plans, but then thought, *"Ah, whatever, I'm on my way to hell so might as well dip into the hand basket."*

9

The Lachine Canal was a short walk from Charles A. As our building didn't have much of a yard, we were allowed an hour each day of free time outside the premises. Gabe and I arrived first. We sat down on the grass in the shade of a towering maple, between the bike path and the water. The Montreal humidity index soared, and storm clouds had begun to appear in the distance, floating surreal-like in the otherwise clear-for-a-city blue sky. I took a smoke from my pack and passed one to Gabe.

"Eh, Gabe?" Gabe nodded and I continued, "Have you ever thought of like, totally ditching this place? Y' know, running and setting up somewhere and just, like, living?"

Gabe paused in thought, "Yeah. But I also like free food and a bed without lice." He laughed and shoved me sideways jokingly.

I fell to the side laughing along with him. "'Kay, guess you've got a point."

Gabe was in the system because he had no one. His parents had died in an accident and there were no relatives to take him in. Shortly before the accident, his mom had left his dad too. Gabe said she was gay[3] and just left one day. He'd blamed gays for a bit, which I thought strange. Out of everyone I knew Gabe was the gayest. Anyway, his social worker and the childcare workers became his lifeline, his surrogate parents, his home. He was one of the few kids doing 'well' in the system. The only reason he was in a medium security group home, rather than low security, was because he had developed a special connection with Dave, our star childcare worker.

Nonetheless, Gabe wasn't perfect and always enjoyed a bit of mischief on the side, under the noses of gullible staff that felt immeasurably sorry for him.

Jack turned up next, guitar strung over his shoulder.

"Eh, man! Ready to rock?!" Jack said with an explosion of enthusiasm.

I laughed, "With that thing? I love some guitar Jack, but the only kind of rock you can let rip with that thing are ballads! Maybe some Cheap Trick?"

Jack examined me with mock insult written all over his face. "No way, man! What planet are *you* from, eh? I can totally make this thing howl. Name a song."

I thought for a second, "OK, how about Metallica's *Crash Course in Brain Surgery*?" I grinned menacingly.

"Some metal. No problem, man. But I'll need percussion and vocals. Who's up?" He glanced at me and started to play. His question was more of a *ready, on your mark, go!* type of comment.

Gabe produced a couple of spoons from his pocket and took on the percussion, so I was left with the vocals.

I observed Gabe and his spoons curiously.

"What can I say, I plan ahead. Spoons are super useful." Gabe smiled, held the spoons together in one hand, and began drumming them on his knee.

Funny the things you learn about your friends along the way. He wasn't half bad at playing the spoons.

I put on my best Madonna voice and gave it a twist—like, shove a Madonna in a car crusher and come out sounding like young James Hetfield. Jen and Wil joined us in time for the chorus. We pelted out *Crash Course in Brain Surgery* in between fits of laughter.

The 'perfect' family that had been picnicking close by got up and left, looking fretful and startled. It never ceased to amaze me how easy it was to scare such well-established people who had it all.

"OK, so now that the Cosby family's left, anyone bring some pot?" Jack winked at me and I couldn't help but blush a little. He could be an ass, but his charming attitude made something inside me melt and I think he knew it.

I dropped my gaze and fiddled with my shoelace.

"Fret no more, Jack-o baby, I come bearing gifts." Wil's smile was secretive, in a guess-what-I-have-under-my-trench-coat kind of way.

Jack raised an eyebrow, "Is that an enormous dube in your pocket or are you just happy to see me?"

Wil produced the dube and motioned for my Zippo. I threw it over, he lit the joint, and took a long drag. I had a flash of my dad tasting the wine at a fine restaurant—slosh, whiff, sip, consider, approve. Wil finally exhaled his approval and passed the joint to me. After I'd also approved, I kept it going around the circle.

"Eh, man ... or, uh, chick or *chic* ..." Gabe drew the word *chic* out with an extra French twist, as if he were referring to a *chic femme fatal.* "We're gonna miss you, you *chee-eec chick*." He winked and blew me a kiss.

"Fuck off, Gabe. I'm no chick. I'm, like, child-bearing age, man—that's like at least a full-grown chicken."

Jack added, sounding way too serious, "If you were a chicken, you'd like be able to fly outa here, eh ... if chickens could fly and all."

I glanced at Jack and wondered about his brain cells. "Eh, Jack?"

He looked at me, "Yeah, Sam?"

"How old were you when you started smoking this stuff?"

There was a brief splutter of laughter between everyone who wasn't Jack. My poke flew right on over Jack's head.

"Dunno. With my mum, I guess ... got into her stash when I was eight. Boy was she ever pissed, eh!" Jack laughed as he remembered. "She like, locked me in my room for a week! Just, y' know, passing me food now and then ... What a psycho. Wasn't like I got into her smack or nothin'! Anyways, smack's fucked up. Never gonna do that shit. That's what got'er in the end. Yup, stickin' to nothin' more 'en pot n' acid—none of that wacko shit for me, eh."

I hadn't known all this about Jack. We all fell silent, not knowing where to take the conversation next.

Jen saved the buzz with, "So you were like born into Cheech. Cool. Or Chong more your thing?"

Jack laughed, "Yup, you got it girl. Cheech for ever more! Or Chong ... whatever. Eh man, pass it here." He motioned for the joint and Jen passed it over.

As Jack was inhaling his freedom from reality, an unwanted guest turned up.

Gini stood over us, glaring at our gathering with disapproval, as was her norm.

"Well, well, look at what I've found. The hot-boxing Adams family. Does Dave know you're here? Or did you not invite him either? Well, don't worry your little hearts out because I've come anyway. And, guess what? I even have a going away present for our pint-sized slanty-eyed bitch over here."

I stared at her, more than slightly worried, considering what she might have on me, but was too stoned to come up with anything.

Wil interrupted my worried silence, "Gini man, uh, I mean chicken, uh, or maybe turkey? ... Is a turkey just like, a humongous chicken? Whoa ... Revelation."

Everyone giggled and then caught themselves and stopped.

Wil continued, "Chill out ... Take a toke. Ganjaman time ... Cloud 9 is callin' ya, man ... chill big chicken, chill."

Gini glared at Wil. "Fuck that. Whatever. *Your* bitch over there ..." She pointed at me, "is a two-faced little twat. You do know that, eh?"

"She's not *my* bitch, man. You miss the class on the hippie revolution or somethin'? She's *her own* bitch." Wil smiled, proud of his wit.

Jack fell backwards, laughing on the grass. "Ho! Ya' burnt, bitch!"

Gini wasn't shaken in the least. She stood, feet firmly planted in place. The smile that grew across her face was menacing, knowing.

Pot-buzzes were two-sided and now the anxiety side began to take hold.

I scrutinized Gini. "What the hell, Gini? You have something to say? Say it! You're fuckin' up our buzz."

That's when the shit really came pouring down.

Gini pulled my journal out of her bag. Pieces of paper stuck out from various pages. She'd bookmarked parts. I thought, *'Oh, fuck. Here we go.'* I desperately wished myself away, but remained in my place, hopelessly stoned, bug-eyed, and about to be squished.

Looming over us, Gini stood erect and confidently in jerk-mode. Her expression was that of a cat that's finally cornered the bug it's been after for ages. She opened my journal to her first bookmarked page and shot me a smug grin before launching my secrets to the world.

Stunned, I sat there fear-ridden, like the tiny insect she thought I was. There was nothing I could do. Gini was a scrapper. She was likely betting that I'd lunge for the journal. That's what she wanted, to put me on my back, to have an excuse to pummel me in front of my friends. But it was either that or let her reveal my deepest thoughts to everyone.

I jumped up and ran at Gini with my hands out in front. My plan was to grab my journal and keep running.

But Gini held on tight, as the smirk grew across her face, and within a split-second I was on my front with her on top of me. She straddled my back, legs on either side, as I lay completely helpless, with my arms flayed out on the grass as if trying to swim myself free.

Pleading with Gini would be futile, so I decided on threats instead. "Get the fuck off me Gini or I'll ..." I couldn't think of anything I had on her, of a good threat.

Gini was a bitch, but she generally didn't break the rules much—well, besides beating on people, but that seemed to be a tolerated right-of-passage in group homes. Every home had an 'alpha' and I suppose she was ours.

Gabe was now standing beside us, "What the fuck, Gini! Get off her!"

Ignoring Gabe, Gini placed the journal on my back, opened it to the first book-marked page, and began to read.

"Dear diary," Gini feigned my voice. I never started like that, but the next part was all me.

"Jesus fuck, if Gabe had any more energy he'd be glowing, like one of those wind-up toys that lights up and zooms around when you release it. He can be such a fuckin' kid.

Especially when he's going on and on about Jack. He's totally got a thing for him. Jack this, Jack that, "Jack's so great, no he's an ass, no he's god-sent, he's such a jerk, he's the best, why is he such a jerk??!" Boo-the-fuck-hoo! What a gaylord. He should follow his mom's footsteps and just come out of the fuckin' closet already."

The group fell silent.

I closed my eyes and chewed on my lip.

Gabe was still for a moment. Then he turned to leave without saying a word.

But Gini wasn't finished. "So, is it true Gabe? You gotta a crush on Jacky-o?" She laughed and no one joined in.

Gabe kept walking.

Jack ran after him and pushed him hard from behind. Gabe fell forwards to the ground but didn't look back. He got up again and resumed walking away.

"Knew there was somethin' fucked up about you! Stay away from me you fuckin' fag!"

Jen stood up and said to no one in particular, "Wow. Bad buzz. You're fucked up, Gini. What was that for?"

The others began to get up off the grass.

Gini rose to the occasion. She jumped up off me, shoved Jen, and Jen tripped backwards. Dripping venom, Gini glared at Jen, "Say that again ya' little cunt."

Wil took Jen's hand and pulled her away from the brewing fight. Jen resisted and turned towards me, "C'mon Sam. Let's go."

"Yeah, *Shopper*. Off you go, little rich girl." Gini paused for effect, "Oh ... don't forget this!" She threw my journal at me, then walked off in the other direction, proud of her ... something or other.

I held onto the book, glad that she hadn't kept reading. Then I got up and followed the group, just far enough behind that I didn't have to interact.

Gabe hid in his room over the next couple of days, only surfacing for meals.

I knocked on his bedroom door on Friday morning before I left.

"Eh ... uh ... Gabe?"

No answer.

I gave it one more shot, "Gabe? Eh man, Ms. Cohen's here. I gotta go."

Silence.

I turned the doorknob and something in me made me pause. I wasn't strong enough for this kind of shit. What would I say? What would he say? I released the doorknob and sighed.

The door stood in front of me like a looming question mark.

I put my hand against it. "See 'ya, Gabe."

CHAPTER FOUR

A Home for Neglected Children

August

Just as my journal was a poor reflection of the way I felt about Gabe, my sentencing to Manny Cottage was a flawed depiction of who I was as a person. If public opinion were to rename Manny Cottage, it would be called *The Home for Neglected Children Who Will Amount to Nada*, because that is the heavy label that teens in Manny Cottage bear. Like jail time, a sentence at Manny Cottage is a branding difficult to escape.

,

I stood naked in the shower block. Betty, a tall muscular woman with pale pink skin and a Lady Di haircut, watched as I washed my hair with a mysterious shampoo that smelled like bleach. When done, she handed me another.

I looked at her, puzzled.

Betty clarified, "This one's for lice."

When satisfied that I was thoroughly sanitized, Betty handed me a towel, watched as I dried myself, then set herself to combing my hair.

She investigated the comb for evidence of infestation while I stood shivering wrapped in my towel. After a few minutes, she nodded decisively. I had passed her louse-free test.

Betty retrieved her clipboard from a nearby chair and checked some boxes. I was a lab rat awaiting an unpredictable fate.

Motioning to a pile of clothes on another chair, she told me to get dressed. "Put those on. They're Bethel unit clothes. Kids all wear the same thing here, so don't worry, you're not special."

I stared at the pile of beige clothes. "Where are *my* clothes? I mean, I'm going to get them back, eh?" The jeans I'd been wearing were the ones signed by Bono. They were irreplaceable.

"Yes. All your stuff will be returned when you leave. Now put 'em on, don't have all day here." Betty switched her attention back to her clipboard and the message was clear: conversation terminated.

When I was beige from head to toe, Betty led me down a hall to a very clean room with a bed, desk and chair. A notepad and pen lay on the desk, along with some pamphlets and a couple of books.

"This'll be your room for the duration of the 3-day induction program[4]."

I stared at her blankly and thought, '*The what?*'

Betty picked up on my confusion. "Oh my, they didn't fill you in, did they? Jeez, they never do." And continued without waiting for a reply, "Every kid that arrives here goes through a 3-day induction program. During this time, you will stay in this room for three days. Your meals will be brought to you. The only time you will leave this room is for washroom visits. You will not be permitted to interact with the other kids in the unit. Upon the completion of the induction program, you will be assigned another room and will be introduced into the general population in Bethel unit. Got it?"

I nodded.

"My office is right here." Betty motioned to the closed door behind her. "When you need to visit the washroom, let me know by knocking on your door and I'll accompany you. I will be supervising you throughout the induction program. Your bedroom door will be locked at all times." Betty nodded as if to say, '*OK, you got it.*'

I looked at her, unsure of how to react.

Abruptly, Betty turned and headed for her office, closing my door behind her. There was a loud *clunk,* as the deadbolt engaged.

I sat on the bed and took in the room.

The walls were pastel green and the Plexiglas window had wire-mesh woven through it. The desk and chair were made of maple wood, which gave the room its only sense of homeyness. They resembled the desk and chair I'd had in my own room as a little kid. My parents loved maple wood. Maple wood and mahogany, all over their house. In fact, the lonely sterile feeling in this room reminded me a lot of home. The anxiety felt a bit different though. At home my mom was always on my back, nagging, shouting, controlling. Here, it was somewhat opposite. No nagging or shouting. Just orders and silence.

My sense of loss of control surged. *That* they did have in common.

My left eye began to randomly twitch, like it does when I've been home for a few days. I pressed on my eyelid with my fingers to stop the twitching and lay back on the bed.

Even the ceiling was pastel green. I was trapped in a green gift box. But who was I a gift to? I imagined the giant in Jack and the Beanstalk opening this box to find me inside. Would he be surprised? Amused at the little trapped and helpless girl inside? Or maybe he'd be disappointed at the lack of fat on my bones. Would he pluck me up and add me to his hamster-cage with all the other trapped kids? Maybe he'd think he was saving me. The cage at least had an exercise wheel, and also bars with air flowing through and no solid walls. If he let me just wander around freely, then what would happen? Chaos for sure.

I had to get out of here. I curled up in a ball and did the next best thing—went to sleep.

9

Betty came in with a tray of food sometime in the afternoon. With no clock on the wall, time had become elusive. She placed the tray on the desk.

"Your chart says that you aren't on the pill. Is this correct?"

"Uh ... yeah? Why?" Was this seriously any of her business?

She pointed at a little paper cup on the tray. "You have to take this."

I glanced at the cup with the tiny pink pill in it. "Oh, uh, I stopped taking the pill because it messes with me, y' know, my moods and stuff."

"Listen, I'm only stating what's in your file. This is not an option. I'm guessing it's because you've been classified as sexually active, perhaps promiscuous. You have to take it in front of me." Betty embraced her inner cop. She wouldn't be taking questions and certainly not protests.

I put the pill in my mouth and feigned swallowing.

"Open up." Betty gestured for me to open my mouth.

I pushed the pill up between my cheek and teeth and opened wide.

Betty looked in my mouth, told me to raise my tongue, and she searched under my lips with her fingers. "Nice try. Now, let's do that one more time."

I swallowed the pill.

Betty gave me an exasperated look. "You girls. You're all the same, every one of you."

She set the tray on my desk and retreated back to her office.

I considered the meal in front of me. Food. Mashed potatoes, peas and carrots, and a pork chop. My stomach clenched. I wondered how much of this food I'd be required to eat. There was nowhere to stash it.

I ate the peas and carrots and half the potatoes, then pushed the pork chop up onto the other half, making it seem like I'd eaten more. When Betty came to retrieve my tray, I lied that I was vegetarian. She scrutinized me for a moment, then shrugged and left with the tray.

Betty never seemed to register the vegetarian message and kept bringing me meals with meat. But she never made me eat it. This worked out well for me, as the meat took up a third of my plate, so I only had to deal with the other two-thirds. I guess she wasn't that observant after all.

Before bed, Betty watched me brush my teeth and pee. She handed me some light green pyjamas. I thought they matched the walls quite well and wondered if the buyer had colour coordinated on purpose. I put them on and instantly felt an allegiance with the walls.

"Goodnight, Sam. Sleep well. And if you have to pee, stamp on the floor. The security guard's office is right below you. He'll come up and bring you to the washroom."

I wondered if he'd watch too. Yup. Pretty sure I wouldn't be needing to pee.

Betty closed and locked the door.

❧

On my second day of isolation, I wrote all my angry thoughts down on that pad on the desk. Then I drew pictures of what I would to do to all the people who'd fucked me over.

With Gini, I'd dig up all the dirt I could on her and scream it out to the world. That bitch would *not* be getting away with reading my journal, that was for fucking sure! I drew a picture of her crying and pleading for me to forgive her, and I scribbled Xs across her eyes like serial killers do in horror movies.

As for my mom, I'd lock her away in this room and give the key to the *Jack and the Beanstalk* giant. I complemented my mom-rant with a drawing of her being squished inside the giant's humongous fist. He didn't much like her either.

And that creep Christien, the one who'd fucked with me and Frankie, he'd roast on a spit over a bonfire, like the pig he is, all bound up and sizzling. His skin would bubble and his eyes'd burst with the heat. All the while he'd be screaming, "je t'en prie! je t'en prie!" *I beg you! I beg you!* And I'd laugh and turn the spit.

I looked at the butterfly tattoo on my wrist. Frankie had one just the same. Christien had given us tattoos that same evening, before shit went sideways. Thirteen, first time drunk, and naive as hell. I'd been so dumb, had even defended him at first ... until he did the same to me while on the run that first time. That fucker was twenty-seven. I cringed. None of it would've happened if it weren't for me. He was *my* uncle's friend, and I had begged Frankie to go to his stupid party. I wish I'd never met that piece of pig's ass.

I scratched at my butterfly tattoo and the pain was gratifying. I began to gouge my wrist with the pen, slashing at that stupid butterfly with blue ink. The pen wasn't sharp enough to break through, but at least I'd defaced the fuckin' tat.

Hot and sweaty, I began to hyper ventilate. I reminded myself to breathe. Anger was like that. Bubbling hot lava, followed by an explosion, then the lava cools again, morphing into something more solid and resilient to being fucked with.

A cold sweat replaced the hot one. Dizzy and suddenly very tired, I folded my arms on the desk and collapsed forward into them. Anger and guilt were exhausting. I studied my irate doodles and frowned. The system sucked. My parents sucked. When would all this end? I tore the pages into tiny pieces so no one could read my thoughts. If anyone saw my doodles and rants, they'd commit me to the Douglas Mental Hospital and ditch the key.

I lay back on the bed. What the hell was this place? All I'd done was run away. A prison for runaways. Nothing made sense. Punishment for wanting freedom was taking it away? Well, they'd better have secure locks on this dungeon because I damn sure wouldn't be staying.

My eye began to twitch again. I fought back tears. No way this fuckin' hellhole would make me cry.

9

On my third and last day in solitary confinement, I read all the pamphlets and the two books.

The *Welcome to Manny Cottage* pamphlet had a map of the whole place. There were eight buildings on the map, and they surrounded a grassy outdoor common area which was encircled by a running track. The school sat on one side of the track and the administration building on the opposite side. The other buildings were units with varying degrees of security. The pamphlet said that each unit was suited to the needs of the kids assigned to it. Although everyone had the right to schooling, the kids from only four units had the right to go to the school building. Bethel, which was the high-security unit I'd been admitted into, had in-house schooling. On the bottom of the pamphlet, big bold letters exclaimed, "*WE* **ARE HERE FOR** *YOU*." I thought sarcastically, '*Wow, what a relief.*'

Another pamphlet, titled *Birth Control is Your Right*, described a women's right to choose. Confused, I thought about the birth control pills I'd been made to swallow.

Then there was the one with a picture of a smoker's lungs on its front cover, and another about gateway drugs. According to those ones, I was already doomed.

The books were more interesting.

The Little Prince I thought kind of cute, but *Go Ask Alice* really grabbed me. Its edges were scuffed, it had obviously been read a million times, for good reason. I wondered if Betty had read it. Perhaps she'd put it in the room by mistake.

Go Ask Alice is a journal written by a runaway girl from a middle-class family who got addicted to drugs after mistakenly trying acid. She'd never done drugs before and couldn't get enough of the experience. Her life soon goes off the rails, she ends up in the slums, gets raped, and it doesn't get better from there. No happy ending in this story. I was definitely doomed. Maybe it was all the fault of drugs ... maybe that's why I was a runaway and rape victim.

I thought back to the first time I ran. Nope, the rape had happened before the drugs. I sighed in relief. Maybe this book's being here was intentional after all. It was sure an effective scare tactic.

Man ... rumination was bad for the soul.

I'd meet my new prison mates in the morning, just a few hours away. The thought made me anxious. What if they were all fucked up like Alice? Druggies never made for good friends. I'd have to watch my stuff and forget about writing. Wasn't going to repeat the Gini incident. What if each one of them was an embodiment of Gini? Gini should really be here instead of me. She's the one who's truly fucked up.

Betty showed up for washroom duty at 8 PM. I'd begun to feel safer locked in my room by myself. Betty never took her eyes off me while with me—listening, observing, jotting things down on her clipboard.

The lights switched off. Day 3 had finally ended.

CHAPTER FIVE

Queen Bees

August / September

I stood in the doorway to my new room, holding my folded white sheets, and took stock.

Two beds, two closets, and a window with a heavy metal grate cover on the outside. The only thing that wasn't white in the room were the plain wool blankets on the beds, which were dark grey with a single blue stripe near the bottom.

I stepped into my designated bedroom and dropped the sheets on the bed with the bare mattress.

Sitting down next to my pile of sheets, I reminded myself to breathe.

I couldn't remember ever being so anxious. The stories I'd heard about Manny Cottage stuck to me like bubble gum sticks to hair. No matter how much I told myself that it wouldn't be so bad—that things would turn out OK, that the stories were only stories, that like bubble gum, a bit of greasing would do the trick—I kept being reminded of the time my mother shaved my head to get the gum out. Sitting there on my bed unusually terrified, I feared that Manny Cottage would be as bad as I'd heard.

A girl appeared in the doorway. She gave me a crooked smile, walked over to the bed opposite mine, and plopped herself down on it. She was very pretty, with light amber-brown skin and short curly black hair. Her demeanour told me she'd been here a while.

"Hey. Tema."

"Uh-m, hey. I'm Sam." I didn't know what to say next, so waited for her to continue.

"See that line, Sam?" Tema pointed to a line that had been made with masking tape on the floor in between our beds and I nodded. "That's a wall. This side is my room and that side is your room. You stay in *your* room, I stay in *my* room. When I'm in my room, I can't hear or see you because of our wall. Respect the wall. Capiche?"

Tema turned away from me, grabbed her book from her bedside table, and lay back on her bed.

I studied her, considering whether to attempt further communication.

Tema glanced at me. "Eh! The wall. Pay attention. You can't see me."

Her tone made me feel like a stupid puppy trying to befriend a hungry lion. My cheeks flushed with heat. I averted my eyes from Tema's side of the room and decided to make my bed.

❦

Tom's office was plain and cold. Everything in it was made of something hard, not at all like Dave's office in Charles A. Tom sat behind his desk and greeted me with a practiced smile.

"Come in, Sam. Have a seat." He motioned to one of two wooden chairs in front of his desk and I complied. "I'll be your Primary Worker while you're in Bethel. Do you know what that is?"

I shook my head for 'no.'

"Well, it means that I'm the person that will help you with anything you need while you're here. If you have any requests or concerns, you can come to me, and we'll sort them out together. OK?"

I nodded.

Tom tried for a warmer smile, but it came across toothy and awkward. "So, Sam ... they tell me you've been sent to Bethel for a few days, because of lack of space in the lower security units in Manny Cottage. It shouldn't be for long, but while you're here you'll have to comply with the rules in Bethel, which were created for higher risk kids. I know you're not in here for the same level of trouble, but it would only cause issues if we were to allow you more luxuries. I hope you understand. As long as you comply with Bethel's rules, you'll fit in fine. Do you smoke?"

I nodded.

"OK, I'll enlist you in the smoking program. Bethel girls have a 6-cigarette limit per day. Cigarettes will be provided to you by me. The smoking pit's outside, in the back. Just follow the others."

I nodded.

"Good. Here's your daily schedule."

I took the pamphlet Tom was handing me.

"Great. Now that that's sorted ..." Tom picked up a small plastic bag from a shelf beside his chair and put it on his desk. "Your things. All gone through, most passed the test. Sorry about the wait, but procedure is procedure. As for your clothes, those you'll get back when you leave Bethel. Same goes for the items that didn't pass the safety test. Is everything understood?"

I nodded again.

Any questions?"

I shook my head.

Tom smiled. "Perfect. I'll see you in the common room for supper at 6 PM sharp." He occupied himself with some papers on his desk and went back to other business, dismissing me without another word.

I picked up my bag of belongings and exited Tom's space.

The office exited right into the common room, which was as sterile and cold as the rest of the place. A few kids sat, scattered here and there, on plastic chairs at metal tables that had been screwed to the floor. As I walked back to my room, also adjacent to the common room, the chatter in the room dulled and eyes watched me silently, with curious if not enthusiastic wonder.

Someone chirped, "*squaw, squaw, squaw*" behind me.

I glanced back and instantly regretted it. The girls watching me were smirking, hungry for new blood. My imagination began to get the best of me, and I couldn't help think of the vampires in that Corey Haim movie, *The Lost Boys.*

The large girl with the bleached hair sucked her teeth and made a barely audible snide remark that I didn't catch, and the other girls laughed. The chatter started up again as I exited the common area into my bedroom.

I put my bag on the floor at the end of my bed and steadied myself. My leg had begun to tremble, which was new for me. Clenching my jaw, I silently ordered myself to get with the game and deal.

Tema broke the silence, "Better man up girly-girl, or yer gonna be shark food."

I bristled with her comment, pursed my lips and glared at her as I aggressively pointed at the tape.

Tema smiled, "Or maybe you'll learn to swim with the big fishies after all."

I rummaged through my bag for my journal, lay on my bed and began to doodle, furiously trying to draw the anxiety out of my system. There was no way I was going to put words to it in this place—I'd learned my lesson about keeping journals. Doodles would have to suffice.

9

Supper was served buffet style in the same common room that I would soon discover hosted almost every event in Bethel—meals, school, movie nights, and occasional visitors. The building wasn't very big, nor was it complicated—16 bedrooms, two offices and a staff room, the common room, and a fenced in basketball court outside (mainly used for smoking, as balls had been labelled as weapons and confiscated long ago). No grass, just concrete everywhere. In a nutshell, prison for kids. Bethel girls didn't mix with kids from other units. Girls in Bethel were considered to be *beyond help*. They were the ones that had *bad* tattooed into their DNA. Bethel was in a sense preparing them for their inevitable future, their *real world*: jail.

On my first day in Bethel I felt as if I'd been swept up in an evil gene pool on a path towards inescapable hellfire.

I served myself the least amount of food I could get away with and sat at the only empty table-for-two. As I was separating the peas from my rice, the larger butchy looking girl with bleached hair came over and sat down opposite me.

"So, what do we have here? *Squaw, Squaw*, not hungry? Scrawny little thing like you don't have space for a few peas?"

I sat back in my chair, trying not to seem defensive but also sure I was failing in that feat. "I'm actually not ... I'm part Asian ... Uh, name's Sam. And you are ...?"

Bleach-brain looked me over as if considering which part of me to gnaw on first. "OK then, chink. *You* can call me Queen Bee."

I responded only by continuing to acknowledge her presence.

She went on, "*This place* ..." She motioned with her hands to emphasize that she meant Bethel and everyone in it, "This is my hive. These are my bees. You are here, therefore *you* are also my bee. Be a good bee and I'll be a good queen. 'Ya get me?"

I nodded and thought *'whatever'*. She reminded me of every other 'queen bee' I'd ever met. Stroke her ego, stay out of her way, do as she asks, and I should be fine. It would only be for a few days. So what if she had brass knuckles and a heart filled with coal ... right?

Bleach-brain shoved my tray and my juice spilled over onto my rice. She flashed me a typical 'queen bee' smirk, got up and went back to join her hive of wannabe queen bees.

I put my hand on my knee to stop it from shaking.

I looked at my plate of food—now a juice soup with bits of rice, a few peas, and cubes of what I'd thought must be chicken floating in it.

Little did Queen Bleach-brain know, she'd done me a favour with the juice. Now I wouldn't have to eat the crap on my plate. Mom calls it a disorder, but it really isn't. I eat enough to survive. It's not like I'm wasting away. Mom's a control freak. She wants to control everything I do, and that includes my eating habits. She has always been like that. In our house *she* is the Queen Bee.

Tema strolled over casually and propped herself against the side of my table, leaning more than sitting on it. The table was small, and she almost touched my tray with her rear.

She turned her head towards me, so she was almost looking at me. "That one'll be fine. It's the quiet Indian next to her that you've gotta watch out for."

I stared at my plate, worried that I may be caught glancing in their direction.

Tema continued, "Noemi. She's the one that started that fire. Y' know, the chick at that foster home that killed those girls? Noemi's real dark. Queen Bee's just her bitch. Noemi's the real Queen."

I looked up at Tema. She made brief eye contact, then continued on her way back to her room.

Bleach-brain yelled to Tema across the room, "Yo yo, blacky! Careful of that one. Chinks are all 'bout sneaky shit, eh!"

Tema smacked her ass, "Kiss it whitey!"

9

Mrs. Lebinsky leant against one of the tables, waiting for us to finish the assigned short story, *The Yellow Wallpaper*, written by Charlotte Perkins Gilman. I'd read it before but didn't want to risk staring at anyone by mistake, so kept my eyes glued to the story as a precaution.

"OK, girls. Who can tell me what this story is about?" Mrs. Lebinsky asked, much more enthusiastically than I'd expected.

Her question was answered with blank stares.

I raised a finger.

"It's ... uh ..." I glanced around nervously, "about how women were labelled as crazy way back when, uh ... but they were actually just reacting to a patriarchal society that kept them powerless." I swallowed hard. That had sounded too smart. And I hated feeling nervous.

All eyes became fixed on me. Heat pumped into my cheeks.

"Very good, Sam." Mrs. Lebinsky was both pleased and astonished.

Bleach-brain mumbled next to me, "Typical chink know-it-all."

Noemi rolled her eyes, held up the story, then dropped it on the floor. "This is so fuckin' stupid. Why's it named *The Yellow* fuckin' *Wallpaper* if it's about crazy women?"

"Well, it's not technically about women being crazy. It's about how social rules and discriminatory behaviours can make people act in ... um ... crazy ways." Mrs. Lebinsky said patiently.

"Whatever. It's fuckin' stupid, and ..." Noemi was agitated and about to boil over.

Tema interrupted, "I get it. So, yer sayin' that our crazy shit is 'cause of system shit?"

Everyone laughed, and Mrs. Lebinsky began to lose control of the class.

She thought fast, "Well, kind of, in a way. Um ... maybe if we take it in sections. Noemi, can you please read the first paragraph." Mrs. Lebinsky picked up Noemi's copy from the floor and handed it to her.

Noemi's cheeks flushed. She gripped her seat with her hands and didn't take the copy.

Mrs. Lebinsky smiled, "Come on, here you go. Only the first paragraph. You're up, Noemi."

Noemi flew off her chair, "I said it's fucking stupid! Fuck the fuck off!!" She stormed out, back towards her room.

I looked at Tema and she shrugged. When no one was watching, she mouthed, "Squaw can't read. She's a real coo-coo." She circled her ear with her finger and crossed her eyes.

Blacky, squaw, chink ... in this place, I suddenly wanted nothing more than to reclaim my stale British identity.

❦

Two weeks inched by and I'd become an expert at avoiding people. Beyond having my food regularly vandalized and being tripped a few times, I was doing OK. Calling Tema and I friends would be a stretch, but so far she'd helped more than hindered my safety ... so, I suppose we were at least *friend-ly*.

Tema and I just spoke in our room, without eyes and ears on us. Tema's makeshift wall apparently had a window that only opened from her side. As long as she began the conversation, we could talk through the wall. I learned quickly that this didn't go both ways. If I began to talk, I'd be talking to the wall. My words were met with silence, as if she couldn't hear me. This place was a hive full of twisted versions of my mother.

When Tema did speak to me, she told me stories about the other girls and why they were in Bethel. I suspected she was trying to scare me or control my fear in some way but nonetheless couldn't stop myself from hanging on her every word. It was like watching a horror movie. Even though you know the girlfriend in the movie is about to be horribly slaughtered, you still watch with anticipation, and are still shocked and horrified when the axe-man, who has been hot on his soon-to-be-victim's heels for the first half of the movie, appears with an axe and chops off her head. Tema's stories were like that—meant to capture your vulnerability to fear and hold it hostage.

Tema's story about Noemi was the most captivating of them all, and she told it like a professional narrator.

"You know the Roch Thériault[5] thing that's goin' on in the news?" I nodded. He was arrested for this insane cult he'd been running. Everyone was talking about it.

Tema glanced at Noemi, who sat unaware in the common room outside our room. "Noemi's his daughter."

I stared at Tema with disbelief. "Com'on, really?"

Tema nodded and launched into the whole history of events that lead to Noemi's incarceration.

"Rumour has it that Noemi was Thériault's firstborn child, conceived during a crazy sex ritual in a barn in the woods somewhere in the Gaspé boonies. Before her release a few months ago, she had spent all her life in that psycho's commune where incest and mass flagellation rituals were totally normal—like going to church on Sunday. But instead of church they'd meet in a barn, where Thériault had built an absolution alter. They'd beat themselves and each other, fuck their siblings, and jack-off and come all over Virgin Marie."

Tema had a flare for drama and she had me hooked.

"And once a year, they'd put on the ultimate sacrifice."

Tema paused for effect, her fingers in her hair, twisting her curls.

I hung on the silence, waiting for more.

"This is where things get super weird. Thériault and his followers believed that the devil came out to play every Halloween and feasted on firstborn babies. The Devil'd then impregnate virgins, so he'd have more firstborns for the next Halloween. The only way to protect the babies and virgins was to sacrifice the mother of a kid older than 8. And that's not even the worst of it. The really horrible part was that the mother must be sacrificed by her own blood, which always meant her children because she didn't have any other relatives in the cult. Apparently, the year before Thériault was jailed, Noemi's mother was chosen to be the sacrificial lamb and Noemi's brother, Abe, was to do the honours."

Tema paused again, still playing with her hair.

"Well ... Noemi was devastated that she herself hadn't been selected for the most sanctimonious honour of killing their mother. She was fuming inside as she watched Abe go through the ritual steps as he prepared himself and the sacred pyre for his and his mother's ultimate rite of passage. It would be his path to manhood and her path to heaven, while Noemi would get nothing and go nowhere, just stay in cult limbo, like a dumbass kid. Noemi wasn't gonna take that shit, eh? So, on the big night—after her brother had bound her mother to the biggest bonfire stack you could ever imagine and doused the whole thing in gas—just as Abe was about to light the fire, Noemi charged him, pushed him onto the pyre, threw a match in after him, and the whole thing went up like a stack of Christmas trees in January."

Tema's gaze reached right into me and I reminded myself to close my gaping mouth.

Spellbound, I waited for her to finish.

Tema continued, "From that point onward, at the tender age of only 14, Noemi became Roch Thériault's High Priestess. They say that when everything fell apart and Thériault went to jail, Noemi had a miscarriage and lost her inbred fetus, which made her even more crazy. A few months later, after endless therapy, drugs, and electric shock treatment, she was put in a foster home. She burned the place to the ground only a few days after moving in, killing her two foster sisters and the family cat. A fireman found the cat nailed to the girls' bedroom door and the girls' crispy corpses were found tied to their beds. She'd completed another sacrifice. But this time her crime would land her right here, in Bethel, with us!"

I shook myself out of my daze, "No way ... Seriously?"

Tema was taken aback with my doubt, "Yes way, man. Cross my heart, hope to die." She glanced in Noemi's direction, "See that burn scar on her throat?"

I looked over at Noemi, who sat at a table in the common area with the bleach-brain bees. The skin on the left side of her neck was pink and kind of shrivelled while also being pulled tight. I'd seen it up close a few times but hadn't paid attention. Staring wasn't something you did in Bethel. The scar definitely appeared to be a burn mark.

Tema emphasized, "She got *that* when she lit up those girls. If it weren't for the fire crew, she would've been roasted toast along with them."

⁹

Tema's story got me thinking about everything I'd heard concerning the Roch Thériault case, and about the fire at the foster home where those girls had been killed. It seemed far-fetched, but what she said rung true. According to the news, Thériault was a psychopath whose whole life was off the rails and far-fetched. And he'd created a community of followers who'd do anything to please him. It was entirely plausible that Noemi was his daughter.

I cringed inwardly every time Noemi came within arm's reach. I feigned sickness, so I could stay in my room without raising suspicion, and I timed my smoke breaks, so they wouldn't coincide with Queen Bee's hive. When I wasn't able to hide, I buried myself in books so the hive couldn't make eye contact, and they wouldn't be able to accuse me of staring.

Tom finally called me into his office with good news in the middle of September: Tomorrow would be my last day in the same unit as Noemi.

Bursting with relief, I had the incredible urge to hug Tom. But that kind of affection in this place would be weird, it wasn't allowed anyway, and the gossip would've taken our hug to broken-telephone 7th heaven. So, instead, I wrapped my arms around myself, squeezed hard, held my tears in, gave Tom the biggest smile that I'd been able to muster in a long time, and mouthed the words, "Thank you".

My shoulders felt light and I couldn't contain my smile as I returned to my room. I even risked a glory-filled glance in the direction of Queen Bee corner.

It had been almost a month since my first day in Bethel. I'd survived. And now I'd be moving on, not quite out yet, but at least on to another Manny Cottage unit where I would no longer have to spend my days scared of being stung to death by a swarm of psycho bees. There'd be other Queen Bees, but none that had taken life.

If only I'd been able to keep my impending transfer to myself.

,

My relaxed facial muscles must've given me away.

Although I hadn't said a word, the next morning there was a buzz in the air that didn't feel right. I told myself it was nothing, that I'd just eat my breakfast, read my book, stay clear of the hive, and be on my way into a much more familiar world tomorrow. All I had to do was abide by my keep-head-low rule and I'd be fine. It had worked for a month, it would work for one more day.

Tomorrow I'd be psycho-free.

I sat across from Tema, watching her scoff down her scrambled eggs. I frowned. Watching her eat made me feel gross. That girl was as skinny as a rake, but oh-boy could she ever eat. I suspected she was throwing it all up again after.

She finished her eggs, toast, and yogourt, and ogled my tray. "Mind?"

I shook my head, "Nope. Eat your heart out."

I was the opposite when it came to food. When I ate, I felt disgusting—as if I was trying to digest all the fucked-up shit in my life.

Done eating, Tema looked at me and smiled, "Grab a smoke with me after clean-up?" Her smile seemed warm ... not quite in character for her.

I briefly wondered whether Tema might actually come to miss me.

I returned her smile, "Yup. Sure thing."

"Great. I can clean. You go get the smokes from Tom."

We weren't allowed to keep our cigarettes in our rooms, nor were we permitted lighters or matches. I stopped at the bathroom, then grabbed a sweater from my room, and went to wait in line at the office. I didn't usually go out into the courtyard while the bees were buzzing around it, but today was my last day and, beyond some light aggression, they hadn't bothered with me much.

Finally reaching the front of the line, I said to Tom, "Two. Mine and Tema's." He handed over two cigarettes and replied, "I'll be out to light 'em shortly."

The concrete courtyard was old and potholed, with dandelions poking up between cracks. There was a grass playing field beyond the tall barbed-wire fence that caged us in. Only the lower security kids got to sit on grass. That was their perk, not ours. Currently, the lucky ones on the other side of the fence were running track and field. Tema sat a short way from the door, with her back against the fence. There were a couple of concrete benches, occupied by the hive.

I walked over to Tema, tossed her a cigarette, and sat down next to her. Tom came out a couple of minutes later, did the rounds with his lighter, and disappeared back into hiding.

Tema took a long drag on her smoke, glanced at me, and casually remarked, "So, out of here in the morning, eh?"

I was surprised by her question. I hadn't told anyone. Trust wasn't something I could afford and informing nut-jobs I was leaving didn't seem wise. I cursed myself for being so outwardly happy, so relaxed. I must've given it away.

Hiding my surprise with a long drag of my own, I replied, "Yup. Being transferred."

I hoped that the warm vibe I'd picked up from Tema during breakfast was real. She was difficult to read and the odds in this place favoured rabid cult junkies.

Queen Bleach-brain stood up from her concrete throne and strolled towards us with Noemi by her side. I glanced at Tema. She was studying her smoke, tapping it, watching the ashes fall between her feet.

Without looking up, Tema smiled. "You know what the best part of setting those kids on fire was?" She kept looking at her feet.

The muscles in my legs clenched and the clench worked its way up through the rest of my body until it reached my brain and held me fast.

Tema continued, "It was listening to the screams of those little rich brats start out high pitch and then get all desperate and hoarse. Like animals begging for forgiveness then realizing there would be none and surrendering to the unfathomable hellfire that was their fate. That was the best part. That was the part that made it worth it."

As if on cue, a girl in the field who'd been running track and field, threw a Zippo lighter through the fence and Noemi caught it. Noemi grinned, then passed the lighter to Tema.

By this time, my brain had been getting tighter and tighter, as if held in a vice grip with Tema controlling the pressure. Was this for real? Was Tema the real Thériault kid? The one she'd said had burned her mother, brother, and those two girls—all alive and screaming and begging?

Tema grabbed me by the hair, pushed my head down and held my face to the pavement. She knelt above me, flipped open the lighter, and holding my head against the pavement, she touched it to my cheek.

"Shouldn't always believe what ya' hear, eh? Think we're that fucked in here? What d'ya say we show the rich brat how fucked up we really are, eh?"

The girls hovering over me sniggered.

I couldn't handle it any longer. My brain and body quit communicating, and my world began to turn, spinning around the reality currently unveiling itself on top of me. Then everything went dark as panic kicked in and fear saved the day.

I woke up to Tema face down on the ground in front of me, Tom on top of her pinning her in place, her arm twisted aggressively behind her back, and roars of laughter in the background. George, another worker, told some uninvolved girls to fetch me a glass of water. He helped me into sitting position.

George surveyed me with what I thought might be pity. "You'll be fine. Looks like you got pranked good, that's for sure!"

His attempt at making things light fell flat and I stared at him incredulously.

He added, "Just the girls' way of making friends. If they didn't like you, they'd never have bothered."

As I walked back to the building past the sniggering girls, Tema snarled, "Better keep an eye open tonight, ya' spoiled chink!" She managed an evil smile even while her face was being held against the ground.

Tom held her in place until I'd gone inside.

I lay awake that night and decided that that would be my last night in Manny Cottage Youth Detention Centre. I'd be transferring myself right out of this loony bin as soon as I hit low security in the morning.

CHAPTER SIX

Tema

Mid-September

"Get me the FUCK out of here!" I yelled pointlessly as loud as I could. "Argh! That fucking spoiled rich twat, Sam! It was a fucking *joke*!!" I threw myself down on the mattress. No bed frame, just a mattress on the floor. No sheets, no pillow. I'd be gifted those at lights-out time, maybe. No nothing, but a fuckin' mattress. *Welcome to the hole, where boredom kills.*

"FUCK! This isn't fair! I was JOKING!!"

I had less than a month to go in Manny Cottage and I'd been sentenced to the hole for 10 days. I mean, what the fuck?! No one gets fucking 10 days! If they decided to extend my stay in Manny Cottage too, I'd torture that scrawny privileged brat for real and make my time in this dungeon worth the effort.

Brown padding covered the walls and floor—a new addition since my last visit. I wondered about the point. Padding was something needed for crazies. I got up and threw myself against the wall to test its bounceability. My impact was absorbed. No bounce, what a disappointment. I slid down the wall and sat on the floor. My thumb hurt from when Tom had restrained me. They had this technique. Grab the thumb, bend backwards, and the arm will do anything you want. Damn effective. I'd be using that one sometime.

I thought of the sequence of events that had happened and laughed. We'd played Sam so easily. She'd been the highlight of the last couple of weeks. Rich brats were such easy targets. Probably shitting bricks just about now, afraid to leave her room. I'd survived the system by being tough, but I was no psycho cult murderer, nor was Noemi. Sam's reaction had been classic. My laughter grew, I doubled over, held my stomach, and rolled on the floor, unable to contain myself.

George, my primary worker, unlocked the door and stepped into my cell. "Tema, what's going on here?"

Oh, please! Was that mock concern I detected?

I continued cracking up, incapable of response. "I ... I ..." I tried to form a sentence.

Hopeless. I didn't even know why I was laughing so hard. I guess it was because of everything. Sam, this room, Bethel, my stupid situation, the reason for me being in Manny Cottage in the first place. The whole thing was a heap of steaming bullshit.

"Tema, I need you to calm down and quit the drama. I'll be in with your meal in a few minutes. You have 5 minutes to expel whatever's going on out of your system, OK?"

George turned to leave.

Quit the fuckin' drama? Why was it that when *I* expressed myself it was *'what a drama queen'* and when *Sam* did it was *'save the fuckin' helpless'*?

I stopped laughing abruptly, "Eh, George?"

George looked back at me.

"Fuck off."

George left the room and locked the door. My meal arrived an hour later, cold and soggy.

❦

Being stuck alone in an empty room with only your thoughts as company had to be breaking some kind of human right. It was fuckin' torture. When your life has sucked in like forever, so too does thinking about it.

I lay on my mattress, biting my fingernails, trying not to think. But, as always, my mind wandered.

My first day in the system was shortly after my seventh birthday. I did the math in my head. 10 years, 6 months, and a day. I was searching for my mom on that street corner near that biker bar, Le Rock. She hadn't come home from work on time and I'd become worried. I knew a few of the local hookers, so thought I'd ask around. The girls always showered me with hugs and kisses and gave me change for fries and ice cream, so I hadn't been the least bit afraid. Many of the bikers were just as friendly. This street corner was home. And if anyone attempted to lay a hand on me, an army of bodyguards would come to my rescue.

But on this particular evening, the corner was vacant. No hookers, no bikers, only a few cops, and some clubbers keeping their distance. Yellow tape blocked off part of the street. That should've warned me of what was to come. I walked up and down the block, trying to locate a face I recognized, but found no one. Even the normal line of parked Harleys was missing. I'd sat on the curb, outside Burger King, and waited, thinking someone was bound to turn up.

That's when the blond lady in the long coat showed up and introduced herself.

Detective Arnault bent down, studied me curiously with a furrowed brow, and said, "Bonjour ... sont où tes parents?" She smiled and waited for a reply.

I stared at her blankly.

"English?"

I nodded.

"It's way past your bedtime. What are you doing out here on the corner so late?"

Scared by her authoritative stance, I sat on the curb like a cornered kitten, looking up at her, waiting for more. Everyone knew well-dressed blond ladies meant trouble.

"I'm Detective Arnault, and you are sitting in my crime scene, my dear. Where are your parents?" She laced her question with a reassuring smile.

I continued to stare at her silently, helpless, hoping my mom would materialize and transport me away from this eerily vacant street corner that had been taken over by serious people in uniform.

The detective waited patiently for my response.

"I'm waiting for my mom. She didn't come home from work." I finally said, so naively.

Detective Arnault's smile remained but had become more forced. I remembered it clearly. That smile. That moment. It was then that I'd felt my life was about to change.

"What's your name?" The detective had said so calmly, like all was good, or at least it might be.

"Temima Williams. Do you know where my mom is?" My voice was shaky, and my world stopped as I waited for her answer.

Detective Arnault's smile disappeared. "Ah, I see. We've been looking for you, Temima." And without elaboration, she guided me over to a police cruiser to wait for social services.

My mother had been shot dead by a cop earlier in the evening, right there on the corner by Le Rock. According to word on the street, she'd tried to intervene in a conflict the police were having with Mad Brad. No one knew his real name, but that's what we all called him. Guy was a total wack job—schizo or something—but never hurt a fly. Merely screamed and shit, at whoever may have unknowingly threatened his bit of sidewalk, covered doorway, or piece of grass, depending on the weather. As long as you respected his space, he was fine, and locals understood this. But, as luck played out, on this day someone (likely some sheltered rich bitch on her way to flirt with danger at the bikers' bar) had got all freaked out and called the cops. The irony wasn't lost on me.

Don't get me wrong. Life as a single young mom's kid wasn't perfect. My mom had issues, which sometimes caused bruises. But she'd never gone the hooker route, always stayed legit, even when hydro cut our power. There were some sicko boyfriends though. She'd put one of them in hospital when she'd found him playing doctor with me one evening. Then there was the recovering addict that never recovered. He was sweet, until he wasn't. The others were mostly OK. I mean they had their issues, but so did everyone. That's what I'd come to know. My mom and those hookers and bikers on our street corner, they were my family. On that day, I lost my whole fuckin' family.

In the system I suffered a whole new kind of abuse.

Placed me in middle-class whitey foster homes a few times, but things never worked out. No one wanted to deal with a fucked up 'mulatto'—that's what some of 'em called me. I kept running, back to the hookers and bikers outside Le Rock.

By age 10, I'd become a permanent resident in Manny Cottage—the idea being to re-program me and keep me off the street corners. By age 13, I'd become a regular in solitary confinement, a smoker and a sniffer of anything that might give me a high—glue, white-out, even some markers would do the trick.

And I ran every chance I got.

Manny Cottage was way out in the sticks. Once, at age 15, I walked for a whole twelve hours before I finally caught a ride to Montreal. I was picked up for hooking on St-Laurent a few days later. A couple of days after that, I was sentenced to Manny Cottage's ultra-secure Bethel unit.

And here I was. Lying on a padded floor in solitary confinement, a month before I'd be transferred to a city group home. What was its name? I couldn't remember. But it would be the last step on my way to freedom. Finally, 18 in a few months. Oddly, that made me kind of nervous. I hadn't lived outside of Manny Cottage in years. I hated feeling nervous. It wasn't me at all. Anxiety was for whinging spoiled pussies like Sam.

I needed a fuckin' smoke. There was just so much wrong with banning smokes to chicks in the hole.

George came in, holding a blanket and sheets, but no pillow.

"You suicidal?"

I shook my head.

He tossed the bundle of 'potential suicide tools' onto my bed.

"Time to brush teeth."

He accompanied me to the washroom and turned his back as I did my thing.

When I was secure in my hole again, George nodded as if he felt my pain and said, "Goodnight, Tema. And, hey … I'm sure you've had it worse."

What was it with fuckin' whiteys? How could anything be worse than being fuckin' locked in isolation until breaking point? Oh, right. Having your mom killed by cops 'cause of that 'black weapon' she must've threatened them with. That's worse.

The lights went out, and I was stuck in the dark, just me and my thoughts. I chewed on my nails and again tried to stop thinking. I told myself I could do this. It would only be a few more days than last time.

9

Day 6 was the worst.

I curled up on the floor. My mind wouldn't stop racing. A squirrel in there was doing acrobatics and I couldn't calm it down. The rodent cackled and taunted me about how awful I was. I deserved all of it. I was a loser daughter of some black whore, a plaything to her perv boyfriends. Maybe that *is* what my mom was. Like the cops said. Maybe she'd been lying 'bout the legit stuff. Just a whore like the rest, and I'd been born with *'Fuck-me'* tattooed on my forehead.

If George would only let me have a smoke, I'd be able to relax, and this fuckin' hellhole wouldn't be so bad.

Where the fuck *was* George?

Why wasn't there a clock on the wall? That was a form of torture in itself—never knowing how long you had 'til your next meal.

What the fuck *time* was it? It must be at least 10 am.

He must've skipped my breakfast. Fuck!

A whine that I didn't quite recognize escaped from me, "George, George! I'm sorry. I'm sorry, George. I didn't mean it. You're cool. Please. I didn't mean it. Please, just bring me my breakfast! I didn't mean it!"

My plea was met with silence.

I grabbed a fist full of hair and pulled hard. The pain felt good. I began scratching myself all over—my arms, my legs, my stomach, my head. I clawed at my skin until blood was drawn. I felt better. Every time I stopped scratching my thoughts came back.

Was I going nuts? This must be what *crazy* felt like. Was the padding in here for day sixes? I kept scratching. I had to stop my thoughts.

My head throbbed. Did I have any happy memories? I tried to find some. Oh, yeah. That time I went camping with my first foster family, the Hendersons. Emily was cool. She'd been my age and had a quirky sense of humour. We'd hit it off great. I thought back to that trip and held on tight.

I remembered the raft we'd built with driftwood. Her dad had helped us tie it together. We'd been so proud. Our raft wasn't strong enough to support us both, but that only added to the fun. The challenge had been to get up on it without it tilting and pitching us off. I smiled at the memory. We'd kept at our challenge all afternoon but had never succeeded at staying on for more than a few seconds. On that day I'd decided that I wanted to stay with the Hendersons forever.

In my dreams I'd pictured myself a Henderson daughter, laughing, teasing, loving each other, with our arms looped together, never to be separated. I never understood why I'd been transferred out, why I had to leave. Everything had been perfect, so I'd thought. But one day I was picked up at their place by a social worker and that was that. Emily and the Hendersons disappeared from my life.

Sadness wrapped itself around my throat and I began to suffocate. My vision blurred and a horrible ringing in my ears penetrated my world. I gasped for air. My chest hurt. What the fuck was happening? I tried to rise up, call for help, but couldn't. I lay in a ball on the floor, helpless, a premature baby trying to breathe. Life was finally going to kill me.

I accepted my fate. Maybe death wasn't so bad. My chest relaxed and air re-entered my lungs. I began to sob.

George came in with my lunch and dropped the tray. "Shit, Tema. Oh. Hey! I need help in here!"

Confused, I peered at George. Then I saw my hands, the clump of hair in them, and the blood on my fingers and arms. I started to yell. The situation, *me*, was all so bizarre. Was this *me*? I watched from some place outside of myself, as this deranged girl who couldn't be me freaked out. Guards appeared and surrounded me.

The guards tried to coax me into standing up, but I couldn't. My legs weren't working. They discussed alternatives among themselves, while I worked on my leg issue.

The short lady guard noticed the bed and said to the tall man one, "Eh, we've got a bed wetter. She's gonna need clean pyjamas. And page the cleaners. The bed's got blood on it too."

The tall one chimed in, "Christ! Why does this crap always happen on morning shifts?"

The short one huffed at me, "Girl, if you don't help us out here, you know where this is going to lead, eh? Now, stand!"

I tried hard but couldn't do it.

They let me fall back down onto the mattress, and I landed hard.

The next moment sped by, as I watched terror-stricken.

Someone heavy, holding a needle, jumped on top of me. I struggled, trying to free myself, but they had my arms pinned down beside me. I yelled, but no one listened. There was a sharp pain in my leg, then darkness took over.

I woke up in the infirmary later that day, to the nurse tending my scratches. Her touch, warm and genuinely caring. My breath caught and I began to tremble. I hadn't cried like this in years.

George advocated for my early return to the general population. Guess he was a white prick with a heart. Someday, when I'm not so angry, I might thank him.

Noemi wasn't so lucky.

When Noemi was finally released from the hole after her 10-day sentence, she spent all her time in her room fixated on the wall. She wouldn't eat or talk or look at anyone. Her roommate, Kendra, said she didn't think she slept either. Noemi would stare through the darkness at her. Kendra said it was really spooky, like having a vengeful Indian spirit passing judgment on her. It had been Noemi's third time in solitary, and they always put her in for maximum time. Eventually, she was diagnosed with something and transferred to the Douglas Hospital, the one for crazies.

CHAPTER SEVEN

AWOL

Mid-September — Sam

My goodbye to Bethel unit, Tema and the psycho bees, was a huge relief. My next step would be escape from Manny Cottage.

As I surfaced, from what had felt like a path to hell, into Manny Cottage's main grounds, I scanned the area, taking note of every possible escape route. The grounds consisted of a grassy square surrounded by brick buildings with a large covered gazebo in the middle. The running track looped around the edge of the square. Although most Manny Cottage units were not enclosed by fences, a barbed wire fence surrounded the grounds behind the buildings. The front gate wasn't fenced in or locked but could only be accessed through the main office building, which was also fence-free.

There were technically two ways out.

Door #1: run during a smoke break. This would require me to climb the fence and manoeuvre my way delicately through the barbed wire at the top. I was quite small, so it might work. Or things could get immensely messy. I pictured myself caught like a fish in a net on top of the fence, kids laughing hysterically, maybe even throwing trash at me, *'Ha! The chink isn't so smart after all! What a loser!'*, they'd shout, as I waited for the rescue crew. From then on, I'd be known as 'Chink Meat' or 'Fishy Chink' or some other twisted nickname that I'd never shake. Nope. Door #1 wasn't going to work.

Door #2: escape through the main office building, which was surely well supervised. I smiled inwardly. I had one big advantage—protocol required that all new unit intakes get a medical check-up at the nurse's station prior to completing their transfer. The nurse's station was in the same building as the main office. And, if I remembered correctly, the whole building had normal windows with no bars. Door #2 it would be.

❦

The nurse's office was as expected, equipped with a cot, desk, chair, posters of the human body (one male, one female), and a bunch of pamphlets on STDs, contraception, and woman's right to choose. And, as predicted, there was an unbarred window. That opened. With nothing but freedom on the other side.

Tom wished me well and left my side as Nurse Esther entered the room. Esther gave me a hard look and frowned, sizing me up. If I had to work in this crazy place for years on end, I would probably do the same to every kid who crossed my path. Part of me felt for Esther. But I also had to survive, and Esther was about to be blindsided—no matter how hard she tried to read me.

Esther picked up her retinoscope, switched its light on and attempted to take a look into my eyes. Putting on my best act, I squinted and backed away as if in pain.

Esther switched the light off and studied me for a moment, concerned. "Hmm. When did your eye sensitivity start?"

I glanced at my knees, "Yesterday. I kinda passed out. When I woke up, my head was hurting. Since then, I guess."

She studied me some more, "You may have a concussion. You should've been brought to me yesterday."

I looked at Esther and nodded meekly.

Esther's eyes softened, "I heard about what those girls did and there is no excuse. You poor kid."

Her kind tone tweaked something inside me. To my own surprise, I broke down in tears and told her what had happened. I hadn't intended on milking the situation in this way, but it did work in my favour.

Nurse Esther put her hands on my shoulders and regarded me with sympathy, "Dear, you need a bit of a break. Do you want to stay here for a few hours? It'll give you some time to collect yourself before heading back to the zoo."

I nodded and thanked her.

A thought crossed my mind—is that what they think of us? Zoo animals? Wild beasts that need to be captured, imprisoned, and forced into submission with the threat of further punishment? Esther had hit it right on the nose, because that's what the place felt like.

I kept my eyes lowered, playing up my depressed and confused state of mind. This act was an easy one as it wasn't much of an act.

Laying down on the cot, I closed my eyes, and feigned exhaustion, then sleep.

Esther left the room.

9

Manny Cottage Youth Detention Centre was nothing like Alcatraz. I opened the window, squeezed through (ripping my t-shirt only a bit), and I was on my way. It was just my luck that the nurse's window led out to the back of the building and not to the front. The riskiest part was making my way from the back of the building to the woods—that were about 100 feet away—without being seen through other windows.

The only way to do it was by mad-dash and that's what I did.

Into the woods I flew, like a wild-eyed deer escaping a hunter's scope. I only stopped for a quick breath when I reached the highway ditch at the other side. Now I'd have to tap into my sixth sense and be patient. The last thing I wanted was to thumb a ride with someone who was going to drive me right back to where I started.

I'd need to judge drivers by their cars and cross my fingers. I figured it best to stick to jazzed-up old Fords and cheap Honda Civics booming with music—they'd be driven by people who wouldn't ask questions. But time was of the essence. I'd have to move fast.

A sky blue Volkswagen bug approached. Its front bumper was crooked, and Jimi Hendrix blasted through open windows. Perfect. I stood up from the ditch and made myself fully visible. I put one hand on my hip and raised the other one with my thumb stuck up, as if I was relaxed and friendly and only needed a lift to the café in the next village.

The guy in the car waved and pulled over onto the shoulder a few feet up the road. I ran to the car, opened the door, and hopped in before he could get his first question out. As long as I was in, I was pretty sure I'd be able to convince him to give me a ride to where I wanted to go. I'd become quite adept at getting what I wanted out of boys and men. Smile sweetly, laugh at everything they say, and play just-dumb-enough. It wasn't *me* at all, and only guys who didn't know me fell for it, like this guy for instance.

I shut the car door after me, turned towards the guy and introduced myself, "Eh, I'm Gabe, thanks for stopping!" A fake name was the best way to go and the first one that came to mind was Gabe's. "I'm going South, as far as you are or as close to Montreal as you can get, whichever works."

The guy slowly observed me through bloodshot eyes. He smelled of pot and looked like he'd been tree planting all day, or perhaps 24/7 for the past month. He was in his early 20s and had blond dreadlocks that I thought may just be natural—a result of not washing or brushing his curls for a very long time, like maybe never.

Dreadlocks finally spoke, "Eh, man ... no prob. Headin' that way anyway."

I laughed warmly at nothing in particular, and he responded with a flirtatious smile.

"Rick." He threw his name out as if it were special, a gift just for me.

Rick turned the music back up and pulled off the shoulder onto the highway. I glanced back at Manny Cottage, breathed in deeply, exhaled deliberately, and smiled. Freedom had never felt so good.

Then I fell asleep for real.

,

About an hour later, Rick nudged me awake and asked, "Eh, man … uh … Gabe? We're almost in town. Where you goin'? Vendôme metro work?"

I nodded, "Yeah, yeah that'll do I guess."

Rick looked thoughtful and hesitated before he continued, "You seem, uh … you got a place to go?"

His question made me nervous, "Yeah, yeah of course. You can just let me out wherever. Like, here is fine." I pointed to the bus stop coming up on our right.

He glanced at me and shrugged, "OK, whatever. I was just gonna say that I know a place you can crash, eh, if ya' need it. It's gettin' late and it's not exactly summer no more. That t-shirt's not gonna do the trick tonight."

I thought about his offer for a moment. I hadn't made plans. I didn't have anywhere to go. The last time I ran away for an extended period, I had stayed with my uncle's friend—who'd turned out to be a real douche—and his gang of mini-douches. No way I'd be repeating that crap.

I decided to trust Dreadlock Rick. What could really go wrong? This guy was about as dangerous as a stoned pussycat.

"Sure. OK. Yeah. I kinda need a place tonight." I'd said it. Done. Now I'd have to hope for the best and take things as they came. I desperately hoped it wouldn't involve any "favours". The Douche Gang had been big on favours.

A few minutes later we exited the highway, drove the loop around and under the overpass, and pulled into what seemed like nothing more than an overgrown field of wild grasses and giant thistles.

It wasn't until I stepped out of the car did I realize we were actually parked on what once was a long cement-paved driveway. Behind a few of the tallest thistles, which were about twice my height, stood an old rickety house that appeared to have emerged out of a Nightmare on Elm Street movie—after Freddy had corrupted it and violently slaughtered all its inhabitants. I stopped by the side of the car, staring at the house.

"That's your suggestion? The place that's gonna keep me safe tonight? Are you for fuckin' real?" I glared at Rick, waiting for his rationalization.

Rick looked at me, amused. "The way that house *looks*, and how it's all thorned in? That's what keeps it off the grid, man. To coppers, this place is invisible. The house is hidden in the bush, looks spooky, and is falling apart, literally. No one bothers with it. In fact, the only person that does bother with this house is Tig. And Tig will keep you safe."

The steps were a rotten timber jungle of very enthusiastic weeds. The plants seemed set on reclaiming the building, and they'd obviously started with the front balcony.

"Guess I can see how the disguise works." I motioned to the thorny weeds, apprehensively.

Rick responded with a *'you haven't seen the least of it'* smile, "Uh ... yeah, sure." And he knocked on the door—one knock, pause, two together, pause, one more.

There was barely audible rustling in the room to the right of the door, and the curtain moved just enough for me to pick up the movement out of the corner of my eye. Then the door swung open and there stood a girl dressed in jean overalls, a stripy long sleeve, and flame-coloured wildly curly hair—Pippi Longstocking's twin street urchin.

She wrapped her arms around Rick, then pushed him away again in almost the same motion, "What the fuck, eh? I've been waiting for days! What happened??"

Rick searched his feet sheepishly for an answer. "Eh, sorry ... I got distracted with some shit. But I brought you something ..." He produced a weed-filled baggy from his pocket and shot her an exaggerated *'please forgive me'* smile.

"'Kay, fine. You can come in. Who's this?" For the first time since she opened the door, Tig acknowledged my presence. She surveyed me—curious, with learned skepticism.

Rick replied, "Tig, meet Gabe."

I fidgeted nervously, "Sam. Not Gabe. Gabe's just a ... y' know, nickname ... for safety."

Rick considered me, respect in his eyes. "Well then, you two will get along just fine. Tig's not *Tig* either, and she's never come clean to me."

Tig scratched her nose and flashed him a timid smile. "So ... what else did you bring me?"

Tig and I would get along well—I could feel it.

While Rick was fetching some things for Tig from the car, Tig gave me a tour of the house.

Peeling flowery wallpaper covered the walls in most rooms. Wood plank floors creaked as we walked over them, and the carpet on the stairs seemed to exhale dust from its steps as we made our way up to the second floor. Here, Tig warned me to keep an eye out for the rotten planks. The roof leaked, she said, and water had rotted holes in the floor in some spots. The place stank of mold, which wasn't surprising because of the leaks and holes everywhere. The windows weren't much better, with mushrooms sprouting from the ancient cracked frames.

Tig called it home. To me, the house just looked like a bit of desperate deliverance ... at the present moment anyway. Home was something I was yet to experience. I hadn't felt at home anywhere in a long time and was fairly sure this wasn't it either.

"So ... uh, interesting place." I was about to follow that up with *'been here a while?'* but realized how lame that would sound.

Tig nodded, "Yeah. You know, it's a shit hole, but a peaceful shit hole. I like it."

Rick came back from the car with a box filled with cans of Chef Boyardee, saltines, and peanut butter.

Tig hugged him again and this time also planted a big fat kiss on his cheek. "You're the best, Rick. Thanks!" And she started to unpack the box into doorless cupboards in the kitchen. She noticed me staring and commented, "You gonna help or what?"

I refocused my thoughts and unpacked the peanut butter.

Rick leant against the kitchen doorframe. "Eh ... uh ... my cash flow's slowin' down ... end of season, y' know, hours cut." He paused. "Means I can't bring much food anymore."

Tig put the last can on the shelf and stood facing the cupboards with her hands on the counter. "Oh."

"Sorry, man. Nothin' I can do, hands tied." Rick thought for a moment, "But, still up for taking you dumpster diving!"

Tig turned towards Rick and smiled. "Thanks, Rick. Guess we'll have to adjust. Totally get it." Then she laughed as if there was no such thing as bad news and went on with thoroughly introducing herself to me.

Tig spoke as if a pause might kill the mood.

I could hardly keep up with her train of thought. What I grasped so far was that she loved peanut butter, hated canned pineapple (and Rick always forgot this), and that she was ecstatic over the fact that she'd be turning 16— legal working age—in three months, which would mean cash to do her own shopping, and maybe she'd get a legit place too. She hated dogs, liked cats, but would get a ferret if she ever got a pet. The mice in this place she thought were pretty cool. She hadn't seen any rats. Did I know that a rat could be trained to follow its owner? She had a friend once who'd trained a rat to fetch too. But she'd still get a ferret if she had the choice. And on and on.

When we were alone after Rick left, I asked Tig why she wasn't in the system, you know, with free food and bed, and she replied, "Why aren't *you* in the system?" And then it occurred to me how stupid my question was.

The living room was the best kept room. Someone had clearly done some successful trash-bin moonlighting because the furniture wasn't half bad, or at least only mildly smelled of Eau de Mildew. A well-worn Victorian sofa and a rocking chair were angled so that whoever was on them would receive direct heat from the old wood stove on the far wall. The curtains, made of faux silk, must've been almost new. The old dog-eaten rug I recognized to be Persian, as my parents had a couple. And there was even a broken cattle scale with a wooden top and iron wheels, which Tig had turned into a coffee table.

"So, what's your story, eh?" Tig smiled warmly, trusting.

This was a question that no one asked in the system. To ask about someone's story was to offer them an exchange of trust—like, I'll keep your secret safe if you keep mine safe. It felt strange to be so easily trusted. It made me feel like trusting her too. But then the little voice inside my head knocked some sense into me, reminding me where trust had gotten me so far.

"Not really that exciting. You know, this and that. Crappy family, kicked out, too young to work. How 'bout you?" I hoped she hadn't caught the caution in my eyes.

Tig began to fiddle with a button on her overalls. "I guess we definitely have that in common. I mean, crappy family and stuff. Dad's a boozer and mum's not around. I can't go home there, so I made one here. Rick's kind of a complicated friend. He helped get me set up here, away from my dad. He knows how batshit drunk and crazy Dad gets. Rick works for him."

Tig opened the door to the wood stove and began to kindle a fire. "Eh, Sam? Pass me some of that wood." She pointed to a stack against the wall under the window.

I studied the pile: painted planks, broken cupboard doors, pieces of frames, and anything else that she didn't need and that would burn and that she'd managed to scrounge up somewhere. Now I understood what had happened to the doors on the kitchen cupboard. I picked up some scraps and handed them to her.

She smiled as she said, "Scrap scrounging day tomorrow. We're runnin' low. Rick's gonna help out. There's a scrapyard a few kilometres down the road where people ditch stuff. IGA dumpster's on the way too. You'd be surprised at the delicacies in that thing. One man's trash, another's stash. You in?"

I nodded. Yup, I could get used to this. I was in.

9

I woke up on the sofa in the middle of the night, shivering. The fire had gone out. I'd have to score a blanket somewhere in the morning. The days in September were relatively warm, but the nights were frigid.

Restless with chills and unable to sleep, I grabbed Tig's flashlight and decided to explore the house a little further. I stopped in the kitchen to grab a can of ravioli in the hopes that food fuel would bring my body temperature up. I found the can opener in a drawer, exactly where expected, opened the can and dug in. Cringing a little, I examined my meal in disgust. Cold ravioli was *so* wrong. I'd go for the peanut butter next time. I left the can on the counter and set off on my mission to explore.

Secrets are always hidden in attics, so that's where I headed. Besides, heat rises. It was a win-win. The ladder to the attic was one of those folded drop 'n climb ladders. I pulled on the string, opening the attic hole and the ladder dropped from up top. I climbed up and surfaced into boxes of family secrets booby-trapped with mouse shit and cobwebs. If I could navigate the shit and cobwebs, I'd be rewarded for sure, I told myself.

My old friend, Frankie, crossed my mind. She'd love all this crap, this intrigue. I felt sad for a brief passing moment. I missed Frankie. But she was living in a different world now. She didn't get how fuckin' great she had it and that pissed me off. Maybe we'd be friends again sometime ... but now wasn't our time.

I opened the first box. Cardboard, nothing special, and filled with Christmas trinkets.

Yup, moving on.

The next box was a little more intriguing as it was made of wood and someone had carved "Pete's stuff" on it. A personalized box of memories. Perfect. Let's see what this guy has to share. I smiled with curiosity—the type of smile that is only ever smiled when you are smiling to yourself—like, *'Ha! Found someone's deep dark secret that no one else knows! What a privilege!'* I opened the box feeling excited but was disappointed when I found only children's toys and an old Ouija board.

I sat on the floor and scanned the area with the flashlight. More boxes, in a variety of shapes and sizes, were stacked up along the walls.

The windows rattled and the roof creaked, as the wind hammered against the house and blew through the cracks. I wondered whether there'd be blankets in one of these boxes. The attic didn't seem to be holding onto the rising heat as I'd thought it might—it was just as cold up than down. I decided to open boxes, scan them quickly for blankets, and leave the rummaging until later.

I hit gold in the second to last box—no blankets but filled with clothes. As I started to unpack the clothes, looking for a sweater, I felt something hard wrapped up in between them. I gently unravelled the clothes from the object in the middle and to my surprise found an antique typewriter.

It was an old black one, with "Underwood" printed above the keys. I turned it over to see if there was an issue date on the back and there it was: Underwood 1918. Wow! I momentarily forgot all about how cold I was. Not many people knew it, but I was a real geek when it came to writing. My fingers tingled with excitement as I explored the old typewriter. Besides some worn keys, it appeared to be in quite good shape. I dug around in the box for ink cartridges and found three, along with a roll of ribbon. I could hardly believe my luck. My creative mind tick-tocked and a business idea began to form.

The clothes were old too, mostly dresses from the 1920s or 30s. They were silky, below-the-knee, sleeveless, bag-like style, with sashes that I assumed passed for belts. I sorted through the dresses, trying to find something I could throw over the clothes I wore. I found a couple of lacy shawls and headbands, some bawdy jewellery, but not much that would keep me warm. I grabbed the baggiest dress and threw it on, then I wrapped the shawls around myself and used a headband as a toque. Still cold, I picked up another dress and added it to my upper body layer. If Tig was to venture up into the attic at this moment I thought, she'd think I was a ghost from the past with a confused dress code. I chuckled to myself and turned my attention to the other boxes.

Tools. More toys. Tarot cards. Books—some classics. A bong (because what family doesn't have one of *those* in their attic?). Family albums. Curtains under the albums. I immediately turned one of those into a blanket and breathed a sigh of relief as feeling flowed back into my arms. And more of the typical stuff you'd find in an attic. No paper for the typewriter though.

Warmth felt good. Encased in clothing, I headed back down to the sofa with my curtain to try for some Zs.

,

The following day started in between the weeds on the front balcony.

I found Tig, sitting with her back against the wall in a ray of sunshine, that had somehow found its way through the jungle and onto the balcony. She was wearing a pink panther t-shirt, smiling, eyes shut, ginger curls even wilder than the day before, basking in the little bit of sun—a ginger-coloured house cat that has found the perfect warm spot. An open jar of peanut butter and a box of crackers lay beside her.

Tig must've sensed my presence because she said, without opening her eyes, "Sorry man, no coffee ... but feel free to grab some food."

I sat down, propping myself against the wall next to Tig. "Eh, have you been in the attic?"

Tig opened her eyes now and took me in. "Yuck. No way. Attics creep me out. All sorts of weird shit goes on in attics. You didn't go up there did you?" She paused and gawked, dumbfounded. "In the middle of the night?! Holy fuck!"

I nodded, "Yeah, well, I couldn't sleep, so ..."

Tig seemed wary but nonetheless curious, "That where you found the curtain?"

I nodded again, "Yup, and there's all sorts of cool stuff up there. I think we could, y' know, create something with some of it. Like, to make some cash."

Tig looked skeptical, and she hesitated for a moment before going on, "What d'ya have in mind?"

I smiled, "I'll show you after breakfast." I picked up the jar of peanut butter.

Being with Tig in this house with these cool treasures and possibilities had revived my appetite. The peanut butter tasted deliciously like freedom. Only a couple of days ago it would've had repression ingrained in it. I savoured the taste of freedom and smiled again.

9

We sat in the attic with my survival plan items on the floor between us. The old typewriter, 1920s dresses and jewellery, a box of tea light candles, some old whisky glasses, a Ouija board, some ancient black and white photos of celebrities wearing similar dresses, some curtains made of yellowing silk and lace, and well, of course, the bong.

When I was finished describing my idea, Tig studied the items, then beamed at me. She said with a little crooked smile, "Y' know ... I have some ideas too. I think we could make this work."

We put our heads together and hatched a business plan.

CHAPTER EIGHT

Slumdoggin' it

Late September

The scrapyard was full of treasures.

So far, we'd scored a king-sized bed (mattress, box spring, and frame), an oil lamp, kitchen table, three wooden school chairs, an old mop, some rags, and a witch's broom. We'd also gathered scraps to burn, which was what we had originally come for. Rick left us at the lot with our pile of treasure while he went off to borrow a trailer from a friend.

Tig and I lay on the bed under a cloudless sky, listening to the birds and enjoying the warmth that only an autumn day can give—crisp, fresh, yet just warm enough—t-shirt and jeans kind of weather. Or, Bethel shirt and sweatpants in my case.

Tig handed me one of the expired *Oh, Henry!* bars that we'd scrounged from the IGA dumpster. "Dumpsters are so underrated." She smiled.

Looking up at the pale blue sky, I commented, "Jeez, I feel like a bum. The first thing I'm gonna buy with the cash we make are a pair of fuckin' Levis."

Tig turned her head towards me and chortled, "Deary, we *are* bums. Bums with treasure, a plan, and the whole slumdog world at our fingertips!" And she exploded with laughter.

Tig was an amazingly positive person for someone who'd had to escape from her dad in the middle of the night, with no plans to return, at the age of 15. My parents were arrogant dicks, but I knew that in the end I could count on them for help if needed. And "positive" was definitely not how *I* felt. But being around Tig somehow made me ... almost positive.

I considered our business plan. "Eh, I was thinking. For our plan to work, we're gonna need some help. I know this guy who goes to that private boy's school ... uh ... St-Andrew's ... not far from here. I think he'd help us recruit some guys, y' know, the safe kind."

I thought about my conflict with Gabe. We hadn't spoken since he'd walked away at the canal that day. Conflict wasn't my thing, but I'd have to figure it out. Although Gabe was only a few months younger than I, he acted like an annoying little brother at times. But he was still the closest friend I had, and I missed him. And I guess I would've been pissed too, you know, if the tables were turned. I hoped Jack hadn't been too hard on him.

"Gabe's school is full of rich D&D nerds with tonnes of lunch money. They're the kind of kids who are always looking for things to do to make life more interesting.

And when they're not playing D&D, their heads are full of Playboy crap. They'd be totally into it."

Tig and I glanced at each other and I winked. "It'll be like baiting chipmunks with a picnic—even with doubt in their minds, they won't be able to resist."

Gabe's description of his classmates made me think of slightly older versions of the boys that Frankie and I had pranked in grade 8. My plan this time around was even better. I smiled smugly with the thought. Boys were so damn easy to predict. Dangle something sexy in front of them, and they'd come running without question.

The rickety-rickety sound of an aging car hauling a creaky trailer approached. Rick turned the corner and pulled up alongside us, towing a trailer twice the length of his poor enfeebled bug.

Rick turned the key and the bug gave a surrendering grunt as the engine quit.

I gawked at the scene. Maybe we'd be pulling the trailer home by hand.

"Holy shit, Tig! Are we seriously gonna load that thing?" I laughed.

"Should've seen our load last week. It was epic, eh! Piled twice as high as the bug. We looked like a dung beetle pulling a load of shit!" Tig roared with laughter.

Rick stepped out of the car and chimed in, "Only thing that'll get this bug down is lack of happy vibes, man. Well, that and lack of pot smoke. It runs on fumes, eh." He studied our pile, "Think ya' might have to leave the bed frame though."

We laughed, then threw all the smaller items along with the chairs into the trailer first. The box spring and mattress went on top.

Rick scratched his chin, as he considered the load. "Yup, bed frame'll be fine. Heave it up, girls!"

The last thing up was the table. We threw it on upside down, then secured our load with old rope.

We all piled into the car, IGA dumpster loot squeezed in between us. Rick turned the key in the ignition and the bug sputtered back to life. He pressed on the gas and we didn't move. He pressed a little harder. The wheels skidded as the little car tried its damndest to pull the weight behind. The bug finally lurched forward, winning the battle, and we were on our way.

We headed back to the soon-to-be less creepy house ... well, depending on one's perspective.

᠑

Rick left us with dish soap and vinegar, and we spent the next few days scrubbing the floors, furniture, and windows. The water was a bit rust-tinged but was running. As long as we didn't scrub anything white, it would do. I'd wondered about drinking it. Tig swore she'd been drinking it boiled, since she'd moved in a couple of months ago, and *she* wasn't sick.

By the time Friday rolled around, we had the place looking, if not exactly fit for an average middle-class family, at least livable ... as long as you didn't mind wind blowing through the cracks and mould slowly devouring the window frames.

Along with a cozy living room, we now had a comfortably usable bedroom and kitchen. The rooms no longer had peeling wallpaper, as we'd pulled it off and smoothed the rough edges with some sandpaper found in the attic. The thick layer of grime was gone from the floors, the dust and spider webs were no more, and we'd scrubbed the mould into submission. We'd furnished the place with stuff that wasn't badly broken, and everything that was badly broken we'd broken up some more and turned into firewood.

I was starting to feel at home. Nothing like the home I shared with my parents. This place felt more like a real home. You know, one that you build with love. For the first time in a long time, happiness bubbled up inside me and I became tentatively positive.

As Tig and I sat at our refurbished, or at least clean, kitchen table on our 'new' and hilariously too-low-for-the table school chairs, we admired our work and fished out the baggy of magic mushrooms that Rick had given us. The ideal housewarming gift for this ol' place.

I looked at Tig who was sitting at the other side of the table and couldn't help but laugh. My chin barely cleared the table, and I peered across it like a little kid.

"Eh man, this stuff make you grow?" I put a pinch of shrooms in my mouth. "Feeling smurfy."

Tig smiled, "I dunno, eh? Maybe. But smurfs are cool, man. I could be a smurf. Imagine, spending life just skipping along, singin' n' dancin'. We already live in a home made of mushrooms. Got that part covered!" She laughed.

Resting my chin on the table like a two-year-old, I smiled at her, "Weirdo."

She smiled back, "It's Smurfette to you. Now pass the baggy, Gargamel."

,

The next day I leant against the phone booth next to Tig as she dialed the number for Charles A. Group Home. Dave would've recognized my voice, so she was doing the honours. When Tig had Gabe on the line, she passed the receiver to me.

"Hi ... Gabe? It's me. Don't hang up! Please, hear me out, OK?" There was silence on the other end, so I prompted him again, "Gabe?"

"What do you want, Sam? Because that's what you're calling for, right? Because you *want* something? If you cared, you'd have called already. So, get to the point. What do you want?" Gabe sounded disappointed and angry, but mostly hurt. At times like these, he reminded me of Frankie.

"I miss you, Gabe ... I'm on the run, and I want to talk, that's all. I'm sorry, Gabe. I don't think you're annoying, or gay, that's just journal bullshit. I write all sorts of things when I'm mad. And I wasn't even mad at you. Just everything else and nothing really. I dunno why I get angry, I just do, and I guess I'm a dick when I'm mad. I'm truly sorry, Gabe."

I did mean it—the apology for being a dick part—but I also did want something from him. Argh, conflict really *really* was *not* my thing.

Gabe sighed, "Fine. I can meet you after school tomorrow. Where d'ya wanna meet?"

Sure that I could bring him around, that he'd get over it and forgive me, I told him to meet me at the bus stop on the corner of Lunder Street and Elm Avenue, the cross street closest to the house.

CHAPTER NINE

Gabe

Late September

I lay on my bed looking up at the stars Sam and I had stuck to the ceiling.

Most of the stars in her room remained there, but the room wasn't hers anymore. Some rough chick from Manny Cottage had moved in. She never smiled. I wondered if it was because she couldn't or whether she was afraid it'd make her human. Likely the latter. Manny Cottage kids were screwed up like that.

My anger at Sam persisted, but I also felt bad for her. I don't think I'd have lasted a week with all those fuckups. Sam was made of some tough shit—a scrawny little thing, but damn fierce. That one could survive anything.

The floor creaked and my door swung open. Nadia interrupted my thoughts.

"Eh, Gabe. Your nose looks better." She gave me a crooked smile, the one in between empathy and laughter.

I touched the bridge of my nose, where Jack had broken it when he floored me. The bandage had fallen off in the shower. Guess I deserved it for kissing his girl? But, honestly, he shouldn't have treated me like a sleazy gay perv. And, Nadia and Jack had only been a thing for like three days. Some guys were *so* insecure.

I looked at Nadia, "What's with that fuck, anyway? He totally freaked me out when he pinned you to the wall. Was he like dropped from a balcony as a baby or something?"

Nadia raised her hand towards the bruise on her neck, then caught herself and scratched her shoulder instead. "I dunno. Jack's Jack, I guess. Super sweet, until he loses it. Then he's a crazy fuck." She shrugged as if to say *'oh well, what's done is done.'*

"I for one am glad he's in Manny Cottage. He's a fuckin' asshole. A charismatic and interesting asshole, but nonetheless an asshole. You can do better, way better." I glanced at her and clarified, "Uh ... the kiss, it was to piss him off. Y' know, for him being a fuck. Just to be clear and all."

Nadia smiled, "Yeah, of course it was." She paused and studied me thoughtfully for a moment. "Eh, I'm being transferred to NDG Group Home. Leaving in a couple of days. Want to go bum around the canal later?"

I nodded, "Yeah, sure. Got anything to smoke?"

Nadia smiled and nodded, then she left me to my thoughts.

Why would Sam write that fuckin' shit in her journal? It pissed me off. Not because she was right or wrong, but because she thought it and then put it in writing. What a jerk! She knew my story. I showed her the letter I found in my parents' stuff. My mom's announcement about our future, her plans on leaving my dad. She'd left a note. And a few days later they crashed and died. Probably because they were arguing. Probably because she'd told him who she was leaving him for. The letter was super blunt too.

Hey Evan,

Me and Bella have hooked up. Been together for a while. Me and you were never really a thing anyhow. You'd be better off with Sal or Jan or someone like that. Best if Gabe stays with you. Sorry about the mess. In a rush. Off to Toronto— took the figure skating job. I'll be back in a few days to pick up the rest and explain things to Gabe.

See you,

Laura

I'd heard them arguing. She said she'd been gay since forever, that she never loved him, and she was tired of pretending for the sake of others. She left us for my nanny, or "nounou" as Bella called herself in French. They'd been in a relationship for quite some time.

There'd been signs, I guess. Like all the extra cheek kissing. Mom had never much participated in the French salute before Nounou Bella came along. And then there was the time they took a bath together to 'save on hot water.' Oh yeah, and when they'd wandered away from me at the Old Port, absorbed in each other, leaving me to watch the fireworks with some old fart and his sausage dog (OK, OK, the guy was a neighbour, but not one *I'd* choose to hang with). Whatever. I truly didn't care anymore—I mean, about the gay part. It was the *jerk* part of Mom that I resented. Jerks can apparently be gay too.

The accident left me completely alone. Just me and an inheritance that I didn't understand. Neither of my parents had family. The three of us—*we* were our only *family*. My anger at my mom sweltered for another moment and subsided again. Someone along the line had left my mom money though, and that's what had got me into an ivy league private school. Well, at least I had *that*. Thanks, Mom.

I think I may be gay. A little anyway. But I'm not a fuckin' perv. And I'm not going to fuck anyone's life up because of it. After the incident with Sam's journal, Nadia told me her uncle's a transqueen. She thinks he's super cool and said she'd be OK with me being gay.

I yelled at her to get out of my room and slammed the door after her. Truthfully though, what is the fucking big deal? Boys, girls, they're all hot in my opinion. Why are straights so fuckin' narrow-minded?! Bunch of fuckin' bigots. Rainbow people rock (exception: jerks).

I rolled over onto my side and felt under my mattress for my forbidden magazines. These were a whole hell of a lot riskier than Sam's journal. I wished for locks on our doors.

I pulled out the *Tarzan Sex Fantasy* issue of Hustle Me. What was great about Hustle Me magazine was that the men were just as hot as the women. I imagined myself slipping between their bodies, Jane and her big greased-up boobs under me, Tarzan on top. I mean, who wouldn't want both? Heterosexuality's so fucked up!

But that was *my* secret. Sam had some apologizing to do. I'd been fortunate. The only one who'd been a dumb fuck about it, besides Gini, was Jack. Sam was lucky I loved her.

I examined the Tarzan & Jane picture and wondered if Nadia might be into it. Maybe her uncle knew a guy.

Dave knocked on my door. "Gabe? You in?"

I jumped and the issue of Hustle Me flew to the floor.

"Hold on! Changing!"

I grabbed the magazine off the floor and shoved it back under my mattress. I lay back on my bed, hands tucked behind my head. Just lying around, nothing to hide.

"'Kay ... I'm decent!"

Dave entered. He looked at me curiously. I was still wearing the same unwashed clothes and obviously hadn't changed.

"Uh ... I wanted to talk with you about Sam." Dave hesitated for a moment, studying me. "You guys are close. I'm sure you're aware she's on the run."

I looked at Dave blankly. His sixth sense freaked me out. I simply couldn't hide anything from him. He could evidently read my mind from his office, because we hadn't talked since Sam had called, yet somehow *he knew*.

"She is?" Best to keep answers short and flat.

Dave smiled, knowingly. "Sam's in some trouble, Gabe. But it's nothing that can't be turned around. Please understand, *I'm on your side*. You can talk to me. If anything comes up, if you get worried about *anything*, you can come to me. I'm here for you and I'm here for Sam. OK?"

"Sure." Short, flat. Innocent smile.

Dave considered saying more but had second thoughts. He smiled again, nodded, turned and left.

Every one of us in Charles A. understood how lucky we were to have Dave. We'd all had our experiences with bad staff. Dave cared for us in ways that few had. Dave fought for us. If Sam was in danger and I needed to tell someone, that someone would absolutely be Dave. In the meantime, I'd have to work harder on keeping his sixth sense at bay.

CHAPTER TEN

Sex Sells

Late September — Sam

Gabe appeared thoughtful, sitting alone at the bus stop, as I walked up and broke the spell. Thoughtful or maybe angry ... I couldn't quite tell. He regarded me, silently. I sat down next to him.

"Eh, Gabe."

He glanced at me, "You're a jerk, you know that, eh?"

I bit my lip. "Yup, so I'm told."

Gabe continued, "Fuckin' *'gaylord'*? Fuck you, Sam. And you didn't even call me."

I shrugged, "You're right, Gabe. I'm an ass. I wanted to call, I really did."

He gave me a hard look, "Well then, why didn't you? I was fuckin' worried. Fuck you, Sam!" Gabe was on the verge of tears, the annoyed frustrated kind.

I decided to shift from my normal tactic—of sprinting from the scene in times of tense emotion—and try something more progressive. I wrapped my arms around him and squeezed until he stopped swearing and hugged me back. I really did miss Gabe.

As we approached the house, he turned to me and stated for the record, "I'm still angry at you, y' know."

I nodded and showed him the way through the brush to the front door.

"Holy fuck, there's a house in the middle of it! This is where you've been? Around the corner from my school for the past two weeks. You are in so much trouble for not getting in touch sooner." He said, half joking.

I knocked the secret knock and waited for Tig to answer. We never walked in unannounced on each other because that's what intruders would do. That's how we identified friends versus intruders. If the door opened without a knock, we'd be out the back in a flash. At least, that was our contingency plan. Tig opened the door, and we followed her in towards the living room.

Tig drew aside the moth-eaten silk curtain that we'd hung in the doorway to the living room, and we entered.

Gabe's jaw dropped, but I could see a smile working its way into his expression. "Fuck me! So ... what's the plan ... exorcisms?"

We'd rearranged the furniture so that the sofa was against the far wall and the cattle scale was in the middle of the room. There were well-worn sitting cushions on either side of the scale. The Ouija board, oil lamp, and bong were sitting on top. And we'd placed numerous tea light candles in old Schwartz's mustard glasses around the room. The glasses were painted with images of hearts, diamonds, spades, and clubs, and reminded me of the ones my mom reserved for child's play.

I laughed at Gabe's comment, "Yeah, we thought we'd exorcise the arrogant crap out of your classmates."

Gabe grinned as if considering the feasibility of such a plan, "Well then, anything I can do to help?"

I smiled, "Yup, there sure is."

,

Gabe brought us a stack of paper for the typewriter, along with some photocopied pictures of 1920s celebrities the next day, and we got to work.

First, we needed to make profiles. Our survival plan was simple: sex sells. And we were going to sell sex with famous ghosts, or at least the *illusion* of sex[6]. Our timing would be perfect, as Halloween was right around the corner. October would be our business blast-off month.

After dotting the ribbon with ink, I loaded the typewriter and crossed my fingers that the ink would show through. I typed in the name of our first ghostly lady of the night, "Marion Davies." The print was faded and uneven, but still legible. Excellent. I smiled, "So, Marion, what shall we say about you?" I began to type as the wheels in my imagination turned.

Marion Davies

Born Marion Cecelia Douras, in New York on January 23rd, 1897.

Hollywood Actress (starred in 48 films)

Nickname: Queen of the Screen

Mistress to William Randolph Hearst

Named one of the top six most beautiful women in the movies in 1930.

Most appealing part of body: her curves - from her tits to her hips, she's everyone's wet dream.

Hair & Eyes: Blond, with dreamy blue eyes.

Hobbies: singing & dancing

Quote: "I did a lot of pictures. I worked harder than I thought I did, but it was a very happy experience. The parties, the dinners, not much rest. But sleep wasn't important. It was one big merry-go-round."[7]

When I was done with Marion, I passed her profile page to Tig, and she glued a black and white photo to the top, next to Marion's name. It was the famous photo of Marion in her white chiffon dress and fur boa, reclined on an antique sofa and looking into the camera seductively—as if she had some hidden magic to offer her admirers. I moved on to the other show biz beauties we were sure would knock the socks off private school twits: Greta Garbo, Norma Shearer, Alice White, Dolores del Rio, Lillian Gish, and just for the sake of *well of course*, Marilyn Monroe.

When we'd finished the profiles, we worked on the invitations.

Dear _____,

You have been specially selected to attend a sensual séance with beautiful ghosts from times long past. The ghosts have been lonely for so long and are aching to show off their wares to sexy boys such as yourself.

Curious? Fill out the form and choose your favorite ghost, deliver it to Gabe, and bring $15 on the day.

Yours truly,
The Ghost Keeper

We handed the ghost descriptions to Gabe, along with five invitations to participate. Gabe would slip the invitations into a select group of boys' lockers. If they took the bait, which we had no doubt they would, they'd need to complete the form that accompanied the invitation and give it to Gabe, who'd deliver it to us. Then we'd set a date. And we'd put our game into play.

Gabe scratched his head, thinking. "I dunno. D'ya think this is a good idea? I mean, what if one of the guys gets all weird and backs out and reports me to the principal or something? I'm pretty sure this isn't legal, eh?"

I shot Gabe a dramatic Marilyn Monroe eyeroll, then puckered my lips and blew him a kiss. "You worry too much, dear."

"I'm serious, Sam."

I sighed, "Gabe, man, the guys'll also be breaking the law. And no way they're gonna risk ratting their friends out. They're not gonna say anything. Worst case, they split without paying up. That's why we've gotta get 'em to pay in advance."

Tig smiled and put her hand reassuringly on Gabe's arm. "We're just having some Halloween fun, eh? It's not like we're scamming or anything. It's a transaction, y' know. We all get something we want out of it."

Tig and I shared mischievous glances. Gabe had his reservations, but I could tell he was also intrigued in a naughty lets-fuck-with-'em kind of way. Soon we'd be rolling in these rich boys' fantasies and the dough they bear. It was a flawless scheme.

Gabe groaned. "Fine. But if things start to go sideways, I'm yelling fire, and we're all getting the hell out of here *fast*. Got it?"

Tig jumped to her feet, "Right out the back into the weeds, babe! Plan finalized. Who wants lunch?"

"Seriously? It's like 5:30. I gotta get home for supper." Gabe got up, grabbed his bag and swung it over one shoulder.

Tig seemed thoughtful, "Eh, Gabe? Can you bring a tomato with you? And, maybe some ham or salami or something?"

"Sure thing. I'll see what I can get a hold of." Then he was off.

"Tomato and ham?" I asked Tig, curiously.

"Makes for better grilled cheese."

During our last IGA dumpster dive, we'd scored stale bread, cheddar cheese that had gone mouldy around the edges, a block of butter in similar condition, a busted package of dried oregano, and a box of overripe apples. The time before, we'd got expired yogourt, instant coffee and Nestle Quik. That, together with what Rick had brought us, made for some interesting meals that even I was eating.

Nonetheless, dumpster-diving wasn't as lucrative as we'd hoped, and food was running out.

Tig cut the mould off the cheese and butter. She laid a slice of bread on a plate and added cheese to it. Then she sliced up some apple and added that too.

She noticed my confused expression. "Apple and cheese works, right? Why not grilled?"

Tig sprinkled the apples with oregano, then put a bit more cheese on top before covering it all with a second piece of bread. I decided, yeah why not, and did the same. Then we buttered both sides and grilled them on a pan on top of the wood stove.

Common sense told me none of this would last, but for the moment, this home of ours sure was sweet—even with the mould.

CHAPTER ELEVEN

Rich Boy Fantasies

Early October

Our first séance didn't quite go as planned, and the hiccups made it even better. Rich private school boys can always be counted on to produce a little idiocy when the moment's ripe for it.

Wyatt, a blond-haired 15-year old on the chubby end of the spectrum, knocked at 3:30 PM sharp and I welcomed him into our coven in the living room.

We'd hung heavy curtains in the windows and drawn them shut. The place would've been completely dark if it weren't for all the little candles scattered throughout the room. Rick had brought over some incense and this we used mainly to create a smoky effect that worked wonders for the spooky atmosphere we'd been trying to generate. The bong we'd left on the table, next to the Ouija board. It was loaded with a mix of hash and magic mushroom that Rick had also provided us with.

We made a business deal with Rick—we'd pay him a bit extra for the hash and shrooms if he supplied us with them as needed. As he had a regular dealer that he frequented anyway, he was only too happy to oblige. We also cut Gabe in on our business, giving him 10% for his help in recruiting clients.

On his form, Wyatt had described himself as tough, with Viking blood, Captain of the chess team, D&D Dungeon Master, and basically a ladies' man. The boys had clearly sent their best to scope the place out. He chose Norma Shearer as his ghost concubine, and I'd dressed the part accordingly.

The plan was for Tig and I to take turns, each focusing on one customer, and I'd be first up.

In Norma Shearer style, I wore dumpster-dive red lipstick, a light rub of blush (multi-purposed lipstick), and smoky eye shadow (ash from the wood oven). I had my hair swept back into a bun at the back with a hairpiece made of Autumn wildflowers (or weeds, depending on your perspective). I'd covered the rest of my outfit with a large shawl, for the sake of our agenda. Under the shawl I wore one of the dresses we'd found in the attic—whitish rayon with silver vines and flowers beaded into a low-dip bust, and lace woven into the skirt. If it weren't for the moth holes and yellowing rims, it would've been a keeper. As it was, it worked well for a long dead concubine, especially in candlelight.

"Eh, Sweetie," I put on my sexy voice, "you got something for me before we start?"

"Oh, yeah!" He took a purse out of his pocket and emptied $15 in small bills and coins on the cattle scale that was now our spirit quest table. "Uh, sorry … uh, about the change and stuff."

I dismissed his concern with a flick of my hand and moved the little pile of cash from our spirit quest table to a shelf on the wall.

Wyatt gawked at me. I motioned for him to sit on the cushion at one side of the table. I already had him hooked and I smiled inwardly. He looked at the Ouija board with negligible skepticism, but sat down as I'd instructed him, without hesitation.

The smoke from the incense wafted up from the corners of the room, giving it a spiritual Halloweeny feeling.

I lit the bong and sucked on the pipe, breathing in and then out its drug-enhanced smoke. I wanted Wyatt to trust me. I passed him the pipe and told him he needed to take two long drags, holding in each one for 7 seconds. Not sure why I chose 7—just liked the number, I guess.

Wyatt took the bong and did what he was told. He coughed and sputtered, but managed a few seconds.

I sat across the table from Wyatt, and we began our journey into the realm of concubine ghosts from times long past.

I gestured for him to put his hands on the table, and I put mine on top of his. "Wyatt Samuel Jensen II, you have signed a contract agreeing that what happens in this room today stays in this room. If anything that you experience today leaves the confines of this room, I can't guarantee your safety from the vengeance of ghosts. Understand?"

Wyatt wasn't sure whether to smile or not, as I might not be joking, so he just nodded, his eyes glued to mine as he tried not to stare at the gap in my shawl that revealed a sensuous amount of skin between my neck and my breasts. The *magic gap*, with treasures hidden beneath, was very much a part of the plan. Keep 'em focused on sex, and they'll gladly be led blindly along any path you lay in front of them. 15-year-old boys were perfect customers.

"That's a good boy, Wyatt." I said in a tone dripping with a seductive *'I may show you mine if you behave'*. Wyatt's eyes briefly fell towards my breasts, but then he caught himself and regained control.

I released his hands.

"So, you've chosen the concubine ghost of Norma Shearer. A boy with taste, I see. Ghosts are moody creatures and Norma's no exception. Our first step is to work on attracting *her* to you. And to do that, we've gotta tell her a story, *your* story, but in fantasy form. She'll only make an appearance if you turn her on, get it? If you *arouse* her. You've gotta be *more* than her knight in shining armour ... you've gotta make *her* want to cum all over you before *you* cum all over her."

Wyatt's eyes grew wide. He nodded vigorously.

Tig had thought that would be too straightforward and that we should take a slower approach, but I disagreed. The only way this was going to work was if we hooked the guy within the first few minutes.

My first time on the run from my parents at the age of fourteen, I'd had to provide some *favours* for the guy who was letting me crash at his place. Sexual taboos hadn't fazed me much since. I also didn't have much respect for stupid boys with sex-crazed brains. To tell you the truth, I was great at *acting* sexy, but deep within me I thought of sex the same way I thought of bullying—it's there for the sake of boys wanting to be 'king of the castle', a castle that's been constructed with selfishness and greed at the expense of girls. I had no qualms about fucking with this boy's head because that's exactly what he'd come here for.

Still holding Wyatt's hands in my own, I squeezed gently and continued, "Wyatt, let us begin."

I began the story-telling segment of our séance

"Norma Shearer! Norma Shearer! This one's for you, pay attention Norma! You have a gentleman caller, and he's aching to please you. Are you there, Norma? His story goes back to the age of the Vikings, when they were pillaging England, stealing beautiful women and turning them into concubines. His ancestors are Viking kings and choose only the best of the best. You have been chosen because you are the best and this Viking I have in front of me would like to be your sex slave." I took a long drag off the bong and passed it to Wyatt.

Wyatt ogled me nervously. I invited him to take a drag, and he did so. Then he returned to ogling me.

I mouthed the words, "She's waiting for you to seduce her." I signalled with my hands for him to begin speaking.

"Oh, ah, oh. Hi, uh, Norma ..."

I whispered, "How strong are you?"

"Oh, yeah, I'm pretty strong. Captain of the chess team. And, uh, related to Thor ... well kinda."

I swallowed hard to keep myself from laughing.

Quietly guiding Wyatt, I added, "Good! What about your, *you know*—how *big* are you?"

"Oh, wow ... yeah, gorilla-size at least." Wyatt blushed.

I motioned for him to take another drag off the bong.

After he'd done so, I whispered, "What can you offer Norma?"

Wyatt pondered my question. He was less nervous. I could tell the pot mix was having an effect.

I stuck my tongue out seductively.

"Uh ... a tongue? Uh, yeah! I want to lick you all over, Norma! You're so hot and sexy and I bet super tasty too." Wyatt giggled. His buzz had definitely kicked in.

I took over, "Oh Norma, ghost of seductresses long passed, will you accept our offering of Wyatt the Viking, with his mighty dick, the size of a gorilla's? Will you let him please you with his tongue? He'd start with your porcelain neck, kissing you under the ear, and then down over your collarbone and your chest, to your breasts. He'd flick your nipples with his tongue and suck them until they're hard, then he'd kiss his way down, down, and down, around your belly-button, and further and further down until ... Well, Norma, you'll have to show yourself to find out more."

Wyatt's mouth hung partially open as he imagined licking Norma's curves. He moved his hands over his crotch to hide the lump that had formed.

I smiled lustfully and then finished my prompt. "Are you there, Norma?"

Tig rattled the windows in the kitchen, and Wyatt jumped despite his best efforts to stay obediently still.

"Looks like we might have company." I placed my hands on the Ouija board. "Norma has signalled that she would like more information from you. We can use the Ouija board to communicate with her."

Placing my fingers on the heart-shaped planchette, I signalled for Wyatt to do the same. He complied and again I smiled inwardly. What an easy catch.

I asked, "Are you there, Norma?" The planchette began to move, with my help of course, towards the top of the board and stopped on "Yes".

Wyatt's eyes were as big as a horny dragonfly's, filled with instinctive lust.

"Thank you, Norma. We are glad to have you with us. What is it that you would like to know about the Viking I have here waiting to please you?"

The planchette began to move again and spelled out the words "V-I-K-I-N-G W-Y-A-T-T D-O Y-O-U E-A-T P-U-S-S-Y?"

Wyatt gaped at me, nodding without speaking.

I whispered across the table, "Say it, Wyatt. You need to tell her yourself."

He paused. I offered him the bong. He grabbed it quickly, took a long drag, and held the smoke in for as long as he could.

Wyatt coughed as he exhaled. Then he glanced around the room as if checking for eaves-dropping friends, "Yes, yes Norma! I like to eat pussies. I'll do anything! Where are you?"

I regarded Wyatt with a flirty smile, and said softly, "Patience, patience. Ask her something. She needs to chat a bit before sex, sweetie."

Wyatt stammered, "What do I ask?"

I shook my head as if he was hopeless and asked a question for him, "Norma, your strong Viking would like to know if you'll eat his dick too."

Even with all the incense smoke and bad light, I could see Wyatt blush. I guessed that was the downside of being so pale—everyone could always tell when you were even the littlest bit embarrassed.

The planchette moved and Wyatt's eyes grew wider for each letter it stopped on: "I L-I-K-E B-I-G D-I-C-K-S I-S Y-O-U-R-S B-I-G?"

This time Wyatt blurted loudly "Yes!"

I released the planchette and said, "OK Wyatt, Norma has signalled her approval of you and wants to meet you. This brings us to our next step. We need some magic to happen in order for her to be able to cross over from the spiritual realm to the realm of the living. Are you ready for magic, Wyatt?"

Wyatt nodded enthusiastically and put his hands down under the table. I wondered if he was trying to calm his hidden part.

We tried to communicate with Norma again. "Are you in the room with us, Norma?"

The answer was "No."

I told Wyatt to close his eyes and concentrate really hard on Norma. As Wyatt complied, I let my shawl drop to the floor, revealing my 'Norma Shearer' dress.

Wyatt opened his eyes and swayed as his vision refocused. He was now quite high. His facial expression was stuck in horny '*I want to believe*' awe.

He gaped at me. "Norma? Norma, you're here. In the room with ... me." His stare turned hungry.

I put on my sexiest voice and replied with my best 1920s movie star accent, "Here for *you* Wyatt. Just me and my pussy and your big delicious dick."

Wyatt tried to get up but was too stoned for such a keen endeavour and stayed on his rear. "Norma? Is that really you? You look ..."

I cut him off, "Don't be silly now, Wyatt. I needed a body to possess, as I no longer have one of my own. It's me, but this is the vessel I'm using to speak with you. That OK with you, sugar?"

I strode around the table to where Wyatt sat hopelessly glued to his cushion, watching the events unfold and control him. I knelt down on all fours, revealing my cleavage, the top of my dress barely hiding my nipples.

Wyatt sat frozen with a lump in his pants that just kept growing. I looked at the lump and he followed my gaze. Suddenly the bulge became a wet blotch. Wyatt's orgasm sigh was a mix of pleasure, surprise, and fear. He jumped up and ran out, letting the front door slam behind him.

I sat back on the floor and held my mouth, keeping my shocked laughter locked up for a few more seconds.

Tig barged into the room and said, "Oh my god, what happened? You light his ass on fire or somethin'?"

That's when I burst. I fell back onto the floor, cracking up so hard that I couldn't form words to tell Tig what had gone on.

Tig started to giggle, "Shit, Sam. You horrible diva!"

I finally calmed down enough to describe what had happened. And what had happened was that I hadn't even had to complete the most tasteless part of our plan—he'd done it for me.

I said, "Holy shit, Tig, I didn't even have to touch him!" I started laughing again as his facial expression tickled my memory. Our intention had been to talk dirty in his ear, while rubbing him off over his pants, but I'd got away with only the suggestion of 'dirty'.

Tig smiled. "Eh man, this guy is like the chief nerd in Gabe's class. I bet his friends are even easier."

9

Super nerd #2 walked in, led by Tig.

Dirk's choice had been Greta Garbo and with her fair hair and complexion, Tig was far more Greta than I was. The kid was tall and skinny with an acne challenge going on.

I was doing a lot of inward giggling today and I let another one slip, putting my hand over my mouth to muffle myself. If I had a witch's wand, I'd turn into a fly or black cat or even a cockroach, and scurry in undetected to watch the fun. I held myself in check and retreated into the kitchen quietly, so I could step on the loose floorboard and jiggle the window on cue.

Leaning against the sink, I listened in on them.

Tig went through the same process as I had with Wyatt— cash, storytelling, rattling window and creaky floorboard,

Ouija board, bong, and the rest. But she'd almost been stumped at the bong part.

"I don't know about this. Are there *drugs* in it?" Dirk drew out the word *drugs* as if he was trying to stretch the thought in his mind.

His question threw Tig off. She replied sweetly in her best southern drawl (just because she liked the accent so much), "'Course there is, baby. Bit o' magic dust has never done no one no harm. We are tryin' to communicate with a ghost, bless your horny little heart. It requires magic."

I heard rustling and guessed that Tig had leaned over the table in an attempt to encourage him to take a drag. "Oh my, oops!" She chortled flirtatiously, "How *did* that one escape ma' booby trap? Just popped out, as if it couldn't even resist ya'! Ma' two melons in there, they just as happy to see ya' as a puppy with two peckers!"

There was more rustling, "Three long puffs, *that's it* sexy—hold for 7 seconds, no less, ya' hear?" Tig waited for Skeptic Dirk to become sufficiently stoned before she began the story-telling.

Mr. Sexy could obviously not handle the suggestion of sex either, and he was soon out the door in the same fashion as the first tough guy.

We spent that evening rolling with laughter in front of the wood stove and getting high on what was left in the bong. Our business adventure had gotten off to a great start.

We'd hit the bored-rich-boy jackpot.

Halloween night, we thought, would be our crowning glory. But our ultimate finale would not go as planned.

CHAPTER TWELVE

Love, Lust and in between

Late October

Gabe sat on the kitchen counter holding his share of the profits. "Jeez, this is only two weeks worth! You think we can keep this going after Halloween? Probably have to shake it up a bit, make some changes ..." We'd made $525. He considered his share thoughtfully. "Maybe we'll have to start targeting the rugby jocks too ..." The cogs in Gabe's marketing mind turned.

I thought about his suggestion for a moment. "I dunno about the jocks ... they might want, y' know, more. Jocks are kinda ... well, jocks."

Jocks worried me. Too much muscle, shaky morals, and tons of arrogance ... it was an explosive mix. There'd been plenty of guys like that at the school I'd attended before ending up in the system. Those guys weren't safe.

"Think I'd like to stick to the arrogant nerds with brains, a few morals, and premature ejaculations." I shot Tig a knowing smile.

Tig laughed, "Guess your right ... nothing beats a minuteman."

Gabe smiled at Tig, "Yeah ... I can see your point. So ... what next then?" He added a wink.

Tig blushed and looked oddly wholesome for a moment, like a kid running through a field of wildflowers in an allergy meds commercial.

Gabe motioned for me to pass him the bottle of Baby Duck that we'd been celebrating with and I handed it over.

Tig's eyes twinkled. "Halloween. We've gotta do a group séance. What d'ya think? We can call it ... I dunno ... maybe *All Souls Nympho Night*? Where we summon the souls of long dead nymphomaniacs or something." Tig smiled reflectively, then added, "It would be like a minutemen orgy." She glanced at me, and we both burst out laughing.

Gabe shook his head. "You two are so mean. You do know that, eh?"

Tig and I let out a synchronized howl as we blurted, "Yup!"

Rick arrived as Gabe was getting ready to leave. He put a brown paper lunch bag on the counter. "5 grams of each, like you asked."

Tig jumped up and kissed him on the cheek, "You're the best Rick! Thanks!"

He shook his head, "Whatever. Just keep me out of it. No details, got it?!"

Rick knew we were up to something and that the hash and shrooms weren't all for us, but also suspected correctly that what we were doing was illegal. He'd help us out with supplies, but he didn't want to be further involved. We had an agreement that if we were caught, we'd leave his name completely out of it. In his mind, I assumed he just wanted to help some poor street girls survive. What Rick was doing was shady, but he didn't *feel* like a shady person to me. His heart was in the right place.

As usual, Rick didn't want to hang out. After only five minutes of chit chat, when he was sure we were doing fine, he said his goodbyes and headed out.

As he opened the door he turned towards Gabe, "Eh, I'm driving your way. Want a ride?"

Gabe smiled thankfully and nodded, "That'd be great, I'm runnin' late. Thanks."

Gabe had some special permissions, as he was in the system for reasons other than misbehaving, but that didn't give him free rein. He still suffered the same consequences as did everyone else if he arrived at the group home past his curfew.

When Tig and I were alone again, I looked at her questioningly.

Tig smiled and said, "What?"

I smiled back and took a swig of Baby Duck, then replied, "You know what."

Her smile grew, "No ... What?"

My eyeroll made a corkscrew rollercoaster ride seem tame. "The wink, that's *what!*"

Tig giggled like a kindergarten kid.

"Seriously?! Gabe?"

Controlling her giggles, she replied, "He's cute, OK! And ... y' know, funny, and he makes me ... feel happy, I guess."

This time I stared at her with wide *'really?!'* eyes. "Gabe is ... well ... he can be so immature. I love him to bits, but he's such a kid, eh?!"

I didn't tell Tig this, but wink aside, I truly did think Gabe was more into boys than girls. I wasn't sure what to make of the wink. Maybe I'd been wrong. Whatever his preferences, he was my best friend and I wasn't sure how I felt about him and Tig hitting it off so well. Was that fuckin' jealousy? I recognized the feeling and it pissed me off.

I suppressed my sense of unease and picked up the paper bag that Rick had dropped off. "Wanna smoke?"

❢

A few days later, we were sitting on the living room floor with candles in the form of a five-pointed star, the bong, and some other props between us.

Gabe had been granted a night pass for a 'sleepover at Wyatt's.' He'd volunteered to be our guinea pig as we rehearsed our *All Souls Nympho Night* ritual. We had invited five boys, one for each point of the star, so Gabe was playing five roles. Totally having a blast at his game of pretend, he kept laughing, which was making it all the more challenging to keep our faces straight and stay on task.

"Gabe, man. Focus! We need to practice. This needs to be perfect. Stop laughing!" I shot him a stern glare and wagged my finger like an old schoolmarm.

Tig burst into a fit of giggles. She was doing a hell of a lot of giggling lately—so irritating.

"Tig! Don't encourage him!"

She put her hand to her lips, in an attempt to hide her glee. "It's just that ... you look ... y' know, with that silk dress and the pearls and the feathery boa ... you're kinda out of one of those old silent comic movies, y' know, wagging your finger like that and moving your lips, but no one's hearing you ..."

Tig laughed hysterically at her own joke and Gabe followed suit. They collapsed to the floor, and rolled on the carpet beside each other, holding their stomachs, trying to add to the joke but unable to speak clearly.

I stared at them in disbelief. "OK, that's it. I'm cutting you guys off. No more bong for you!"

If they didn't want to be schoolmarmed then they should both just grow the hell up. Maybe they *were* suited to each other. I gave up and went to grab some munchies.

Take 2.

Gabe and Tig gained control of themselves, and we gave it another try, without the bong.

Tig took on the role of High Priestess this time and I did effects. Our idea was that one of us work the room's atmosphere while the other distracts the boys with charisma and stories of lustful bouncy-boobed lost souls searching for a fuck-partner. As Tig summoned the spirits,

Gabe acted out possible scenarios that might come up among the boys—like dealing with skeptics and requests for specific spirits.

Gabe peered at Tig, one eyebrow raised, impersonating a privileged brat used to getting what he wanted. "What do you mean you can't summon Cleopatra? What's the difference between her and Marilyn Monroe? I paid money and I want Cleopatra!" He said dramatically, putting his hand on his hip like a pissed off middle-aged woman.

Tig tried not to laugh, she pretended to become faint and confused. I pulled on a long string we'd wound around the ceiling fan, making it turn a few times, the wind causing the candle flames to dance.

Tig put her hand up to her forehead and said in a soft voice, "Shh! I sense ... I sense ... she's scared ... worried that our séance has been infiltrated by another spiritual realm that is far stronger, far more ancient. A realm from a distant past ... long before the 20th century. This spirit is so full of want and lust ... she can smell the lust in this room ... oh ... she wants it so badly ... but she's scared. She will only present herself when the room has been secured against souls from other realms. Are you ready boys? Ready to secure this sex space so that our 20th century brothel of only the most beautiful babes can make the journey safely through to our ultimate soul-searching orgy?"

Tig bent forward and gazed longingly at Gabe, lips pouting, boobs almost exploding out from the bosom of her dress, batting long eyelashes, asking for someone to please spank her because she'd been *naughty*. She was an aphrodisiac in human form.

Gabe gaped, dangling on Tig's every word, every movement, like a hypnotized idiot.

I studied him, thinking, confused. Perhaps he wasn't gay.

Gabe found his voice. "Oh. My. God. Girl, you had me spellbound! You're a natural! Those guys are gonna be drooling all over themselves too much for any doubt to get in their way. You're like the Queen of Lustful Souls Looking for a Fuck." He laughed.

OK, I was back to considering the possibility he might be gay after all. Why did it matter to me anyway? I felt annoyed at … myself? Gabe? Or was it Tig? I watched them laugh and joke and poke fun at each other as if they'd known each other forever. *Argh! Whatever!*

"OK! Enough with the crap. I think we're ready. Pass me the damn bong."

Tig and Gabe fell silent. They looked at me, glanced at each other, and then shared a super annoying 'hidden' smile.

Gabe said, "Sam, chill. You know we love you. But you'll just have to accept that sex-craved ghosts from the 20s are the ones who are gonna get screwed this Halloween. Well, them and some horny dweebs from my school. So, you'll just have to get over yourself."

I rolled my eyes for the umpteenth time that day—Gabe and Tig's friendship made my stomach cramp up—and replied, "Go fuck yourself, Gabe."

,

While Gabe and Tig stayed up late giggling on shrooms in front of the fire, I decided to crash. Well, kind of crash. *Be alone* would be a more accurate description.

I lay on our humongous bed under wool curtains and stared at the peeling paint on the ceiling. Someone had once stuck glow-in-the-dark stars up there and there were cleaner spots where they'd been—star fossils, memories of some other world. I wondered whether the kid who used to sleep in this room would've ever thought that someone like me could be doing the star gazing in it one day. Some fucked up homeless chick playing sex games with rich boys' imaginations.

I put my arms over my face. I hated the crying feeling and told myself to stop it, to think of something else. My parents always popped into my head during times like these and there they were—pop!—in my fuckin' head again. I banged my head with my fists, trying to beat them out of there. I felt myself losing control. I needed my control back.

Tig and Gabe came in, lay on either side of me, and began playing with my hair.

"You know you're our true nympho queen, right?" Gabe said and kissed my cheek.

I kept my eyes on the ceiling.

Tig hugged me from the other side. "I'm so happy to have met you two. You're the best, Sam. As for Gabe, he comes in a close second."

I smiled, "OK, fine, whatever. You're both forgiven. Now, where are the shrooms?"

They both laughed and Gabe bounded off the bed and out of the room the way only Gabe can. "Coming!"

Moments like these made everything OK.

CHAPTER THIRTEEN

The Devil is in the House

October 31st

Well before kids began trick or treating, scaring the neighbours with thrown together parts of the spookiest bits of their imagination, pagan religions in Scotland and Ireland practiced an *All Souls Feast for the Dead* called *Samhain* (pronounced Sah-wan). The aim was to worship and appease ancestral spirits, to bring prosperity to the village and fertility to the land. All sorts of myths and legends surround Samhain, from sky gods to harvest spirits to witchery. The myth we'd chosen to focus on was the one where the dead come back to life on October 31st. We'd added a few twists ... but hey, what's a good story without some unique ingredients?

On the last day in October the dead would rise for a huge orgy with the living. But to access this orgy—to attract the dead to specific people—a special ritual had to be held. This ritual had several stages, the first being the sharing of Mother Concubine's blood and flesh, in the form of wine and hash brownies.

Mostly, we were just making it up as we went along, but some of it had a basis in truth. Gabe checked it out: wine and candles were commonly used in Samhain ceremonies. As for the rest, well ...

When it came to belief, atmosphere was everything. Tig and I spent Halloween morning re-organizing the living room into a perfect receptacle for lost souls looking for some fun.

We nailed a big woollen curtain up across the window, under the lacy curtain, and another to the living room doorway, to ensure complete darkness and silence. We emptied the room of furniture, moving it all into the bedroom. As before, we arranged tea candles and musky incense around the room. Then we worked on our five-pointed star, about half the size of the room, also made with candles, and drew a circle around it with chalk.

The string to the ceiling fan was looped around the fan and then over the curtain rod. It hung right down to the floor, ready to be pulled for our spiritual breeze effect. Gabe would remain hidden in the kitchen, prepared to rattle windows and make the floor creak on cue.

Our séance was scheduled for 7 PM, and we were ready to go well before. In the meantime, we tested our new Popeye pipe. Rick had brought it over with his last hash delivery. It was one of those long curved pipes that detectives smoke from in old movies, and beautifully carved from what looked like ebony wood and some kind of bone. An engraving of a beautiful woman was etched onto its tobacco bowl. It would fit into our story line very nicely.

Gabe walked in around 5 PM. "Got the brownies!"

"Oh my god, Gabe! Didn't Dave smell 'em?" I gaped at Gabe, astonished.

Gabe laughed, "I'm not *that* much of a badass! I made these at a buddy's place." He took a paper bag out of his school bag, along with a cheap bottle of cooking wine, and placed them both on the kitchen counter.

I opened the bag and took a whiff. The brownies smelled delightful, hash-infused chocolate with a hint of vanilla. "Mmm ... this'll be perfect."

Tig put her hand in the bag for a tester piece and Gabe slapped it away. "Eh! None of that 'til work starts! We need to be lucid."

We arranged the brownies into one of the two bowls we owned, opened the wine bottle, and placed both on the cattle scale table. Then we got dressed up.

The clock struck seven, and we heard the bustle of people manoeuvring their way through the tangle of tall weeds outside, then up the steps onto the porch. The candles were lit, and the room was ready. The boys paused for a moment, whispering among themselves, then they knocked the code-knock Gabe had given them. This was it. Tig and I glanced at each other, took a deep breath, and smiled.

"Ready?" Tig said and I nodded.

And so began the night that would change everything.

9

The five-pointed star glowed as the light cast by the candles connected each line. The boys entered the altered mood in our séance room and fell silent when they saw Tig.

Tig had modelled her look off Marilyn Monroe and wore a bright red dress that was revealingly low and tight around her breasts, fire engine red lipstick (scored in the Pharmaprix dumpster), and even styled her curls appropriately. Although a redhead, she was still the most convincing 'Marilyn Monroe' I'd ever seen. The boys obviously thought so too because the sight of her stopped them in their tracks, and they stayed glued in place until she ordered them twice to sit.

I had dressed as the voluptuous Yvonne De Carlo, in an old dress almost as appealing as Tig's. However, for effect, I remained covered with a large shawl until the time was right.

As instructed, each boy sat around the five-pointed star on the outside of the chalk circle. Acting as High Priestesses, Tig and I stood on the window-side of the circle at the tip of one of the star's points.

When everyone was sitting and quiet, Tig began.

"Y'all have been inva*h*ted here this evening to call on the lost souls of long passed sex babes to join us in givin' alms to the gods of passion and ejaculation." Tig maintained her sexy Southern drawl.

One of the boys giggled and Tig continued in her most seductive tone, rounding each word in her mouth as if it were a lollipop filled with *come-hither.* "This is a circle of lust and trust. For anyone who ain't here to *cum-hither,* you will interrupt the spirits' crossin', so please git on outa here now." Tig pointed at the door dismissively and the boy stopped giggling.

"OK then, *mah* sexy angel-*ahd* boytoys … Let's git this party started." Tig winked at the group and the boys seemed to momentarily stop breathing.

With hardly a word, she'd cast a spell on them with her pouty red lips, bouncy boobs, and kissable tone of voice.

I lit the pipe as Tig went into a bit of Samhain folklore— the sexy bit of course, which actually didn't have anything to do with Samhain, but embellishing never hurt anyone. I was once again amazed at how easily some boys could be manipulated by a beautiful big-tittied girl.

I passed the pipe around and each boy took a drag, as they'd done previously with the bong. They were not new customers, they knew the drill.

"This is a special n*ah*t, with special requests. Before we begin, y'all must say thanks to the Earth spirits for orgasms that have passed and orgasms to come. Accept the blood and flesh of Mother Earth in thanks." She put the bottle of wine up to her lips, licked the rim, and took a sip. All eyes were glued to her lips, then to her tongue, then back to her lips.

The wine was passed around and each person took a swig. The bowl of brownies followed.

Every time Tig began to talk about a new spirit, she placed a picture of the woman inside the five-pointed star. When she had finished her story-telling, there were five pictures in the star: Hedy Lamarr, Joan Bennett, Lauren Baccal, Marilyn Monroe, and Yvonne De Carlo.

143

Tig let her eyes drift around the circle of boys, pausing briefly on each one, before she began to speak again.

"Boys, now's the time for us to summon the spirits we have placed within our star. This star is a portal. When a spirit chooses to show herself, she will do so within the portal and may only step out of the star if she is in*vah*ted. But beware, *mah* highfalutin' playthings, wanderin' souls are unpredictable and can be deathly dangerous. For our own safety, we will not be in*vah*tin' spirits outside the star. Y'all hearin' me, *mah* sexies?"

The boys all nodded, like robots obeying their master. Hooked. Absolutely hooked. And quite stoned by now too. They watched Tig, craving her next step into the beyond.

"The first thing y'all must do when lurin' a spirit outa the netherworld and into ours is convince her that you are worth her trouble. When the pipe comes to you, 'ya must share a personal story that will make your chosen spirit *want* you and only you."

The boys glanced at each other, then at me, then back at Tig, this time shaking their heads. Tig just smiled as if this was only a minor glitch, easily fixed.

"Boys, boys, boys ... y'all not afraid of *turnin' on* these gussied-up lost lady souls, are ya? Well, that would be something for the history books: hotties like you afraid of the ladies." Tig seemed thoughtful as she studied the boys for a moment. "Oh, *Ah* see ... it's each other y'all scared o' sharin' with."

The boys glanced at each other again.

"How 'bout this: *Ah'll* pass 'round these little scraps o' paper ..." She picked up a stack of scrap paper and pencils next to her. It was all in the plan. "... and ya each write how *you* would please your chosen spirit and why she should bother with ya, got it?"

They all smiled, relieved.

Tig passed around the paper and pencils. "When y'all done, you can light your paper on fire and put it in this bowl. Secret kept." Tig picked up an old chipped flowerpot and some matches from beside her and placed them in the middle of the star.

I lit the pipe again and passed it around the circle. By the time the orgasm part came about, these boys were going to be too stoned to remember if they had or hadn't.

The next bit was the trickiest bit. This is where all the props and illusions came into play. The incense in the room was working well, creating a hazy double-vision effect, especially with the help of the pipe. As the last paper was burned, I pulled the string attached to the fan and the candles flickered with the breeze.

Tig put on her satisfied look and said to the empty star, "Someone is there! Who is there? Make yourself known! We are here for your pleasure and to be pleasured by ya. Show yourself!"

Silence.

Tig closed her eyes, as if trying to concentrate.

"This spirit. *Ah* can sense her. She's here, in the star, but refusin' to show herself. She's not convinced yet."

Tig instructed the boys to close their eyes and concentrate hard on summoning their chosen lost soul from the other side. "Y'all must work together on this, pull her in with your most lust-filled thoughts, ya hear?"

The boys smiled, surely feeling a bit silly by now, but they all closed their eyes.

Unseen, I dropped the shawl from my shoulders and stepped into the middle of the glowing five-pointed star. I wore a long green evening gown made of transparent voile, a shorter slip underneath and under that, a pointy Wonderbra (with extra padding) for effect. The dress was torn around the bottom, which added character. I'd painted my lips with tangerine lipstick and my lashes with blue mascara. The only part of me that didn't scream Yvonne De Carlo were my brown eyes, but these boys would be too stuck on my other parts to notice. And anyway, it wasn't like they really knew who she was. They only knew what we'd told them.

Right on cue, the floor creaked and window rattled, and the boys' eyes shot open. They looked first in the direction of the noise, then back to the star, where the apparition had 'just appeared'. Two of the boys instinctively yelped and jumped backwards, then laughed at themselves and re-joined the circle.

"Holy shit, chill man!" One of the boys blurted giggling.

Another responded, "Screw off, man! I just jumped 'cause of you. Stop messin' with my make-believe."

The first one chortled, "Yeah, whatever, ya doorknob."

Tig let out a loud "Tshhht!" and they all fell silent again. Total control. Now it was my turn.

I feigned confusion, as if suddenly plucked from another planet and deposited in this room. I asked, "Where ... where am I?"

Tig replied, "Yvonne ... Yvonne De Carlo? Is that you?"

I nodded, "Yes girl, well of course it's me! Who else would it be?" I pretended to fix my hair, "And who are *you*?" I asked and then smiled seductively. "Lust drew me to this room, but I see only *you*. Tell me now, *where* are the *stallions* that asked me to come and promised me pleasure? Or was it the other way around: asked me for pleasure and promised to cum? ... Anyway ... All these clothes are making me sweat and sweat makes me horny. I demand that you show me the boys and stop hiding them away for yourself!"

Tig bowed her head to the Yvonne-me and said with reverence, "*Mah* dear Yvonne, Queen of Sex, thank you for gracin' us with your presence. Indeed, the boys who summoned you are present. They await the pure pleasure that only you can give. What would ya ask of them?"

I leant seductively towards Tig, "Perhaps, it is not the boys that I want ..."

One of the boys blurted, "Oh! Yeah, baby!"

Another stifled a giggled.

With a sheepish and slightly shocked expression, Tig replied, "Whatever do ya mean?"

Knowing Tig, I was sure she was trying as hard as hell not to burst with laughter. We'd had a hard time getting past this part during rehearsal.

"Come on … Marilyn … I know it's you. Stop pretending. Don't you think these boys are smarter than that?" I glanced around, finally acknowledging the boys. "Let's give 'em a show, dear. Like only you and I can." My smile said I wanted to kiss her all over and then eat her up.

The boys were the perfect stunned audience waiting for more.

Tig rolled her eyes, "Yvonne, ya gave me away! *Ah* was just gettin' started, toyin' with these sex-crazed stallions. But ah've missed ya so … *Ah* would like to help ya with your sweat issue … you should really take off a layer …"

I blew Tig a kiss and presented her with my dress zipper that ran down my back. Marilyn-Tig smiled bewitchingly as she stepped into the star's perimeters, unzipped the voile dress and began to pull it off, over my shoulders, my hips, and into a heap on the floor. I now stood in the middle of the star dressed in only a slip and stuffed Wonderbra. The boys adjusted their sitting positions and covered their crotches with their hands, but kept staring, transfixed.

That's when shit went sideways.

There was a screech of tires outside and some loud aggressive cursing mixed with pleading and scuffling— the kind of interaction that comes only from men.

Tig and I looked at each other, fixed in place and terrified.

Someone had found out about what we were doing. As I pulled my dress back on, the boys leapt up and ran for the back door, away from the noise, disappearing out into the thick spiny thistle. I briefly felt sorry for them. They probably didn't get far, but kudos for trying.

Rick was first through the front door, followed by a huge burly man with a hammer.

I screamed, "What? What? What the fuck?!"

The big man with the hammer responded, "Come'er you littl' whore! I got ya' pegged. Don't even think 'bout runnin'! Yer comin' home wit' me now."

He came into the living room, heading towards Tig, but swinging the hammer in my direction—a warning for me to stay out of it. I screamed again and ran for the kitchen.

Gabe stared at me stunned, unmoving, wondering what to do, where to go from here.

Rick was panting, holding onto the kitchen table. "Fuck, fuck, fuck! Tig's dad. I couldn't stop him. He's nuts. We gotta get outa here!"

I studied Rick, trying to comprehend the depth of what he had just told us.

Tig's dad, the drunken psychopath that Rick had saved Tig from? The guy who was worse to live with than living alone on the street in a decrepit rotting house, eating mouldy cheese? This lunatic was in our living room swinging a hammer at his daughter, our amazing friend, a great person who no doubt had a star-studded future in film! SHE, Tig, was about to die if we didn't help her.

I began to open drawers, searching for a weapon.

"Gabe! Rick! Grab a tool! Something heavy!" My adrenaline was sky-high, and I was panting. "Fuck! Grab a pan, a bottle, can of ravi-fuckin-oli, something!"

Gabe stood by the table like a zombie, not registering my words.

Rick took off out the front door, yelling, "Going to find help!"

I grabbed Gabe by the shoulders, shook him and shouted, "Gabe!! Wake the fuck up!!"

"OK ... OK ... OK! I'm OK! Oh, Christ! Give me something heavy!" Gabe's voice was hoarse, and he sounded terrified, but from his expression he was ready for action.

I pulled a small iron pan from the drawer and tossed it in his direction. I scrounged through the flimsier pots, pushing them aside, looking for another decent weapon. I was shaking, nothing looked strong and heavy and lethal enough to take this guy down. I tried to calm myself, to stop panicking, to start thinking again.

Things were being thrown in the other room, stuff was breaking, people were breaking. I put both my hands on the counter to steady my shaking and the thumping in my head and whispered to myself, "Wake the fuck up!" And then I shouted it.

Gabe was gone from the kitchen, into the room with Demon-dad.

No, not Gabe. Not Gabe. Please don't break Gabe. I'd sent him in there to die while I remained frozen in time.

That was the thought that finally pumped energy back into my limbs, rationality back into my brain. I became focused again, grounded again, strong again. No one was going to hurt my friends with me around and get away with it. Fear hung close, right on the brink of courage. With a violent howl I silenced it and charged into the living room, into the fighting arena, into the place where my friends were *not* going to die today.

Tig's dad held her by her hair and Gabe lay on the floor next to the window with blood on his face. Dollar bills were scattered all over the place, and the bowl they'd been in lay broken beside Gabe's head.

Demon-dad had his back to me and was yelling at Tig, "You fuckin' whore! Is that what you left me for, eh?! You think you can just leave ME?! And go fuckin' whorin' 'round the neighbourhood like the little slut your mother was? You belong to *me*, whore! I should bend you over right now and give it t'ya good."

Tig's dad was not human. His face was purple with rage and he spat with every word uttered. He pushed her down onto the floor and began to undo his belt. Tig was just lying there, crying, her body trembling, her hands over her ears, not fighting, surrendered.

This was bad.

A fury filled me like lava in a volcano bubbling up towards a life-threatening eruption. Something inside me, a monster I'd never known before, leant down and grabbed the bong by my feet, and in one swift coordinated movement, with all the force I could muster, I swung my weapon at Demon-dad's head.

And, to my horror, he didn't go down.

Demon-dad swore loudly as he turned towards me and tried to stand up. "You little fuckin' shit!" He wobbled slightly, holding his belt in his hand.

I was instantly drained of my fearless powers. This guy was an unbeatable super villain determined to crush me.

Demon-dad put his hand on the wall to steady himself and shook his head to clear his vision. At least I'd knocked his marbles out of whack a little. Maybe he'd swing and miss.

Abruptly, Gabe was back on his feet. As Demon-dad cleared his vision, Gabe swung the frying pan hard and, with bull's eye precision, hit him square on his temple, knocking him cold to the floor.

Everyone fell completely silent and time stood still.

"Is he ... is he ..." I tried to ask the question that we were all thinking but couldn't get it out.

Gabe walked towards Tig's dad cautiously, leant down, and felt for a pulse. "He's alive."

My body began to shake again, and my voice trembled as I instructed Gabe to watch him.

Frantically, I gathered up all the dress-up scarves we had. We were going to have to tie this guy's hands and feet together before he woke up. We couldn't risk him causing more damage or killing us before we had time to escape. We'd have to call the cops. I loved this place, I loved living with Tig, I loved that Gabe and I could hang out outside the system's cage. But this demon had to be stopped.

"Tie his feet, Gabe!" I tossed some scarves his way.

As Gabe started to wrap the first scarf around Tig's dad's ankles, he mumbled and moved his arms.

Gabe jumped up in fright.

I lunged towards Tig and pulled her to her feet. Fuck the scarves, we'd have to run! I grabbed a few bucks off the floor to help us through the night.

"C'mon Tig! Gotta go, NOW!"

Tig whimpered, "OK. OK. I can walk."

Demon-dad put his hands to his head and grumbled something inaudible.

"Fuckin' run!" I yelled at Tig.

"I can't!" Tig's legs were all wobbly. She was having trouble walking.

Gabe ran over to her, "Hop on!"

Tig struggled herself up onto his back, and he piggy-backed her out and away from the house.

We got as far as the bus stop. Gabe put Tig down on the bench inside the shelter.

"Gabe, I'm going to go to the pay phone. We need help. Stay with Tig. I'll be back real fast."

Tig curled up on the bench, held her knees to her chest, and rested her head against them. Her hair covered her face, and we could hear her crying softly.

Gabe nodded at me, "Sure thing. Go."

As I walked back to the bus stop after calling the cops, I began to panic about something else.

I couldn't go back to those nutcases in Manny Cottage. I needed a plan, but my mind was too scattered to come up with anything but the obvious: run. Run far, far, away and just keep running. But that was a plan bound for a crappy ending too, right? I stopped walking as I considered my options.

As backwards as it may sound, all I really wanted at that moment in time was to be a little girl again, at home curled up under my puffy down comforter in my Princess Canopy Bed with my overbearing mother making all the decisions.

I couldn't abandon Gabe and Tig, like I'd done to Frankie way back when she'd needed me. I'd fucked up there.

When I arrived back at the bus stop, Gabe and Tig were sitting side by side. She seemed slightly less distressed.

"Eh guys, we gotta split. We can't be here. The cops ... who knows what they're gonna do with us." I paused before continuing, "Gabe, you haven't missed your curfew yet. You go home, OK?" Gabe started to object but I interrupted him, "Stop. Just listen, OK? I'm gonna bring Tig to my parents' place. My mom's got her issues, but I'm pretty sure she'll just be happy to see me right now. I've been gone for over a month. I'll tell her that Tig's dad's drunk and dangerous, and she can't go home. Which is true anyway. She'll feel sorry for her, y' know, and want to fix her or whatever."

Gabe peered at me with skepticism. I'd told him all about my mom and hadn't painted her as a very caring person.

I continued, "My mom's complicated, OK? Just, trust me. It'll buy us some time. And we can clean up and stuff."

Energy too drained to object, Tig nodded solemnly. She was a shell, her soul absent. I took her hand, helped her up, and gave her a long hug. The sound of sirens could be heard in the distance, just as Gabe's bus pulled up.

I hailed a cab and prepared my mind for Mom.

CHAPTER FOURTEEN

Oh, Mother

October 31st – November 1st

Tig and I exited the cab onto the curb in front of my parents' Westmount bungalow. From slumdog heights to upper crust bubble, we stepped out of one world into an entirely different universe.

I pulled a $20 from my over-sized Wonderbra and paid the driver.

Tig stood still, staring at the house perched on its impeccably managed piece of land.

Bungalows are often portrayed in books and on TV as quaint little cottages some place in the country where retirees or newlyweds escape to, or at least that was the image that popped into my mind when I heard the word *bungalow.* My parents were intent on calling their home a bungalow ... and perhaps it was, when compared to some of the mansions in the neighbourhood ... but when compared to the houses in the next neighbourhood over, our house was a haven of luxury that most could only dream of. An aesthetic mix of stone, oak, and iron, the only difference between our "bungalow" and the mansion next-door was the number of rooms. Westmount embodied wealth, end of story. And sometimes, like right at this moment with Tig beside me, it was incredibly embarrassing.

"Is this where you live?" Tig glanced at me, then resumed staring at the house.

I didn't know what to say, the answer was of course obvious. We'd just been dropped off at my address, the address I'd given the cab driver, the address I'd said that was mine when the driver had asked me to point out my house.

Tig continued, "Why don't you like living here?"

I regarded Tig thoughtfully, not sure how to respond to this. Coming from a wealthy family made me feel like a poser. As if I didn't deserve to be unhappy or troubled or 'socially challenged'. As if I was just a whiny rich kid who thought it cool to be in the system, who wanted to be seen as *bad*, who wasn't who she said she was.

And I wasn't.

I never told anyone about where I lived, about all the *stuff* I owned, about my pink princess birthdays, and my endless music lessons, and all the holidays we took to exotic southern beaches. The way I spoke often gave me away though. I could disguise my body, but my 'dapper' vocabulary was harder to hide. Tig was the first friend from my system life that I'd brought home.

I had no response for Tig. I took her hand in mine and squeezed.

She gave me a crooked smile. "Your mom must be a real basket case."

I smiled back and nodded, "Something like that. But she'll be bearable for a couple of days. I think."

Some trick-or-treaters ran past us and up the driveway. Mom opened the door for them, dealt out some sweets, and was about to close it again when she caught sight of me.

Holding the bowl of sweets in front of her, she said, "Sam? Is that you?"

For a brief moment I thought her voice had been shaking, like the kind of shake that happens with emotion, but instantaneously she became herself again.

"Where were you? You get in here now, you hear! You've had the whole world looking for you and worrying about you. You have no right to toy with people like that." As I approached the door, she looked me over, "What *are* you wearing?" And when she saw past the clothes, "At least you put on some weight. You were looking like an AIDS victim last time I set eyes on you."

I stared at her, already exhausted with *home*. My eye began to twitch.

Mom noticed Tig behind me and, assuming her to be a trick-or-treater, she pulled me into the house and asked Tig, "Where's your bag, dear?"

To give my mother the benefit of the doubt, Tig did look like a zombie with her torn dress and bruised faced. I pinched my leg and kept my voice steady. "Uh, Mom? This is Tig. She needs a place to stay for a bit."

Mom's eyes grew wide with shock, but she moved aside and let Tig enter.

9

We sat around the kitchen table with the first aid kit open, a plate of muffins, and a pitcher of freshly squeezed orange juice. I accepted some juice but turned down the muffin. Mom had changed her tone towards me, as she usually did when guests were over. I thought it a positive sign that she considered Tig a guest whose opinion mattered.

"My my, what have you girls been up to?" She didn't wait for a reply. "Whoever did this to Tig needs to be held accountable. No one should be hitting a girl like this."

Tig winced as Mom cleaned the cut under her eye, but I could tell she was also happy to have someone caring for her. Tig was safe, and that mattered a lot. That was good. I could put up with Mom for that.

As Mom finished up, Tig's gaze dropped, and she fought back tears.

My mother took Tig's hands in her own and said soothingly, "Tig, dear, you can talk to me. Tell me what happened."

Mom *never* spoke to me with this kind of gentle urging, gentle caring. Part of me steamed with resentment, but I was happy that Tig was safe. I reminded myself again that *that* was what mattered.

After some coaxing, Tig told Mom about her violent father and begged my mother not to call the authorities, as she was convinced she'd be sent back to him. Mom agreed but called me into the kitchen before bedtime for a private catch-up.

We sat across from each other at the table. Now that Tig had left the room, Mom became her good ol' controlling self again. She pushed the muffins towards me, "You must be famished, Sam. Eat."

I moved the muffins to the side, out of her reach. "No, really, I'm not hungry."

She pursed her lips, "Fine. Play your game. It's *your* health, you know."

I glared at her. This argument we'd had a million times. "Mom, can we just ... you know, talk normally for a bit? I'm tired, Mom. I'm really, really, tired."

She sat back in her chair, "Sam, you've been off the grid for a month, and you want to talk normally? None of this is *normal*. Not one smidgen of your life is *normal*. Start explaining or I'm going to call the group home right now, at this very moment, you hear?"

Mom was a hound when it came to lies. I had already decided on my story. Mostly truths, with some stretched stuff and some stuff left out entirely, usually worked out well.

I told her about my scary experience with the Manny Cottage psychos, embellishing it just enough to freak her out. I explained how I'd thumbed a ride into town, and "no" I didn't catch the name of the driver or his license plate number. I said I'd met Tig in the east end, and we'd been staying here and there, until her dad showed up and beat the crap out of her. I told her that we'd called the cops on Tig's dad, but he had a history of being let off easy. He was probably home again.

Mom drilled me with questions.

"No," he didn't know where we lived.

"No," I hadn't been doing drugs.

"No," I hadn't been prostituting myself—the dress was a Halloween costume.

"Yes," I was still an underachieving selfish bum with neither goals nor direction.

"Yes," I was *that* slutty girl with a reputation.

"Yes," I knew how much of an embarrassment I was to my family.

"No," my choice of clothes didn't help my situation.

"Yes," I knew that my future was doomed.

"No," Tig wasn't a drug addict or thief who was going to cause all sorts of trouble in the middle of the night.

And "no," I hadn't been staying with Frankie while on the run.

Every time I ran away my mother assumed I was somewhere getting high with Frankie. Funny that she should blame Frankie for my actions, as that girl was an angel compared to me. And anyway, Frankie and I were done. Last time I saw her was when she'd told me to stay the hell out of her life, about an hour before I'd almost been squashed by that train. Like I was going to fuck off with Frankie.

I rolled my eyes, "We done, Mom?"

My mother studied me, her forehead tense and wrinkled. "Fine. Three days, Sam. Then we've got to talk next steps."

I nodded and headed down the hall to join Tig in my room.

⁊

Tig lay on my bed in between all the pillows and teddies, under the silk drapes that made up its canopy. She asked again, "Why don't you want to live here?"

I collapsed onto the bed next to her and replied partly to her but mostly to myself, "I hate my mother."

I closed my eyes. Tig reached for my hand and held tight.

"I hate my father."

I studied Tig for a moment, worried. Her eyelid had turned purple. "Sorry, Tig. For your father, I mean. I'm sorry you have such a difficult dad."

Tig shook her head, "No, don't, it's, it's … let's just sleep. Been a fucked-up day. I'm tired."

I squeezed her hand in response and, without another word, we fell asleep side by side.

⁊

When Tig and I came down for breakfast in the morning, my dad was sitting at the table with The Gazette's business section open. He'd had his breakfast and was doing his habitual 10-minute scan of the newspaper while he finished his coffee, before running out the door. He didn't look up or acknowledge me until we sat down at the table.

Dad glanced at me and gave me a quick nod with a curt smile, accompanied by an expected, "Hi, Sam. Nice to have you back."

He went back to scanning the paper without acknowledging Tig.

When his predicted 10 minutes were up, he rose from the table, put his dishes next to the sink, went into the hall, where he put on his coat and his shoes, picked his car keys out of the stone bowl on the chest near the door, and left without saying another word.

My mother, always immaculately groomed and a natural *boss*, sighed, "See what you do to your father, Sam?"

Tig glanced at me, and I noticed a flicker of understanding in her eyes.

It was best not to engage with my mother. Engaging always made things worse, more heated. Engaging made my brain hurt. So, I sat silently while my mother made fake happy information-gleaning small talk with Tig, as she prepared a fried breakfast for us all.

"So Tig, I see you've found some decent clothes to wear."

Tig nodded, "Sam lent me some clothes … I hope that's OK."

She wore sweatpants and a hoodie I'd lent her. Tig was taller than me and much more gifted in the tits department, and these were the only clothes I had that fit her.

"Well, of course it's OK. You had to get out of that hideous outfit. Halloween is over, dear!" My mom laughed as if she'd made a funny joke. "So, tell me, have you been missing school too?"

Tig nodded.

My mother continued, "And what school were you at before you and Sam met?"

Tig turned inward, considering my mom's question. My mother was clearly trying to figure out what neighbourhood Tig came from. My mom was all about social class.

Tig caught on quick though. "Val David High. I live in Val David."

I smiled secretly inside myself. Val David was a little rural town known for its mix of social classes. There was no way my mother would be able to make a social class judgment based on that place. Tig told me later that she'd been to Val David once and wanted to move there someday because of its anonymous feel.

But my mother wasn't done. "And your dad? What does he do?"

Strange question. I had the urge to reply, *'You mean, what does he do when he's not beating his daughter?'* But I knew she'd asked because she was still trying to figure out Tig's social class. She wanted to be able to *read* Tig, to make assumptions about her, and she couldn't do this without knowing the social standing of her family and about her upbringing.

"My dad? Uh ... he owns a construction company. He's a boss, I guess." Tig sounded drained.

"And your mother?" My mom couldn't leave anything be. She had to have her answers.

"My mom ... she died. My mom's dead." This was a lie, but I guessed it was easier than telling the truth.

"Oh. I'm sorry to hear that, Tig. I had no idea. What happened?"

My mother was unbelievable. *'What happened?!'* It was still all about her digging into Tig's life. That question had nothing to do with empathy. I felt embarrassed. I wanted to scream at her. But I knew about the earthquake that I'd cause if I let loose—the aftershocks would last all day, possibly all week, so I bit my tongue and gulped down my freshly pressed juice.

"Cancer. It was cancer. It took her quick." Tig lied again.

There was a pregnant pause. Mom, only semi-satisfied, still wasn't finished. More was coming.

"Does your dad get angry at you a lot?"

That was it. I couldn't take it any longer. I stood up and yelled, "MOM!! Stop prying ... please mom!" I added the "please" in an attempt to limit the tremors that were sure to follow my outburst.

"Sam! Sit. Down. Now. You don't yell at your mother like that. After everything I've done for you and continue to do for you. I'm only being friendly, trying to get to know *your* friend who is in *my* house." She glared at me as I shrank back down into my seat. "Now missy, you are going to be polite and eat the food that I spent the morning preparing for you." She kept glaring at me as she pushed a plate of waffles towards us.

The last thing in the world I wanted to do was eat.

"Eat Sam." She pointed at the waffles and fixed her eyes on me.

She wouldn't stop looking at me until I took a bite. So, I began to eat.

Mom continued, "Tig. Sorry about that. Sam is jumping to conclusions. I only want to help you and that's why I'm letting you stay, OK? Now, where were we?"

I had difficulty swallowing but kept eating slowly to appease her.

"Um ... my dad's an angry person. He's ... Uh ... Maybe he can't help it. He drinks too much and loses control sometimes." Tig was being honest this time. She truly did think that he couldn't help it. That's what she'd told me too. I felt sad for her.

"Well, most of us lose control at times. Raising kids isn't easy, you know. I'm sure your dad loves you."

My stomach churned. I couldn't listen to her any longer.

I exploded, "Love? *Love*?! Fuck you, Mom! Just fuck you!! You have no idea what the fuck love is!"

Words left me then and I stood there fuming and voiceless, my emotions bubbling out through my every pore. I stomped out of the kitchen, through the hall, to the bathroom, where I shoved my fingers down my throat and emptied my mother's overbearing love into the toilet.

❦

Tig was reclined comfortably in my hammock chair, when I finally surfaced from my regular cry-space in the bathtub and entered my room. The bathrooms were the only rooms in the house with locks. Mom said that as long as she paid the bills, my room was as much hers as mine (hence the flowery wallpaper and canopy bed). It was far from a safe space. She waltzed in, like the Queen she was, whenever it pleased her.

Tig had found my flute, assembled it, and was in the process of trying to figure out how to get sound out of it.

As I approached, she observed me affectionately, "So ... I think I get why your mother drives you nuts ... you OK?"

I fell back onto my bed and put my hands over my face, "Tig, I dunno. I dunno if I'm OK. She's a special case. But maybe she's right. What's wrong with me? Why can't I ..."

Tig cut me off here. "Stop. Sam, you're a great person. She's the weirdo. Shit, your dad won't even talk to her. In fact, the only person I noticed talking to her was *her*. She hardly lets anyone else in on the conversation. She's like one of those pull-string dolls that asks questions and tells you how she feels but never listens for your answers or cares about how you feel. Got one of those from my dad on my sixth birthday. That's what your mom reminds me of. She's a pull-string doll with an attitude, Sam." Tig smiled at me.

I considered her allegory, picturing my perfectly groomed mother with her run-on mouth, every kid's nightmare doll, and started to laugh. Yup, definitely a heartless doll with an attitude.

"Do you really play the flute?" Tig tried again to blow a note.

"Yeah ... been a while though. Mom got her knickers all twisted up in knots when I quit."

I thought back to the day I'd stopped practising. I'd had enough. I'd fallen out of love with music. She went ballistic and tried everything to encourage me to play again— bribing, guilt-trips, rage, crying, grounding, grounding, and more grounding. I'd been banished to my room indefinitely, not allowed contact with friends, especially Frankie who was of course to blame for corrupting my innocence.

Sometimes I wondered whether my mother had any friends, because she seemed to put all her emotional energy into *me*. Perhaps she just needed a friend. I smiled at the thought. It felt good to feel sorry for her.

I rose from the bed and took the flute from Tig. "You have to blow in but also a bit across the hole in the mouthpiece. Like this." I blew a crystal-clear B note.

Tig looked impressed. My mom had left for work, so I played Metallica's *Master of Puppets* for her. I'd learned it at Charles A., on the flute my SW had dropped off in hopes that I'd do something productive (likely at the bidding of my mother). Bored and restless one day, I'd given in and learned a new tune. Master of Puppets seemed fitting, as I often felt like a puppet in a show controlled by others.

"Cool! That was fantastic! Can you show me how?"

I nodded, "Sure. I can show you *Hey Jude* if you manage to blow a note." I handed the flute back to Tig.

Tig tried a few times, positioning her mouth and lips differently, trying to get the right angle, until she finally blew a clear note.

Tig through her hands up in triumph. "Yay! Right on, got it! 'Kay, show me *Hey Jude*." She exclaimed, so proud and happy, as if the day before hadn't happened, as if it had all just been someone else's bad dream.

I spent the afternoon teaching Tig how to play. It was an oddly normal experience. Like we were back in school, doing *normal* teen things, on a *normal* weekend, in a *normal* house, in a *normal* neighbourhood. Doing things that we *should* be doing. But it was all an illusion. A bubble that would burst at any minute. And when it burst, we'd be back to pop-up futures determined by puppet masters.

I asked Tig, "Uh, your dad ... he's kinda like ... nuts, eh?"

Tig frowned sadly and nodded.

"Tig, I'm pretty sure my mom's going to turn you in. I mean, she's gonna have to report my return to my social worker and, when she does, I'll be taken back into custody."

Tig averted her gaze, out the window, thinking.

"My mom nicknamed me 'Tig', when I was real little. *Tigger* from *Winnie the Pooh*, 'cause I was always running and jumping and never just walking. My real name's Heather. Heather Macklin. It's my dad's last name ... Macklin. And Heather's his mom's name ... my Grandma. Never met her though ... she's long dead. The only name I have that's part of my mom is Tig. I can't go back to my dad, Sam. I gotta run ... but I'm new at this street thing. I don't know anyone. Where am I gonna go? Rick's probably not up for getting involved again." She looked at me for suggestions.

I had no good solution though, no solution that would fix things and make the shit in life disappear.

"The street's really not much fun. I mean, we had fun, but that was luck, eh?" I thought for a second, then added,

"Listen Tig, don't run. When my mom reports you, you'll have to speak with a social worker before they decide on whether to return you to your dad. Tell her the complete truth, 'kay? Tell her about everything that happened before you ran away from home and what happened when your dad found you at the house. Tell her how scared you are. Tell her you think he's going to kill you. They'll never send you back if you tell them all that, I'm sure of it. I mean, I was in less danger, and they didn't send *me* home ... although I'm also part criminal. Maybe ... also tell them you shoplifted some of that food?"

Tig nodded more vigorously now.

I put my arms around her, "It's gonna be OK. Group homes are not so bad. You're going to be OK. Maybe you'll even be in the same one as Gabe. Maybe we all will." Or maybe I'd be back in the psycho ward with the crazy fire-wielding cult bitches, but I decided not to go into that bit.

,

Alas, my mom concluded that she couldn't wait until her 3-day deadline was up. She arrived home with two police cruisers her tail.

As we were being escorted out the front door, Mom put her hand on my shoulder and said, "Dave called me at work, Sam. I couldn't exactly lie now, could I?" She paused as she deflected my glare. "Don't you give me that look. Someone else gave you away. Dave had heard all about your shenanigans, and it wasn't from me."

I stared straight ahead, avoiding eye contact.

"Whatever, Mom. See ya."

I squeezed my arm, firmly implanting my nails in it. The pain kept me calm.

Another stint at Manny Cottage was a thought I couldn't deal with.

I focused on Tig, and mouthed silently, "Remember what we talked about—you'll be fine."

Tig looked terrified but nodded in acknowledgement.

We left in separate cruisers.

CHAPTER FIFTEEN

Dave

Early November

Judge Beaulieu's office was as expected. High ceiling, big window, oak furniture, framed photos of her shaking hands with local politicians, flowers on the windowsill, and a glass cabinet filled with memorabilia that represented the system through time—an *old boys club* office inhabited by an old girl.

I sat before her desk in one of three chairs. Tim Reid, a representative from Youth Protection Services, occupied the chair beside me. The other chair awaited Sam's social worker, Abi Cohen.

Judge Beaulieu read through Sam's file, silently.

I studied the stuff in the glass cabinet. A framed picture of Weredale Home for Boys[8] caught my eye. A group of smiling boys stood on the steps, with an extra proud childcare worker by their side. If I didn't know better, I'd have thought they were a happy bunch at some normal school in Normal Land. The kid in the middle stood out.

He wasn't smiling like the rest, he looked tired and fed up with the charade. Now, *that* was more like how I felt when I had lived there. I wondered how many of those kids in that picture line-up had welts on their behinds from being whipped with a belt. I still had scars on mine.

"*Alors, allons-y.* I have a hearing in 20 minutes. Tell me why you're here and be quick about it." The judge peered from behind her desk, slightly exasperated. She wasn't one to take any shit, and she sure as hell wasn't going to waste her time on a system brat.

The judge's attitude reminded me of the cold-hearted jerks that worked at that home when I was a kid. No matter how much I tried to stay calm and focused, this judge always made me sweat.

I forced myself back into the present and cleared my throat, "Samara Long, Judge. She has been located and is in the custody of Youth Protection Services. I would like to recommend she be returned to Charles A. Group Home."

Before I could continue, Tim interjected. "Judge, Ms. Long is a serial runaway. If we put her in a city group home, she'll be on the streets again within a week." He smiled almost flirtatiously at the judge, as if saying 'you get me, I *know* you do.'

Judge Beaulieu glared at Tim and, thrown off guard, he shifted nervously in his chair. Had she been she offended by his ease? I hoped this would work in my favour.

"It is true that Sam ... uh, Ms. Long ... has a history of running away, but I believe I have a solution and I'd like to try it out." I waited for the judge to signal for me to go on.

Tim grinned arrogantly, "Oh, com'on, we all know nothing works with these kids. Stop wasting the judge's time. Ms. Long should go back to Manny Cottage. The only thing that'll contain that one are tall walls and a barbed-wire fence. I'd also add that it is quite unorthodox for a *childcare worker* to be part of this decision at all. Dave is here out of courtesy, that's it." Tim said the word "childcare worker" as if it were the most insignificant position of all.

I couldn't figure out whether Tim was burnt-out from work-overload or a power-hungry asshole. Either way, he should've changed jobs years ago. It was well-known that Manny Cottage used questionable disciplinary tactics. It was no place for a harmless runaway. And, anyhow, locking a kid up is no way to teach trust and respect—a recipe for disaster is what it is. I would not lose Sam to Manny Cottage. How would youth protection ever move out of the dark ages with guys like *Tim* on board?

I responded calmly, "Listen, Ms. Long ran away because she was scared, due to being physically threatened. Sending her back to the place that terrifies her is not the answer." Tim tried to interrupt, and I cut him off. "We've had some success with her at the group home, and she has a support network there. The kids at Charles A. Group Home have a kinship. My idea ..."

Tim spoke over me, "Facts are facts. Ms. Long is a runaway. That's a fact. We put repeat runaways in Manny Cottage. A fact and also our policy. So, what is the issue here? Save the group home bed for someone who's going to appreciate it. Messed up kids don't just fix themselves because someone cares!" He sounded annoyed and frustrated that I'd been allowed to speak for so long.

Then Judge Beaulieu surprised me.

The judge put her hand up and, looking at Tim, she said, "Stop. I want to hear Dave's suggestion." And she motioned for me to continue.

Abi opened the door, entered quietly, and stood behind Tim and I.

Judge Beaulieu raised her eyebrows, "Well, nice of you to finally join us Ms. Cohen. Please, take a seat."

Abi sat down in the empty chair. "My apologies, Judge. I got caught up with another case. My phone never stops ringing. We could do with a few more social workers in this city." Her voice trailed off as she said the last bit.

The Judge swung her attention back to me. "So, on with it, Dave."

"Thank you, Judge. When I was an orphan in the Weredale Home for Boys I remember the sense of hopelessness I felt. I was there because of events that were out of my control, yet it seemed being an orphan had automatically labelled me as a 'lost cause' and 'criminal-to-be.' The system was not set up to help orphans succeed. We had to fight to survive. By 17, I'd become a street scrapper and was stealing cars just because I could. I was angry, and I was heading towards a life of incarceration. I couldn't see a way out. That life was everything I knew, and the adults around me expected me to follow that path. No one had faith in me, so neither did I."

Tim scratched his chin and checked his watch.

The judge listened, composed and patient.

I continued, "Then I met a detective who thought differently. I was up on car theft. But he saw something in me and gave me a chance. He asked me what I wanted to be when I grew up. Half joking, I told him I was good at fixing people up after fights. He said *'you know, hospitals hire people to do that. I will see what I can do for you. This may be your one and only chance. The ball's in your court.'* It's difficult to describe what it feels like to be trusted by an authority figure when you have never been before. At first, I was skeptical. But then, a few days after the hearing, someone approached me with an offer to train me as an ambulance technician. It was then that I realized I could control my destiny. I had choices. I didn't have to be crippled by my past. My path could be filled with passion instead."

The judge glanced at the clock on the wall. "OK, OK, I get it. What's your idea for Ms. Long's case?"

I smiled, "Sam loves to write. She's a natural at it too. I've read some of her short stories. I want to organize a youth newspaper and I want her to be editor in chief."

Abi's face brightened, "Wonderful idea! Sam's so creative. We could add the newspaper as a requirement to being accepted back into Charles A. You know, that along with no tolerance for running away, of course."

The judge lent back in her chair, thoughtful. "What about funding and publishing?"

Tim struggled to contain his exasperation. "Yeah. Funding. No money available on our part, that's for certain."

I ignored him. "Already taken care of. I've got a friend in publishing who's willing to support the project."

Judge Beaulieu nodded and looked at Abi. "OK, then. Ms. Cohen, you and Dave sort the details out and call me before Ms. Long's court appearance. If everything looks good, then I'll approve a trial period."

And that was that. Tim appeared shocked. He'd been silenced. This was not the conclusion he'd expected. I wanted to shout out in triumph but settled for a warm smile and nod at the judge. The judge dismissed us with a wave of her hand.

,

Abi Cohen held the door for me, and we exited the building together.

She stopped me on the steps.

"Dave …" She hesitated a moment. "I think what you're doing for Sam is fantastic. She needs this. They all do." Another pause, then a smile. "I was in the system too … in an orphanage during the Duplessis era. You know, when the church and government conspired and labelled us all *'nuts'* for profit?" Abi laughed nervously.

I nodded in acknowledgement. I didn't know how to respond. Past lives could be a touchy matter. Mine definitely was.

"Anyway, it's hard to talk about. There was a lot of abuse. Nuns make horrible mothers." She laughed uncomfortably again. "I was a lucky one. You know, I was given a chance, like you."

I smiled supportively and nodded. "I'm glad you survived it, Abi. Kids in the system are fortunate to have you on their team."

The Duplessis scandal[9] was all over the news. From what I'd heard, Orphanages that had once been set up by the Catholic church to house pregnant teens and re-home their illegitimate children, had been closed and the orphans were sent to asylums as asylums were more profitable for the government than were orphanages. The orphans had then been re-labelled as "mentally ill patients", as the church received more funding for a "patient" than they did for an "orphan." The re-labelling also gave way for psychiatric experimentation on orphans under the pretense it was a treatment for sin. The list of abuses was long and included physical and sexual abuse, lobotomies, electroshock therapy, isolation, and more. Many orphans never made it out and those that did were often unable to function in society, due to trauma and an inability to read and write. A mass grave containing the remains of Duplessis orphans had recently been discovered.

It was quite something to be standing next to a Duplessis orphan who'd *made it*. I had so many questions but kept them for another time.

Abi studied me for a moment. "Something interesting happened this morning. Just as I was leaving my office, my boss stopped me. She'd been told that I'd been poking my nose into Manny Cottage business. A couple of kids had told me some pretty horrific stories about being confined alone in an empty room for days. When I asked Manny Cottage staff about it, they gave me the run around."

I shook my head, "Yup, been there, done that. I tried to pry too and was shut down quick. Some of those detention units are not much more than jails for kids. I was horrified when I'd heard Sam was in the Bethel unit. I just don't get the logic behind using restraint and isolation on kids, or anyone for that matter. I mean, what does it accomplish, other than anger and more rebellious behaviour?"

"There must be others asking questions. It's incredible that this kind of punishment is still going on. I've been told to lay off and leave things to my superiors." Abi was disappointed and I could completely relate.

"Getting through to those guys up top is like trying be have a conversation about morals in the front row at a Rolling Stones concert. No matter how much you try, your opinion won't be appreciated nor heard. The best thing we can do is record everything we hear, keep sending our reports and suggestions, and try our damndest to keep kids out of Manny Cottage."

Abi frowned. "Yeah ... Hey, do you have time now to chat about your idea for Sam?"

I glanced at my watch. "Sure. Coffee at the Plaza?"

Abi nodded, "Sounds great."

CHAPTER SIXTEEN

Second Chances

November/December — Sam

I stood before the judge, exposed. Emotionally naked. Here I was, *me* the fuck-up, for all to see, waiting for judgment. The same old wrinkled judge scowled from behind her podium. My file, containing all my dark secrets, emotional breakdowns, and street adventures, lay open in front of her.

Judge Beaulieu frowned and shook her head. But she'd seen it before. This judge was well acquainted with teen fuck-ups. Each of her wrinkles represented a time when she'd seen it before. And perhaps that is why this turned out to be my lucky day.

"Well, well, Samara Long. Here you are again. Last time you were in front of me, didn't we agree that we would never see each other again?" Without waiting for a reply, she continued, "Your social worker is recommending that, for some odd reason, I should go soft on you and not send you back to Manny Cottage. Now, tell me Sam, why should I go soft on you?"

I thought quickly and began, "I, uh, I'll never go AWOL again. I want to ..."

Judge cut me off, "Never go AWOL again? AWOL seems to be your back-up plan for everything. Why should I believe you?"

I started again, "Manny Cottage ..."

And she interrupted me again, "Uh-uh. Don't go there. I don't want to hear excuses. You should thank your lucky stars that you have a good lawyer, a great social worker, and parents that never give up."

I stared at her, wide-eyed and hopeful.

Judge Beaulieu continued, "There's a catch though. I'm busy as all heck today, so I'm going to leave it up to Ms. Cohen to explain everything. When she does, you'll need to sign a contract with her agreeing to the terms, OK? If you don't sign or if you break the terms of the contract, you'll be sent back to me. I won't be so generous next time. Do you understand?"

I nodded, trying to keep my joy from disturbing my I'm-taking-you-very-seriously face. No Manny Cottage! Holy shit! Fuckin' A! I felt like I'd just escaped certain death.

When the judge dismissed me, I turned to search for my mom in the back row where we'd sat waiting our turn. Mom drove me crazy, but she deserved a thanks for the role she'd surely played in this. But she was nowhere to be seen.

Ms. Cohen interrupted my search. She placed her hands warmly on my shoulders and held my eyes with hers, "This is excellent news, Sam. I'm so happy for you. We can discuss the ruling, and the contract, on the way to the group home. Your mom had to go back to work. I'll be driving you."

I wasn't surprised that my mother had left, but it hurt nonetheless. I was her failure, that's what she thought. Sadness tugged at my insides for a moment. I brushed it off with a silent, *'fuck you too, Mom'* eyeroll. And I followed Ms. Cohen to her car, wishing that I had a mom who was more like her.

❡

Gabe lay in the hammock on the group home's porch. Plugged into his headphones and absorbed in music, he didn't notice me until I climbed the steps and stood on the landing next to him.

"Sam! I knew you'd be back." His hair was messy in a 'just woke up' sort of way and his smile was warm and partly mocking. He must've been immensely comfortable in the hammock, as he usually greeted me with way too much energy. A fleeting thought occurred: this laidback version of Gabe was kind of hot.

Shocked at where my mind had gone, I refocused. "Yup, back to the jungle ... or from the jungle ... or something ..."

Gabe grinned, and I wasn't sure what to make of his expression this time, "I'm glad you're back, Sam ..." He hesitated, then added so only I could hear, "... 'cause this place got *way* worse over the last few days."

Before I could ask what he meant by that, Ms. Cohen was pushing me through the front door. "You two can catch up later, Sam, after we finalize this contract. Dave's waiting."

As we entered the building and headed for Dave's office, the trouble Gabe had been referring to hit me head on: Tema stepped out of the office.

Dripping with bogus sweetness, she exclaimed. "Sure thing! Thanks, Dave!"

Forget my contract, the real catch to not being sent back to Manny Cottage was going to be more time with Tema. At least I'd have Gabe as back-up.

Our eyes met. I froze. She relaxed. I felt like a doe come face to face with a mountain lion. Blood pumped into my cheeks. The deer inside me wanted to bolt, but I knew I'd have to deal with her, and learn to avoid her bite. I hated feeling like a deer. That bitch was going to pay for her bullshit, one way or another.

She sauntered past me, then up the stairs she went.

Ms. Cohen motioned for me to follow her into Dave's office.

"Welcome back, Sam. So glad to have you with us. Have you gone over the contract with Ms. Cohen?"

I nodded, Ms. Cohen and I had talked about the contract in the car. Then, preoccupied with the Tema issue, I resumed my habit of chewing on my lip when nervous,

Dave studied me thoughtfully, puzzled by my nervousness. "Ah, Tema. You were in Bethel together, right?"

I nodded again.

"Sam, I don't know what your relationship with her is or how things went in Bethel, but I can promise that you are safe here."

And nodded again. What was there to say? Not like I had any choice in the matter.

"I've assigned you room #8, the one beside Gabe's. Would you like to go settle in, unpack?"

I nodded, "Yeah, sure."

"OK. Ms. Cohen and I have some things to discuss. Come down when you're done."

I headed up the stairs to my new room.

Gabe caught me on the stairs, "Eh, just so you're, y' know, not surprised and shit ... The scary Manny chick moved into your old room."

"Nice." *And another eyeroll saves the day. Thank god for flexible eyeballs.*

"But I rescued your stars." Gabe shot me a cheer-up smile.

I kissed him on the cheek, "Thanks, Gabe. Now let me unpack."

The room wasn't so bad. A bit smaller than the other one, but other than that it was quite similar. Bed, desk, chair, chest-of-drawers, fire-escape, white walls.

I threw my bag on the floor, made the bed, then I went back down to talk with Dave and Ms. Cohen.

9

"So all you have to do is start a newspaper? Shit, girl. You must have friends in heaven." Gabe was lying on his back beside me on my bed, head on my pillow, looking up at me. I had my back against the wall with my knees bent.

I stared at Gabe, "*All* I have to do? That's no small task, wiseass. I gotta get people on board. Ya' think the smart asses in the system are gonna just be like *'yeah, sure I'll spend my precious time away from doing nothing in particular to spill my guts onto paper for the whole world to read! Sure thing Sam, I'll get to it right away!'* I'm screwed, Gabe. There's no way this is gonna work. I may as well head back to Manny Cottage today. At least that jerk Tema isn't there." I held my head in my hands, feeling hopeless and miserable.

Gabe put his hand on my ankle to get my attention and gave me a *'you got this'* look. "Listen, you are *not* leaving me alone with Tema. We can do this together. You've got writing and business sense. I can add some happy energy, along with my shiny new marketing skills. *We* got this, babe!" Gabe winked at me.

I regarded Gabe with doubt. "System kids are nothing like those gullible dweebs at your school."

"Nope, but system kids are also not as busy as those gullible dweebs. We just need to work on their motivation—feed their mojo, yeah?" Gabe said this way too optimistically.

I considered demolishing that super annoying positive vibe he'd been possessed by but thought better of it. I guess there'd be no harm in *trying* to make the newspaper work.

But first I'd need to locate my mojo.

I called for my mojo. Nothing changed. So much for that.

Maybe Tig could help me find it. "We need Tig in on this, man."

For the first time since he entered my room, Gabe frowned. "Still haven't figured out where she is. Dave says it's confidential."

"D'ya think they sent her home ... to her dad?" This was my biggest concern. It was unlikely, but who knows.

"Dunno." Gabe paused, thinking. "Perhaps we need to investigate ... you know, like reporters ... for our paper?" He smiled.

"Good one, Sherlock. We can find her with our Star Trek teleportation device. Then we can write all about her troubled life to make other system kids *feel* better. Tig would be totally on-board." I shot Gabe my best *get-fuckin-real* eyeroll.

Gabe laughed, "Got a point."

9

The week crept by like a centipede with digestive issues.

Tema was brewing a stew filled with evil intentions, I could *feel* it. But I couldn't make out what she was up to. She'd tried to befriend my other headache, Gini, the one who'd read my secrets to the world just before I'd been sent to hell. Gini was not a befriending type though, and had told Tema to go hell—no room for two lead witches in one coven apparently. That was my highlight of the week. Maybe they'd fight to the death, leaving no extra strength to torment the rest of us. It crossed my mind to play them against each other, but that'd be a dangerous gamble given their appetite for skinny Asian chicks. I'd likely end up in someone's cauldron.

It took a few days before Tema turned her hungry glare into words. It happened on a Tuesday, while the two of us were on supper duty, cutting veg for the stew. '*How fitting*,' I thought, '*the witch is on cauldron duty*.'

Without looking at me, Tema said in a low voice, "If you get real close to it, burning hair makes your eyes water like onions."

I stayed quiet and repeated my promise to myself that I would not engage.

She continued, "Have you ever smelled burnt human flesh, Sam?"

What a nutter. But her craziness was weirdly intriguing. In other circumstances, like if she wasn't holding a knife and living under the same roof, I'd have liked to quiz her to figure out what the hell's going on in that fucked up brain of hers. But in the present situation, I kept cutting and let her talk.

"Smells like a mix of scorched beef and rotten fish. Probably 'cause of all the shit people eat." Tema glanced at me, hoping for a reaction.

I stayed quiet, kept my eyes on my chopping board. Why was she discharged from Manny Cottage? And, shouldn't she be in some kind of locked-in mental ward? The logic of the youth judicial system never ceased to confuse me. Put an innocent kid in with the criminal crazies and put a crazy in with the comfortably naïve innocents. What the fuck? I decided that *that* would the topic of my first article in my new newspaper: The idiocy of mixing hardened criminals with runaways ... I'd call it something catchy ... like, '*Fuck You, Kids*.'

❦

As I was working on my article that evening, Gabe came into my room and handed me two drawings and a poem.

"Poem's from Alex ... he says they're lyrics, but just looks like bad poetry to me. The doodles are from Chris and Pete." He collapsed on my bed next to me. "Told 'ya I'd get some material for you!"

I studied the drawings. Chris' was a copy of the Iron Maiden zombie skeleton trying to escape the paper it was drawn on. Not bad. Pete's was more design than depiction. More Pink Floyd than Iron Maiden. There were lines and shapes and squiggles and starbursts and lots of bright colours, like a light show gone mad. He'd probably been doodling while high.

"Cool, thanks."

I read through Alex's lyrics.

Fuck the system
Smash it down
The four horsemen
Are comin' to town

Crushing heads
Kicking 'em in
No more meds
I'll live in sin, sin, sin, SIN!

So fuck you
Fuck you
Fuck you too!

Screw your jail
And your rule
I'm gonna bail
You fuckin' tool!

"Uh, Gabe? What the fuck? We can't print this." Picturing the reaction we'd get from Dave if we tried to include this poem, I started to laugh. "Shit, man. Is he for real?"

"Yup. He was pretty real about it ... Should I tell him to stick to singing and playing? Or he could model? He's kinda cute." Gabe seemed serious for a moment. Then we both burst out laughing. Alex's poem was a stretch, but him with his twiggy legs, carrot-coloured unwashed long hair, and permanently stoned expression, trying to model was absolutely hilarious.

In between fits of laughter, Gabe exclaimed, "Holy frignibbles! I have an idea! He could be our rock star mascot!"

We rolled on the bed with laughter. But it wasn't a half bad idea.

Gabe held my arm as he tried to simmer down enough to continue the thought. "Totally! He'll totally do it, Sam. With that bod and hair, he could be like our very own Axel Rose!" Gabe paused, and obviously trying to control himself, said with a dramatic flare, "Introducing, *Alex Rose!*"

Containing myself for a moment, I added, "I dunno man, think that would break copyright laws?"

Gabe shoved me playfully, "Fuck off. Alex's way too unique to break any copy laws."

"Got a point. Ok, so, we have a couple of drawings, a bad poem that Dave will never allow to be published, an article on better practices in the system, possibly a photo shoot with *Alex Rose*, and ... we need more ... What about a column or something? Like for advice, eh?" I looked at Gabe for suggestions.

"Yes! That's it! I wanna do it!" Fireworks went off in Gabe's eyes as his imagination went wild.

And there it was: the birth of *The Montreal System Rat*, my greatest achievement as a delinquent and also my biggest headache ever (excluding a few criminal hiccups).

Our first print was cause for celebration.

With his magical power of recruitment, Gabe had squeezed out two articles, five drawings, two poems (that didn't contain swearing and dying), and a full page spread photo of our teen rock mascot, *Alex Rose*, playing his guitar in the park (we tried for the graveyard, but Dave wasn't quite ready for that).

Gabe had worked hard on his advice column, which Dave was wildly unsure about and was going to monitor closely, because of confidentiality issues and blah, blah, blah. And then there was also my own article, now heavily edited to avoid encouraging a full-on rebellion, which would result inevitably in Dave being out of a job, as Dave put it. Dave could be such a wuss.

It took us two weeks to gather all the material, put it into an order that made sense, and prepare it for printing. Through a friend, Dave organized a tour of The Gazette for me and Gabe, where we learned all about the steps needed to prepare a newspaper for printing. We also had the opportunity to seek advice from a reporter on interview tactics, which was awesome.

When the printing day finally arrived and Dave came back from picking the paper up at the printing press, we were all sitting uncharacteristically well-behaved at the table eating supper. Well, at least we were when Dave walked in. That'd been the deal—he'd pick up our newspaper if we could behave like 'adults' in his absence. There were other childcare workers in the group home, but the only one that had earned our respect enough for us to 'behave like adults' was Dave.

He walked in and put the box on the table. I felt like a little kid at Christmas time, waiting for Santa to get on with it and give me my gift before I exploded and could be good no longer.

Dave smiled at us, with his hands resting on top of the parcel. My heart sank a bit. I thought, 'damn, that's his speech look'. If he started talking, it could be half an hour before he finally opened the box.

"You guys should be proud of yourselves. This paper took a lot of effort and each one of you helped in some way. Whether through writing, drawing, posing for photos, taking the photos, or supporting the effort in some other way, everyone here participated in the creation of this paper. And that is something to be proud of."

Dave looked at each of us in turn, taking us all in, including us all in his visual pat-on-the-back.

His gaze paused on Gabe and I, "Sam and Gabe. You two should be especially happy with yourselves. This paper could not have happened without you. I had my worries in the beginning. It was a huge task with a lot of responsibility, but you did it. You handled it. I have no more doubts, I *know* you and your team can do it again. So, let's open this darn package and celebrate the first edition of *The Montreal System Rat!*"

We all cheered. Even Gini and Tema were acting as if they understood the meaning of team pride. Gini had done the photography work for Alex's photo shoot and Tema had advised him on rock star style and posture and had also gone mad on him with hairspray. Which made him look more like Jon Bon Jovi than Axel Rose, but anyway.

Dave took the copies out of the box and passed them around. They were perfect. I hadn't been so proud since ... I couldn't remember when. Although the newspaper wasn't in colour, the fonts and pictures were beautiful, as agreed upon. We'd used Dave's computer to type up the articles, and the font was borrowed from the printing press.

I walked over to Dave and, for the first time, gave him a hug. Alex snarked, "fu ... riggin' Jesus! Sam's lost her bananas—call a shrink quick! She's huggin' someone!" I wasn't known for my affectionate ways.

"Frig off, Alex." I growled playfully back at him. "Go tease your hair or pluck your eyebrows or something." I replied sarcastically, referring to the 'Alex-*Axel* Rose' photo that he'd prepared himself so carefully for.

Alex laughed, "Yeah, whatever. Deep inside, you *know* you want me. I'm Alex Rose, with cool clothes and hair that blows!" He did a little pirouette and bow. Alex was an idiot and a questionable poet, but his charm was ... unmatched? Unique? Different in a *not bad* way? Or ... something? I couldn't figure him out, but the place wouldn't have been the same without this '*Fuckin' A*' smartass. I couldn't help but smile, and just to keep his ego in check, I added a big fat Sam-stamped eyeroll.

That's when the phone in the hall rang.

This phone only rang when an approved call came in for one of the kids. The call would've already gone through the group home's main operator, Sally, whose office was next to Dave's. She was also a childcare worker, and one of the regular ones, but she seemed to prefer the paperwork side of the job, as she only surfaced from her safe space in times of desperate need. Like for coffee in the morning, after we'd all left for school. That was the rumour anyway, that she surfaced for coffee. Jen had seen her one day when she'd stayed home sick. Sally had recently dyed her blond hair auburn, and none of us had noticed for days.

Alex was first to the phone. He was dating some non-system chick from his school. Although, she did appear to be just as problem-prone, with her leather jacket, Dr. Martens boots, black clothes, black makeup, and black mood.

He picked up the phone hastily, then switched gears and put on his typical laidback attitude, "Hey there, what can I do you for?"

My eyes hit the sky again as I thought, 'what a cheese.'

Alex turned towards me, letting the receiver drop from his chin, "Eh, Sam—for you." He turned his attention back to the phone, "So ... Tig, eh? I've heard 'bout you. Those séances ..."

I grabbed the receiver and scowled at him, "Beat it, lover boy!"

Everyone knew everything about everyone in this place, or at least they thought they did—sort of like living inside a broken telephone.

I could hardly believe it was Tig. We'd asked around but hadn't managed to locate her. A whole month had passed since we'd parted. Relief had never tasted so sweet. I tried to keep my voice quiet and level, so as not encourage eavesdropping by the two alpha crazies sitting at the table only a few feet away.

"Tig! Oh my god! Where are you? How are you?"

Gabe was now by my side, mouthing the words, "I want to talk after, 'kay?"

I nodded, and he sat on the floor with his back against the wall by my feet.

Tig sounded tired, she hesitated before answering, "Eh ... I'm ... I'm back at my dad's place." She paused again, "I was in a shelter, but my dad swore to the judge that he'd given up drinking. The judge ruled that we should try again. Anyway. I miss you and Gabe."

This news was terrible. I didn't know how to respond. There was nothing I could say that would make Tig feel better or make her situation better. Back with her dad? The guy who beats her and maybe worse?

"Tig, is he hurting you?"

Tig hesitated once again, as if picking through possible responses in her head, "He's my dad ... He makes mistakes. I stay out of his way. He likes it when I make him supper, keep the place clean ... I keep him happy and he's OK. He fired Rick though. I never see Rick anymore. I wish we lived closer ... I'd come to see you then."

"You've gotta get out of there, Tig. We can figure something out. I mean, shit man, *I'm* in a group home, it can't be so hard to get you committed too! Did you tell the cops about ..."

Tig interrupted my line of thought, "Sam, I know you and Gabe want to help me, but as long as my dad wants me home I don't think the judge will commit me. That's what it sounded like, anyway. I turn 16 in a month. Then I can find a job, eh? The judge said that I can legally move out then too. It's only another month. I'll be fine. Don't worry 'bout me 'kay?"

Among all the feelings and thoughts running through me at that moment, 'OK' was not one of them. I was far, very far, from 'OK' about all this. Tig could not live with *that* guy, the one I saw beat her silly and then throw her to the ground and undo his pants. Tig's dad was the devil incarnate.

"No Tig, I'm not OK with this. You need to jump on the bus and come back to town. I know places you can stay. We'll work this out together, 'kay?"

Gabe couldn't take the heart-breaking conversation we were having. He rested his head on his knees, as he listened quietly. Then he got up and left, up to his room, to get away from it.

Tig ended our call suddenly with, "Gotta go, he's back." And she hung up without waiting for my reply.

I leant back against the wall, biting my lip anxiously, reflecting on our conversation and feeling helpless. It occurred to me that I forgot to get Tig's phone number. I jumped up and headed to Sally's office, hoping she had recorded the number. She informed me curtly that it wasn't her job to record numbers. After some begging, Sally passed me the phone book, so I could look Tig up, but no Macklins were listed in the Manny Cottage area. So, that was that. I'd have to wait until Tig called again. Completely helpless.

I knocked on Gabe's door, but he wasn't in his room. I found him sitting outside my window on the frost-bitten fire escape, smoking a cigarette, blowing broken rings, thinking. The window was propped open with my geography textbook—just enough for him to fit his hands under the bottom and pull it up again. I grabbed the blanket from my bed, pulled the window up, crawled through with the blanket, pushed the window back down again, and sat next to Gabe on the step. We sat there silently, wrapped in my blanket, sharing a cigarette, then another, practicing smoke rings, as we contemplated our lack of power.

Gabe finally broke the silence, "Life is so fucked."

I nodded in agreement. "She'll call back. We need a plan, before she calls back."

,

Our first fall snowstorm started after midnight on December 2nd. Most of me was unaware, as I slept somewhat soundly. But some part of me must've sensed the wind howl, the trees creak, the ice pop, and the snow pelting against the window pane, because I had the strangest dream.

I was back in the house, the abandoned one that I'd stayed in with Tig. But I wasn't *normal me*. I was tiny like a bug, clinging to a beam, watching life through compound eyes.

The wind was blowing hard outside, which made the old roof creak and the windows rattle in their rotten frames.

Tig and her dad were sitting below me, across from each other, conversing. As the storm grew outside, Tig's conversation with her dad became heated, almost as if they were arguing about the storm. Tig's dad kept pointing at the roof and Tig responded by shaking her head. I tried to yell at Tig, to tell her to run, run now while she had the chance, but my voice was too tiny, she didn't hear me.

With a loud *BANG!* the roof instantly gave in to the wind, blew right off and away into the night. The snow now pelted down into the living room and the wind whipped the curtains around wildly.

Tig's dad lost it. He began shouting at her, telling her the storm was her fault, that she was a whore, and pumping the air with his fists. He ran at Tig and she dodged him, but he caught her the next time he lunged. I watched, powerless, as he beat her, a spectator unable to move from my perch on the beam. I closed my eyes and began to pray for help.

When I opened them again the scene had changed. No longer on the beam, I'd moved down to a spot on the wall. Tig and her dad were gone, only to be replaced with Frankie and that creep Christien. Frankie wasn't fighting, she was hardly moving, and Christian was ... doing stuff, the stuff that Frankie had told me about, the stuff that I hadn't wanted to believe, the stuff that ended our friendship.

I tried to fly away, escape the memory, but an all-mighty force held me fast. I couldn't move, couldn't be heard, all I could do was watch, and be useless.

In the next moment, I was down in the midst of it, under Christien, held by fear. He was grunting and drooling and telling me not to worry, that this was something I *wanted*, something I *deserved*, something I *owed* him. I stared at him, eyes wide, unable to scream, defenceless.

I woke up panting and drenched in sweat. I didn't help Frankie. I couldn't help myself. I had to help Tig. I just had to. Gabe and I would make it happen or die trying.

But how do you help someone when you don't know how to find them?

My mind raced, I got no sleep, and I still felt useless in the morning. I considered skipping school. I hated school, and it was even less tolerable when tired and stressed. But the idea of being sent back to Manny Cottage was worse.

,

"Gabe, we've gotta use the paper. Write an article that will save Tig or something. Use our voice, eh? That reporter at The Gazette does it all the time." I said this to Gabe as he ate breakfast the next morning. I hadn't got my appetite back since I'd been home again. My mother had that effect on me.

Gabe looked up from his bowl, "Like what? An article that tells the whole friggin' world Tig's secrets? I think it was you who said that was stupid, *Sherlock*. Oh no, hold on, maybe we could write an article about the time her dad turned up at our sex séance and get her committed to Manny Cottage with the quackos!"

Sarcasm didn't suit Gabe. He was hardly ever sarcastic, not in a mean way anyhow. But his current tone was full of *get fuckin' real*.

"OK ... so, not an article?" I said, feeling stupid for suggesting it.

"No, genius, not an article." Gabe said way too grumpily.

"What's your problem? This isn't my fault. Take it easy." Now I was getting grumpy too.

Gabe put his spoon down and lowered his voice to out-of-Dave-range, "Sorry. But what the fuck are we supposed to do? We can't do anything. We're like ... stuck ... while Tig's at home with that fucker! *What the fuck can we do?*"

There wasn't an answer to this question. We had to do something, to fix the problem, but we didn't have the means in our toolbox.

"We've gotta convince Tig to run. That's what we *can* do." I said, not entirely sure of how we'd do this, but that's all I had, so I'd said it.

Even if we did convince her to run, where would she go? Wasn't like it was warm enough for the streets. She'd need a place to stay. And the only people I knew with places to stay were creeps that'd want something in return. I was quite sure Private School Gabe here didn't have those kinds of connections either.

Hope twinkled back into Gabe's eyes. "I know this guy ... his parents are caretakers in an apartment building on Côte-des-Neiges. Anyway, they renovated the basement of the place and made it his room. It's real big, and he's got everything down there. The place might as well be an apartment. His parents go away a lot, he's held whole parties in his room. That's where I met him, at one of his parties. He's super cool. I think he'll be open to helping Tig out ... y' know, if we explained the situation."

It was nice to have *Hopeful Gabe* back. *Grumpy Gabe* had been a new, strange, and highly uncomfortable experience.

9

Tig called again the following week, and we pitched our plan to her. Between the two calls, we did ample research and came up with a decent runaway plan. The biggest obstacle would be Tig's own resistance. But we had a plan for that too.

Gabe took the phone this time, "Eh, Ti ..." Tig must've cut him off because he fell silent, listening.

I sat on the floor by his feet, prompting him to give me a hint to what was going on. Concern was written all over his face. I nudged him, mouthing the word, *"What's wrong?"*

He put his hand up, making a *'stop, wait, quiet'* gesture.

My heart sped up as I ran through possible causes for Gabe's stress concerning Tig. Was she scared? Was she hurt? Or worse? Could it be someone else on the phone telling Gabe some horrific news? Did her father finally completely lose it on her? I shook Gabe's leg in a *'tell me now!'* gesture, but he remained quiet, listening, with an annoying unexplained worried expression.

I couldn't take it any longer. I seized the receiver, "Tig? Is that you? What's wrong?"

At first, the line was silent. Then there was a sniffle.

Tig replied, "Sam? I ran. Early this morning. He went nuts last night. Came home drunk and just went batshit." Tig paused, sniffled again, and said in a trembling voice. "It was like he used to do to my mom. I was so scared. When he fell asleep, I ran. I thumbed a lift to town. So, I'm just up the street, at Guy Metro. Where do I go, Sam? I have nowhere." I could hear in her voice that she was trying hard to not break down in tears.

Our dilemma was that we hadn't planned for her to escape before Saturday, the day that Gabe and I had some extended unsupervised time. We were house-bound on weekday evenings. This was the worst time for her to need our help. Our plan would need some innovative thinking. I asked Tig to hold for a second while Gabe and I had a whispered brainstorm session.

Dave walked by and peered at us suspiciously. We smiled innocently and he said, "Uh-huh." And continued on his way.

"OK. We have an idea. You can come here while we work it out." I gave Tig the address and instructed her to climb the fire escape on the back of the building to my bedroom window on the third floor.

She agreed, we hung up, and I looked at Gabe. "Shit. You call Vincent, I'll go up and wait for Tig."

Gabe nodded and I headed for my room.

I waited 15 minutes and then crawled out onto the fire escape, worried that Tig would change her mind. She turned up around the back of the building after a couple of minutes. She stood stiffly, frozen, in her summer runners, jeans and hoodie. It was -9C out with 10 cm of snow on the ground, and she was dressed for a summer night. I threw a snowball to get her attention and signaled for her to come up.

When Tig reached the landing outside my window I couldn't help but stare. Her face was hollow, as if she hadn't eaten for days. She had a fresh bruise on her neck, but her black eye wasn't new. She'd had so much joy in her when we'd been living in our slumdog house. But now she seemed empty and scared and powerless. Like a depressed hummingbird that had lost its ability to hover and hum and dive and play. She was Tig without the Tigger.

I tried to put my arms around her, to give her a hug, but she flinched when I touched her. "Oh my, Tig." I didn't know what else to say.

We climbed through my window and into my room. There wasn't a lock on my door, but no one ever checked the rooms before bedtime. I was sure we'd be fine, we wouldn't be discovered, as long as we stayed quiet. We sat on my bed, with Tig wrapped in my blanket, holding hands in silence.

Gabe knocked the secret knock and came in. He also tried to hug Tig and got the same flinched reaction. His eyes moistened and turned pink. He put his fingers to his mouth and squeezed his bottom lip, like he did when nervous and couldn't think of what else to do.

He whispered to me more than to Tig, "Vincent's on his way." He looked at Tig, "He's a good guy. He'll take care of you, OK?" Gabe paused, and when he continued there was a shake in his voice, "I'm sorry we weren't there for you, Tig. And I'm sorry we can't be with you tonight. I'm so sorry, Tig. I'm so sorry."

I'd seen Gabe emotional, but never like this.

Tig gazed at him, with the faintest glimmer of hope in her attempted smile. "I'm fine, Gabe. I'm fine. I'm out now. In a month I turn legal, I can get a job, I can do whatever I want. Now, stop blubbering all over me, 'cause I'm fine, 'kay?"

I'm fine. Those two words, that spec-sized sentence, must be the most underrated sentence of all time. So laden with meaning, yet easily dismissed. Like being given permission to move on, to not think about *it* further, because *it* doesn't affect *me*, it's *someone else's car crash—thank god.* Tig spent the remainder of December being 'just fine', while we stood by and watched.

CHAPTER SEVENTEEN

There's More to the Grinch

December

Tig greeted Gabe and I with a big warm smile on Saturday. She'd only been staying with Vincent for a couple of days and was already back to her more typical bubbly self. I shared a relieved glance with Gabe and took a seat on one of the two sofas in Vincent's space.

The room was impressive, with personalized graffiti covering the walls, a huge kite hanging from a high ceiling, and a jamming stage in one corner. An artist and musician, Vincent's room reflected his talent, imagination, and dreams. He was a student at Beats High, a fine arts school downtown, also my old school, but we'd never hung out. After meeting him for the first time the day before, I couldn't help but wonder how we'd managed to miss each other. He was exactly *my type*. I tried not to ogle him as we made small talk.

Tig talked most of the time, as usual. We could always count on Tig to fill uncomfortable silences with chatter. She always had something to say, something to laugh at. It felt odd watching her smile and laugh and joke around, with that ugly bruise around her neck and a black eye. The happiness and the bruises contradicted each other. If I closed my eyes and just listened, or if I'd been blind, I would not have guessed that she'd been so recently beaten up by her dad. She amazed me. If only I could heal so quickly, be so relentlessly vibrant and positive in the shittiest times.

Tig raved over how great a musician Vincent was, "If I hadn't seen him playing with my own eyes, I swear I'd have thought the music was coming from the stereo. He's crazy good." She said to me and beamed at Vincent. She added enthusiastically, "You guys should play that Metallica song together ... uh ... what's it called, Sam?"

"*Master of Puppets*?" I smiled a little, hoping deeply that Dream Boy Vincent would be up for it sometime. "I'd need my flute, though."

Vincent smiled back at me and something purred inside me. He said, "Sure, I'd love that! Maybe I can even find a flute for you somewhere, eh, if you can't bring yours."

Yup, this was going well.

Gabe interrupted Tig's *Vincent-is-great* session, clearly annoyed by it, "'Kay, so ... anyone for pizza?"

Vincent replied, "Already ordered. Should be here in a few minutes." There was a knock on the window. "*Et voila!* Magic! Mention pizza and so shall it appear."

Vincent rose from the sofa to retrieve the pizza through his bedroom window. While he was up, Gabe took his place beside Tig. Which turned out well, as it meant Vincent would be sitting next to me now. I purred some more and smiled to no one in particular.

Vincent came back over with the pizza, placing it on the floor between the sofas. We all grabbed a piece. Then he reclined back on the sofa next to me and said, "So Sam, flute, eh?" He smiled that sexy *I'm-into-you-and-listening* smile of his.

I'd definitely be bringing my flute next time.

Tig leant over to grab a napkin. "Sam's a *wild* flutist. You guys'd rock the house down together." She slid off the couch onto the floor, to sit by Vincent's feet. Gabe was left alone on one of the couches. "I can do the dancing." Her smile was voluptuous.

"Sounds like a good plan to me." Vincent shared his sexy smile between us.

Gabe's eyeroll sped over Vincent like a hit and run. He chewed on his slice of pizza as if it was made of cardboard.

❡

Gabe sat on my bedroom floor, piecing our next newspaper issue together with violent intensity, shoving the articles and drawings and photos around as if they'd wronged him in some way. I tried to ignore him as I read his replies to the queries he'd received for his advice column.

"Gabe! Stop tearing the pages. Vincent's totally into me, man. He's not into Tig. And Tig's into you. Chill, man!" I motioned to his responses in the advice column, "And you've gotta change some of these replies or you're gonna get a target plastered to your head. I mean, '*Stop being a gullible frignibble, she's a fake and a cheater, just leave her*'? And, '*If you think he's into you, get friggin' real because all he wants are your tits*?' Seriously Gabe? Who are you replying to here? 'Cause it doesn't look to me like it's got anything to do with the questions, '*I've been with my girl for a year and I think I want to marry her. Am I too young?*' And '*Will my guy bolt if I tell him I love him?*' I mean, really Gabe?"

Gabe peered up at me, clearly annoyed at my interruption of his demolition of our newspaper. "I offered advice, not patience. Those questions were the stupidest questions ever. I mean *who* wants to get married when they're like 16? And, love?? What a load of shit. What is '*love*' anyway? It's just something Hallmark made up for losers who ask stupid questions like this!" He got up and left my room, slamming the door for effect.

I thought, '*OK, then.*' And took his place on the floor, puzzling our newspaper together. We had two days before it went to press, and although Gabe was having issues, I quite enjoyed my role as Chief Editor. The theme of my story was dealing with Christmas music when everything sucked. I called it, '*There's more to the Grinch*'. We'd also added a games section this time, with a Creative Swearing crossword and a 'Whodunit' riddle, compliments of Dave who was full of riddles.

The doorknob squeaked behind me and I assumed it to be Gabe coming back to apologize. He was like that with his emotions—fiery but apologetic. I continued fiddling with my pieces of newspaper and waited for him to speak. The door shut and I could sense him standing behind me, watching, waiting for me to acknowledge him. But this was his emotional mess, and he'd have to start, so I did my thing and waited.

"You're not so special, y' know."

Tema, not Gabe.

I spun around and stared at her, surprised and more than slightly worried that we were in a room alone together with the door closed. She had her hands behind her back and the panicky part of my brain wondered if she had a weapon in them.

Tema continued, "You think you're all hot shit 'cause of this paper, but you're really just a dumb rich chink brat. I could squash you in a second." Tema said all this very matter-of-factly, as if only pointing out the obvious.

"Tema ... anything I can help you with? Is there something you want from me or did you just drop in to say hi?" I felt a bit more secure dealing with her in *my* group home than I had in Bethel, which had been *her* lair. And I needed to get back to my papers, so thought I'd move the conversation along and get to the point.

Tema tensed, scowling at me quietly for a moment. I could hear some crunching of paper behind her back. Then she relaxed her facial muscles just enough to speak clearly, "I wrote a short story. A murder mystery. And you're going to put it in your paper." She produced the folded sheets of paper she had hidden behind her, unfolded them and smooth them out.

If I hadn't known her better, I'd have thought Tema was actually nervous. Perhaps she was? I pondered the thought for a second, and decided it was a conundrum not worth my time. Tema held the story out towards me and I took it.

"I'll take a look at it. I can't make promises though. Everything goes through Dave, eh?" Actually, I was quite clear on what was allowed and what wasn't, and I was the first in line with the power to approve and reject content. But, in Tema's case, I'd be blaming Dave if I had to reject her work.

"Nope, not good enough. You have a decision to make: either publish this or I fuck up your life—capiche?" Tema was definitely direct. I hoped desperately that her story was publish-worthy.

"Gotcha. You done or can I help you with something else?" No point trying to explain 'acceptable content' to her. I could do some editing ... maybe she wouldn't notice. I mean, how many people re-read their piece after it has been published, right?

Tema grimaced at me, then turned and left, slamming the door behind her. I breathed a sigh of relief, rolled my eyes and thought, *'What a psycho'*. I was glad that the anger I held inside wasn't as horribly tormenting as hers. I flattened out Tema's folded story and began to read.

9

Tig tapped on my window that night, shortly after I switched my light off, catching me by surprise. I listened at my door for possible approaching staff, then opened the window and let her in. I wouldn't be joining her on the fire escape in this kind of bitingly cold weather.

"Shit, Tig! What's wrong? What are you doing here? We've got about 10 minutes before Dave makes his rounds." If I was caught with Tig in my room, I'd surely lose privileges, and I had a jam session date at Vincent's on the weekend.

Tig smiled awkwardly, "Promise you won't be mad at me?"

Not sure whether to nod or shake my head, I did this unsure rotating motion instead and asked, "Why?"

"Me and Vincent ... we kinda ..." She started.

I interrupted, "What the fuck, Tig? Seriously?" I shook my head and said more to myself than to her, "This is such a fucked-up day."

And, Tig's nonchalant behaviour after going through all that crap with her dad was even more fucked-up. She seemed happy, like it never happened, like her life was *normal*. She was just a normal kid screwing another normal kid under perfectly normal circumstances. It confused me, and she wouldn't share, so I had no clue what was really going on in that fiery-haired head of hers.

Her smile turned guilty with a tinge of defence, like she'd been caught stealing coins from the swear-jar. "It was just once! He's hot, OK? I don't really want to go out with him or anything. He's just hot. Trust me ..." She winked at me, "I was only warming him up for *you*."

My jaw clenched, "What if *he's* into *you*, eh? And what about Gabe? You can't screw with guys like that, man. Guys can't take that shit. Anyway, Vincent's *my* mark, you slutty tease." I said the last bit half-jokingly.

Tig started to laugh, "And now you can have him!"

I *'pfffed'* and chortled, "Keep your leftovers. But I'm still jamming with him. And don't tell Gabe, OK? Gabe is into you in a more, y' know, *loving* way. He was all weird today, like he's got some kind of 6th sense goin' on."

The floor creaked outside my room. Tig hit the floor and shimmied herself under my bed. Dave opened my door, said goodnight, switched my light off, then shut the door again without an ounce of suspicion. I looked up at the glowing stars that Gabe had plastered to my ceiling as a '*welcome back*' gift and thanked them for being my lucky ones.

Tig pushed herself out from under my bed and gazed at me thoughtfully, "Yeah ..."

"'Kay fine, tell me about Vincent. How was it? He as sexy under all those senseless layers of clothing?"

Tig crawled into bed with me and told me all about it, as if she'd won a prize date with a porn star from *Hustle Me: Women's Edition*.

She was still talking when I fell asleep, and had left by the time I awoke the next morning.

9

My jam session with Vincent went as well as it could go, with me knowing his and Tig's sexy little secret. I was glad that Gabe had decided to stay away, as *that* could've been way more awkward. I wasn't into guys as 'boyfriends' anyway, I reminded myself. Sex is sex. Right? Yup. Tig had the right idea. Sex is *just* sex. And I'd be having a serving of Vincent before the New Year.

"Eh, Sam, that was fantastic." Vincent said to me as his band members put down their instruments and headed for the fridge. "We've never played with a flute before.

You added spark—it was cool, unique." He studied me, gracing me with that cuddly smile of his, "You want to play with us at my New Year's Eve party? That would be awesome ... to have you along for the ride."

I thought, *'Yup, I'd love to ride you ... uh ... I mean hop on board ... uh ... meaning come along for your ride ...'* But I caught myself and said, "Yeah, sure thing. Let's play together." I returned his flirting smile and felt all hot and tingly inside. According to Tig, he even went down on her.

Tig overheard us and winked at me. No jealousy. Just a happy *'go for it'* wink. I wondered whether I should be concerned. But *sex is sex* ... right? Normally I'd talk to Gabe if I had concerns about Tig.

,

Our Christmas edition of *The Montreal System Rat* hit the press a week before the holidays began. Whereas our first edition had only been available to a few select group homes, this edition was distributed to all group homes and detention centres that had put an order in. It was our big launch, and we were thrilled.

Dave pasted each page of our paper up on the wall in the hallway, in celebration of the work that we had each contributed. I'd never seen him so happy with us. If he'd been scheduled to work this holiday season, I'd have chosen to stay in Charles A. for Christmas. Dave was far better company than my parents. But he had a family. The staff during the holidays were always the younger on-call ones.

Christmas Holiday for system kids was sure special, but not in a positive way.

No kid in the system had a 'normal' Christmas. Some went home to unwelcoming families, some stayed in the system with staff who wished they were home and not working during the holidays, while others went AWOL and ditched traditional Christmas festivities all together. And, there were always some Christmas hazards, usually within the groups of kids who went home or hit the streets.

Christmas for system kids was like walking through a dangerous jungle filled with unexpected events and emotions that hunt to kill. The only system kid I knew of that ever looked forward to Christmas was Gabe. But with all this Tig stuff going on, even he was apprehensive this year.

I stood in the hall beside Gabe, as we stared in delight at our paper now plastered to the wall, reading all the bits and pieces over again.

Gabe paused as he read Tema's story, "Did you edit this?"

My cheeks flushed, "What? Well ... I'm the editor, so ..."

He looked at me, "You edited this *a lot.*"

I shook my head, "No ... well ... not a lot, a lot ... Y' know ... some spelling, grammar ... changed the murder victim ... tweaked the setting ... just a bit."

Gabe raised an eyebrow, "And you think Tema's going to be fine with this?"

"Gabe, man. I couldn't let her violently bludgeon a staff member to death in her story. Trust me, the changes were for the better ... even if she re-reads it and notices. And if she does, I'll blame Dave—say the changes were his decision."

Just then, Tema wandered into the hallway on her way to the office. We both promptly turned our backs to the wall, covering her story, as she steamrolled her way past us.

"She'll never notice." I said only somewhat confidently to Gabe.

He glanced at me sideways and replied, "Uh-huh."

,

The holidays arrived on Friday with my head still connected to my neck. Tema hadn't noticed my editing changes. Luck remained in my court, for which I was glad. I'd need lots of luck as I tried to navigate safely through my parents' holiday schedule.

It would be home for me this holiday season and I wasn't looking forward to it in the least. I'd prefer to spend Christmas hidden away at Vincent's with Tig, but that'd count as an AWOL, which would mean back to Manny Cottage for me. So, I enjoyed my last evening with Gabe, before reluctantly allowing myself to be sucked up into my own family holiday mayhem.

I lay on Gabe's bedroom floor as he decorated his room with the leftover ribbons and baubles that Dave had given him. Dave had invited him over for Christmas dinner with his family on the 25th, which had flipped Gabe's mood again. He was back to his carefree Christmassy self. I think part of him had given up on Tig. He'd stopped talking about her anyway.

"Gabe?" I asked and he nodded. "We're still doing that skating thing together, eh? On Christmas Eve?"

He nodded again.

"And that ..." I was abruptly interrupted by Tema, who stormed into Gabe's room fuming with anger.

"You better get your explainin' ready, you little cunt! Who said you could go change my story, eh?!" Tema ran at me, grabbed me by the hair, and attempted to pull me up to my feet.

"Ow! What the ... let me go!" I tried to turn towards her, to push her away, but her grip was too strong and painful. My only option was to follow her pull up until I stood on my two feet, at her mercy, bent down in front of her. I grabbed her legs with the intention of pulling them out from beneath her, but that scenario proved much more successful in theory than in practice. She stood there, her legs like steel rods screwed to the floor. She was a machine in human-form and I was Barbie trying to kick the machine over with my stiletto. All I could do was hang there from her fist, like a bauble on a Christmas tree, and succumb.

Tema held me there for a minute, enjoying my pointless efforts at escape. With satisfied glee in her voice she said, "From now on *you* are *my* bee." She let me go and swaggered out of the room.

Gabe sat on his bed looking stunned, his mouth hanging open. "Jee-zus ... that was fucked-up. But girl, you so fuckin' deserved that." Gabe let out a shocked laugh. "What d'ya think she meant by you being her *bee*?"

I sat on the floor, dragging my fingers through my hair, comforting myself while checking for bald spots. "Damn. Fuckin' psycho. Shit, maybe I deserved it a bit. Should've stuck to basic editing." Heat rose behind my eyes and the lump in my throat began to grow. "She's why I ran from Manny Cottage—where Ms. Queen Bee rules the hive."

Sensing my stress, Gabe shuffled through the box of decorations on his bed, found some mistletoe and dropped to the floor in front of me. He held the mistletoe above my head, put on his silly smile and said, "All I want for Christmas is a big ol' smackaroo from *you*, darlin'."

Returning his goofy smile, I rubbed the dampness from my eyes, and puckered up. Although I knew it to be his idea of a perk-me-up joke, it was the most meaningful kiss I'd ever had.

❧

I arrived back in my room to find the other alpha bitch, Gini, sitting on my bed. My fight or flight reflex kicked in before I could check it and I jumped despite myself.

"Fuck! What do you want? Get out of my room!" Two in one day was too much.

"Jeez, quiet down. Dave's gonna hear you. I'm not here to fight."

Gini sat by my pillow with her knees bent, her back against the wall. She fidgeted with the ripped hole in her jeans, and wouldn't look directly at me, which made her seem weak. Not a side of Gini I'd ever seen. I wasn't sure whether to be on my guard or not, so I remained by my open door, leaning against the frame, ready for a quick escape.

"Something up, Gini?" I said, trying to sound like I cared.

She studied the hole in her jeans, thinking through what she was about to say. "I ... I like the paper. It's good. Uh ... I was gonna write in to Gabe's advice column, eh ... But ..."

Gini started to tear-up and empathy began to sneak its way into my heart. Gini had made it her mission to make my life hell, so empathy was not something I'd ever had for her before. It was a strange feeling, and rather than letting my guard down, I became more wary.

"Did something happen, Gini? Uh ... do you need ... uh ... my help?"

That question sounded so weird coming out of my mouth—like a detached voice asking an inanimate object whether it needed something. Gini and I had never had a relationship that extended beyond seeing each other as annoying barely human entities.

"I can't go home. I mean, I have to, but I can't. My mom's like ... she's gonna be high. She's ... she wants me home, but only sort of, eh? She puts on this act. Like, everything's fine. But she's fucked-up, and I don't know how to help her." Gini's voice became stunted as she started sobbing more heavily. "She needs me there ... but it's all so fucked and I'm ... I'm just tired. I don't want to go." Gini glanced at me, totally vulnerable.

I relaxed and went to sit beside her on the bed. "Did you tell Dave? I mean, do you want to stay here?"

Gini shook her head, "No way, man. I can't tell anyone. My mom's my mom. And that's her secret. I just don't wanna go home. I gotta figure this out. What can I do? How do I be with her but not be with her? I'm all she's got. If I tell Dave, I may never get home privileges again. Holidays with her are just extra bad. Like, real extra bad."

I thought about her dilemma for a second. "Well ... uh ... me and Gabe are meeting up on the 24th ... Do you wanna join us?" I regretted my offer as soon as it left my lips, but it was said and I'd have to deal with it. And now, so would Gabe. I cringed inwardly. He'd kill me when I told him.

Gini brightened up a bit, "Eh, sorry for ... y' know. I'm just ... not great with people."

I smiled with effort, "Yeah well, I guess ..." And I trailed off, not knowing how to respond to that. Gini was a bitch. She read my journal to the world. She'd fucked with my happiness *a lot*. And now I'd invited her into my own holiday mess. I thought sarcastically, *'yay for new friends!'* But I also understood not wanting to deal with a nutso mother, so ...

𝟿

My mother put the groceries on the counter, fished the oatmeal cookies out of one of the bags, arranged some in a perfect circle on a plate, poured me a glass of milk, and said "Here dear, eat." All within 5 minutes of arriving home. I sat at the table in front of the plate, my hands by my side. She began to put the groceries away.

Taking in the room, I asked "New décor, Mom?" The whole house had been re-vamped for Christmas, everything in cream and gold this year. The lights on the trees outside were a traditional antique white—as always—but the inside décor was new. In past years it had been shades of green and white, with bits of red here and there. This year it looked more like something out of an Arabian prince's palace.

"Yes, new. We needed some *new* in this house. Besides, green, white and red were becoming tacky. Gold is the new green. I wanted gold and purple, but your dad preferred the cream. Do you like it?" She asked, without looking at me. Her question was more of a habitual add-on to the end of her commentary, rather than a question that required a response.

"Yeah, I guess it's OK." I replied, but she didn't acknowledge it. Instead, she kept her back turned to me, while she did food things. I got up and headed for my room.

As I exited the kitchen, she called after me, "Sam, you didn't even touch your cookies. You're going to waste away!"

I kept walking, ignoring her.

My room was as ridiculous as always. The least she could've done was redecorate it to suit my age while busy turning the house into her Christmas Palace Of Joy. I collapsed on my Princess bed. Pink, white, lace, flowers ... I mean, seriously? I felt more at home in the bathtub.

When she called me for supper, I ignored her. And when she came to get me, I feigned sleep.

❦

After a couple of lonely days hiding in my room among my enormous array of pillows and teddies, Christmas Eve finally arrived.

I met Gabe at the Bonaventure skating rink an hour before we'd planned to meet Gini. He'd been pretty pissed about the compromise. If there was anyone in the world he disliked more than Gini I'd be surprised, but he also had a big heart with room enough for paused judgment. So here we were, pausing our judgment, as we smoked a joint on the steps of an emergency exit, listening to the

Nutcracker Ice Capades soundtrack beating out from a tinny speaker above the doorway.

"This stuff better last, man, 'cause that girl's no walk in the park. Jeez, what were you thinking? Gini with blades on her feet ... it's like giving a hungry lion weapons, beyond the claws and teeth it already has." Gabe chuckled. "Whatever you do, don't piss her off, or maybe don't talk at all, or she may just skate all over your cheeky ass!" Gabe laughed, obviously trying to picture the scene—me and Gini having it out on the ice, hungry lion fighting angry Bambi, slipping all over the place, trying to walk on each other with skates.

"Gabe, man, get your mind out of the gutter and stop fantasizing 'bout chicks scrapping. I am way too civilized for fighting to the tune of the Nutcracker." I took another long toke, and spluttered it back out immediately with a poorly contained laugh. "Shit, Gabe, what have we done?"

"What have *we* done? Nah-ah, Gini's *your* problem. I'm just gonna skate quietly behind you guys and enjoy my buzz." He gave me a huge self-satisfied grin.

I replied with a shake of my head, an exaggerated eyeroll, and called him a "fuckin' wimp." His smile grew, as if saying '*yup, and?'* I gave him a shove, then laughed along with him.

Gini turned up as we were lacing up. She sat down beside me and put her bag by her feet. "Eh. Almost didn't make it, but I'm here." She sniffed the air around my head and smelling pot said, "Guess I should'a come early." Then she glanced at Gabe's skates and smirked ever so slightly, "You gonna do ballet or somethin'?" Gabe wore his black figure skates.

Without responding to Gini, Gabe took off onto the ice.

I turned to Gini and, summoning my caring side, asked, "Things OK with you and your mom?"

Gini avoided my gaze, and began to lace up her skates. After a moment, she replied, "Fine. Just Fine." She tied her skates, stood up, and entered the rink without another word.

As I followed Gini onto the rink, Gabe skated up from behind, caught my arm, and pulled me along after him. Gabe was born with skates on. He skated with elegance, fluidity, and control, like a happy dolphin showing off its tricks. Gabe's mother had been a professional figure skater, and he was the goalie on his high school hockey team. Drop a hockey player and gymnast in a mixer and you'd get Gabe. He let go of my arm and flew along the ice ahead of me, then did a double spin, exiting it backwards.

Gini skated up beside me, "Think you were right, eh? 'Bout the gaylord thing." She was referring to my journal entries and trying to bc funny, but it grated on me.

Eyeing her sharply, I snapped, "I wasn't right. And ... even if, who the fuck cares?!" I swallowed the rest of what I wanted to say to her about that episode, and the way she had exposed my lame journal babbling about my best friend to my best friend. I began to fume with the memory. I skated away from her and worked on calming myself.

I did a loop of the rink with Gabe, then he skated up ahead into the centre of the rink and did a perfect axel spin.

Gini caught up with me again, "Eh, uh, I'm gonna go."

I glanced at her, then away again. "OK." I considered trying to convince her to stay because that would be the nice thing to do, but I honestly just wanted to skate with Gabe. "Guess I'll see you after the holidays."

Gini nodded, turned away, skated off the rink and left.

As I watched her leave, guilt nudged me.

9

Every once in a while, holidays with my parents brightened up during dinner parties that included extended family and friends. This wasn't because I necessarily enjoyed the company of others, but rather because it meant that I wasn't alone with my mother. The 28th of December was one of these days.

The party happened at my parents' place and everyone from my Great Uncle Harry to Dr. Short, my childhood pediatrician—who also happened to be our neighbour—was in attendance, sipping homemade mulled wine and spiked eggnog while they gossiped about those who'd missed out or hadn't been invited. I attempted to avoid my mom by hiding in the group huddled around my Aunt Lucy who, after a few drinks, became the community gossip queen. She somehow knew everything that went on in the community and loved to share. After parties where she had been in attendance, the rest of the community knew all the details too.

Aunt Lucy flirtatiously flicked her long straightened hair away from her face and smiled mischievously at her listeners. She'd been talking about the family feud that the Richardsons on Elm Street had going on with the other Richardsons on Hugo Street. One twin had apparently betrayed the other one with someone on Huntington Street. Aunt Lucy's eyes were wide with the heat of her story as she stood in the spotlight that everyone had gifted her.

"... so, Mary just turned up, on June's doorstep, with a bottle of *apology* bubbly, she walked right in without even knocking, all ready to make up and get on with life, and came face to face with butt naked Jason, his pecker sticking right up high saluting the heavens! I tell you, I'd have loved to have been a fly on the wall! Poor June, she was a mess when she told me. Mary took that bottle and whacked that hard-on right to Kingdom Come, so to speak." Aunt Lucy winked and the group closed their mouths back up and started cracking up as they pictured the scene.

My Aunt was a real piece of work. Never boring, easy to chat with, but not someone you'd want to confide in. Yet, strangely, everyone seemed to confide in her. And even more interestingly, although she knew everything about everybody, not many people knew much of anything about her.

Mom came around with a plate of hors d'oeuvres. She held out devilled eggs and crackers with cheese and offered them to each huddled group. Everyone but me helped themselves to a couple of pieces. As my mom turned from the group I sat with she commented, "Oh yes, please excuse my daughter. She's intent on turning herself into one of those bony zombies in that hideous Michael Jackson video. Kids these days." She chuckled as if my state of mind was so obviously ridiculous.

I flushed, partly with anger and partly with embarrassment. The seed of hatred I had for her grew a little more.

The table with the drinks on it was presently unattended, so I wandered over casually and filled the tallest glass available with mulled wine, then added some rum as no one was watching. My happiness index desperately needed boosting.

As I stepped away from the table, I noticed my dad leave through the back door with the beautiful young dentist who lived a few doors down. I thought, *'huh, so that's his secret to staying happy.'* It should've bothered me, but it didn't. Whether my parents broke up wouldn't make a difference in my life whatsoever. I wondered if my Aunt knew about it. Probably. Perhaps the whole community knew about it.

I headed for my room with my tall glass of happy juice.

,

I sat on my bed, looking up at the absurd fit-for-a-princess canopy hanging down from above, falling elegantly around me. Was I *just* a spoiled rich brat? At least I didn't have Gini's mom. That little voice in my head wouldn't shut up. It kept telling me I didn't have the right to feel this bad, this sad.

I ignored the voice and chugged my drink. There was a harsh pang in my stomach as the sugar-infused alcohol filled its emptiness. But then the numbness kicked in and I lay back on my pile of pillows, enjoying my short mental vacay.

CHAPTER EIGHTEEN

Flirting with Death

New Year's Eve

I went with the Cher look for Vincent's New Year's Eve party.

I squeezed into the black leather laced-up dress, bought on my mother's dime, and then threw on the tacky Christmas sweater I'd added to my cart to hide the dress. As far as she knew, I wore an oversized sweater with a short tight skirt, which was barely acceptable in her eyes, but she'd held her tongue rather than argue. Wise choice, as we'd have argued but I'd have worn it anyway. My choice of makeup on the other hand would've surely ended with me tied to my bed, so that part I tucked away in my bag. Tig and I would do each other's makeup at Vincent's before the party started.

Tig's birthday gift lay on my dresser. It was a silver anklet with a *Tigger* charm attached to the clasp. I'd had the charm engraved with "Tig 16." I placed the bracelet in my change purse to keep it safe. Tig had finally turned legal working age.

As I put on my coat, Mom positioned herself in front of the door, blocking my exit. I braced myself for the emotional vomit she was about to spew all over me.

Mom peered at me with ingrained resent, "Sam, you have to eat something before you go. You can't just … do god knows what on an empty stomach."

I stared at her and didn't respond. The best way to make a quick getaway was to not converse.

My mother put one hand on her hip and resumed her charge, "Why do you do this to me? What have I ever done to you besides help you? Tell me, Sam! Why are you so intent on making my life miserable? Why are you so selfish? All I've ever done is dedicate myself to making you into the best version of yourself. And all you ever do is throw it in my face. You know what? You can just go, Sam. Go!" She opened the door for me and signalled for me to leave.

As I stepped out of the house, she yelled after me, "Don't eat for all I care! Be a ridiculous skeleton! Waste away! You've even managed to confuse your Aunt Lucy! *She* doesn't even know what to say about you!"

Despite my relief that I'd escaped the house, on my way to a happier place, my heart jumped as she slammed the door behind me. I stopped on the front path for a moment, gathering my thoughts, trying to focus forward into the night rather than back into my mother's world. I took a deep breath and continued on my way towards Tig.

The person I really wanted to speak with was Gabe, but he'd decided to skip the party. Still angry at Tig and Vincent, he'd accepted an invitation from Dave to celebrate the New Year with Dave's family. I was happy I'd be seeing Tig, but she'd changed since Demon-dad had crashed our séance. Lately, I often felt as if I was communicating with a Tig possessed by a wild party animal that didn't care about anything but sex, drugs & rock n' roll. Fun for a while, but Gabe made more sense.

,

I sat on the toilet seat in Vincent's bathroom, while Tig decorated my face with silver eye shadow, black liquid liner, pink blush, and blood-red lipstick. My hair, relentlessly straight, needed quite a bit of teasing. The whole process took close to an hour. Beauty was an art, and art should never be rushed.

Tig examined me, impressed with her work. "*Et voilà* ... A babe to be reckoned with." Then she turned towards the mirror and looked at herself. "I'm gonna go for the big-haired Stevie Nicks look." She said this mostly to herself, as she was the gifted artist, not me. I'd help her with her makeup, if she needed it, but that'd be unlikely.

Tig fished through her makeup case and pulled out a tiny baggy. She carefully dumped its contents onto the cover of the *Circus* magazine that lay next to the sink. Coke. She took a Joker playing card and a dollar bill out of her pocket and divided the little white pile in half. Making two neat lines with the card, she rolled the bill up into a tight tube, and passed it to me.

I was a 'badass' in many ways, but coke had never been one of them. I'd tried it once, and another time had a suspicion that a joint I'd toked from may've been laced with the stuff. But other than that, I'd stayed away from drugs that have the power to possess.

But today was Tig's birthday ... and New Year's Eve ... and ... eh, fuck the world, right?! I took the rolled-up bill from Tig, smiled, said "Bottom's up!", and snorted the line.

⸴

Vincent was prepping the stage together with the other musicians, when we entered his room.

Today I had *my* flute with me. I'd 'given up' music—as far as my mom knew—but my flute meant too much to let it go. I kept it at my parents' place because I'd be devastated if it got damaged or stolen at the group home. I could just imagine Tema or Gini using it in some evil revenge tactic. No flute sounded better to my ears, and I'd begun to really enjoy playing 'flute rock' with Vincent and his band. The difference between the flute Vincent lent me and my own was like comparing a dove's song to a robin's. Although a dove's tune is somewhat soothing, a robin can hit crystal clear notes that the dove just wasn't made for.

I held my flute safely against my chest and smiled.

Vincent and I would rock this place to the ground this New Year's eve. And then I would *rock his world*. It was all part of my New Year 1988 plan, and after that line of coke, I became unstoppable.

As we approached Vincent, Tig whispered "Eh, uh, I think Vincent's chick is coming by later tonight. They're on and off, and pretty sure it's off at the moment. Just a heads up."

I glanced at Tig, flashing her a cocky smile. "Guess I'll have to do him sooner than later then."

Unstoppable, invincible, indestructible, at that moment I was a superstar and Vincent was about to be my biggest fan.

Vincent greeted us with his typical sexy *'join me in my spotlight'* smile. Without gawking, he took every inch of us in with his eyes. I felt caressed with his attention, and he hadn't even said anything yet.

Still smiling, he finally said just one word: "Wow."

He walked casually over to us, kissed us each on both cheeks, perused me with his dream-boy eyes, and added, "*We* are going to rock the house tonight." Then he touched my nose, brushing something off the tip, "Got more of that too ... if you want some before the show."

,

We kicked off the party with Iron Maiden's *The Trooper* and ended our set with Aerosmith's *Dream On*. I'd never been so exhilarated! When the last note died, I threw my arms around Vincent, and we kissed each other without a second thought. My veins pumped with the excitement and his kiss made my heart throb.

We let go of each other, gave the crowd a mock bow, and the band headed off-stage into the storage room where our instruments would be kept safely away from drunk people. I was the last to deposit my instrument and as I put it down, the door closed behind me.

Vincent leant his back against the door, his hair stuck to his face with sweat, his eyes eager and committed. He opened his mouth to speak, but didn't get the words out. I put my finger to his lips, signalling for him to hush.

"It's all part of tonight's plan." I giggled softly, and he smiled.

"Is it, now?" His smile widened, and he touched my face.

A moment later my hands were in his hair, his on my neck, and we were kissing more passionately than I'd ever before. He shoved me backwards, up against the wall, his hands everywhere, my dress pushed up to my waist. We slipped down to the floor, and now his lips were everywhere too. I thought, *'Fuckin' yay for storage closets and boys who aren't afraid of cunnilingus!'* Which I'd only just learned the word for, thanks to the *Hustle Me* magazines Gabe had hidden under his mattress. I smiled and enjoyed the trip.

,

We freed up the remainder of the night for partying with the crowd.

The place buzzed with laughter, horseplay, and people dancing to music thumping through *Marshall* speakers. The air was smoky, beer abundant, and everyone was high. Or, at least I was. Same same, right? I laughed to myself as I made my way around the room, between groups, taking a toke here and there, searching for Tig. With no sign of her, I grabbed a beer from the fridge next to Vincent's bed, and extended my search. Where had she got to? I checked the whole place but couldn't find her, and no one had seen her since our gig. I started to worry. Had she left? Where would she go? I mean, the party was *here*.

The only other place to check was outside, where the temperature had dipped to at least -20C. I couldn't imagine why she'd feel the need to exit into that. Was she annoyed at me for the stage kiss or for disappearing after the set? Had she gone looking for me? Had Vincent's ex shown up and kicked her ass 'cause of her own adventures with him?

My buzz turned anxious and jittery. My mind raced towards a brick wall with *'what ifs'* and my brakes were failing. I threw on a random jacket and opened the door to find Tig lying on the steps, her head resting on folded arms. It appeared as if she'd put her head down to relax for a moment and fallen asleep. She hadn't even thought to put a jacket on.

I tried to wake her, but she didn't budge. She was really cold, her lips tinted blue, and white frostbite circles had formed on her cheeks. Trying to contain my panic, I covered her with my jacket, ran inside, grabbed the first big guy I could find and ordered him outside to help me bring her in.

"Holy fuck. Is she fuckin' frozen?" Big Guy #1 said as he leant down to help pick her up.

Moving an unconscious person proved to be more difficult than we'd envisioned.

I yelled for more big guys. "Eh! We need help here! Uh, Lucien! Kev! Someone strong!"

Big Guy #2 showed up. "Jee-zus! Wow. This is one fucked up chick if I ever saw one! She get lost or something? Fuckin' girls." He laughed and shook his head, as if this type of behaviour wasn't surprising in the least, coming from a girl.

Why were so many 'big guys' so small-brained? Annoyance simmered. I shut it down and focused on Tig.

With effort, we got her through the door and back into warmth. As I ordered people to bring jackets to cover her with, she moved and opened her eyes.

"Stay still, Tig. We're going to warm you up. What the fuck were you thinking? It's fuckin' cold out! You got a death wish?" I laughed nervously, more because of anxiety than because I thought the situation funny. Laughing during highly stressful situations was one of my personal glitches. Thought Mom would kill me when I couldn't stop cracking-up at Granddad's funeral. Then again, to be fair, him with makeup on *was* pretty funny.

I covered her with jackets, scarves, and the hallway rug.

"Sam?" Tig glanced around, trying to place herself, confused. "Wha-z ... I'm tiy-red ... Where ... Wha-z goin' on? I gotta go, Sam. Sam? Sam?" She looked at me but didn't see me. "T-iss place. T-iss fuckin' world. Sam! Gotta go, 'kay?" She stuttered, then started to whimper. Tig attempted to push herself up off the floor but hardly lifted her head. "Gotta go, Sam." She pointed at the door but couldn't keep her hand steady.

I leant down next to her, and held her hand gently in mine. "It's OK, Tig. I got you. I'll always be here for you." My voice trembled. This was all so fucked. I should've seen it coming. Tig was far from *fine*. I should've seen it.

Tig's hand lay limp in my own. She was so weak. Her lips gained colour, but her skin remained ghostly pale. I crawled under the pile of clothes and cuddled up next to her. Body heat made sense. Saving a friend while high was like sitting an exam for a course you hadn't taken—it was all guess work and panic.

I told Big Guy #1 to call a cab. Tig needed more help than we could give.

Big Guys 1 & 2 carried Tig to the curb where the cab waited. As we made our way down the slippery walk, I saw a face that I hadn't seen in months. Frankie paused on the path in front of us, taking in the struggling huddle of what she likely thought were drunk people keeping other drunk people from falling flat on the ice. I followed the group, hiding myself from her line of sight. Frankie? What was Frankie doing here? Then Tig spoke, and my question was answered.

"Oh, fuck! Yer Fwan-kee! In d'photo! Hi!" Tig said this as if she'd been waiting forever to meet her.

I didn't hear a reply from Frankie, but imagined she was giving Tig her '*What the fuck?*'' glare. I thought, '*Well, at least Tig is feeling better.*'

Tig continued, "Yer a luck-ee duck-ee Fwan-kee. Vince's a jeww-wel. Tasty, tasty. G'd catch! Tanks fer sharr-ring." Tig giggled. She'd said too much.

Damn. Vincent's girl was Frankie. Now I'd definitely have to avoid her. And him. I couldn't decide which would be more unfortunate. I supposed it was him, as she didn't want much to do with me anyway.

Frankie ignored her, or at least didn't respond. She walked around us, her eyes straight ahead, looking towards the door where Vincent stood. Boy, was he ever going to get it at any moment. Frankie had totally missed me walking behind the group. I breathed a sigh of relief, and my head tightened with guilt.

"Nope. No! Ain't goin'!" Tig struggled and tried to resist as we helped her into the cab. She'd figured out where we were taking her and didn't want to cooperate. I finally convinced her to get in with a promise that I'd lie to the doctors about her identity.

Little did Tig know, events on this night would change her life forever.

CHAPTER NINETEEN

Tig

Early January

Sober voices floated like ghosts in the air around me.

A man's question penetrated the fog. "Alcohol? OK. Anything else?"

The answer came from a voice I recognized. Sam. Sam was here with me. But where was *here*? A lot went on around me, yet I felt oddly detached. *Me* was contained within a cloud, while everyone else shared clear sky.

A bump disrupted my haze, and I began to move forward. I was lying on a cot. The puzzle began to form. Lights zipped by above. Green and white robed people hovered over me. A hallway. I was moving through a hospital hallway.

Then my world shifted.

The hallway and people disappeared. I ran through a dark tunnel, away from something horrifying. The thing behind chased me, growling, getting closer with every step.

Abruptly, I found myself in a room with no doors. A familiar woman knelt calmly on the floor in the middle of the room. Her hands rested on her knees, and her eyes were closed. She seemed peaceful. It was my mother, but without the fear, blood and bruises.

I called out to her, but she didn't hear me. I tried to go to her but couldn't move forward.

Something held my feet. I looked down to see them chained to the floor.

Hostile laughter began as a low rumble and grew louder. The kind that had nothing to do with humour. My dad's laughter, as he approached breaking point. I began to sweat. I fiddled with the chains desperately, trying to find a way out. I called to my mom for help, but she remained unresponsive, safely contained within her made-for-one escape pod. How could she have done this to me? How could she leave me with this monster? Why wasn't she helping me? What was wrong with her, sitting there, safe and peaceful, while I was about to die?!

Death. Was that what was happening to me? I didn't want to die. Or maybe I did. Was that where my mom was? Dead. Was that why she looked so serene, so carefree? Was death her escape? No. I would have heard him kill her. I'd have seen her body. She wasn't dead.

I glared at her angrily and shouted, "Why did you fuckin' leave me, Mama?!"

She continued to kneel silently, an island in the middle of my prison cell, motionless and unaffected.

Dad's laughter got louder, until he'd materialized in the room between me and Mama.

Dad embodied his normal hulking, threatening self. Nothing could touch him, and he knew it. Charming to everyone but those who'd been caught in his trap. The difference between me and my mother was that she'd been caught and those caught can escape. I'd been *made* in his trap. I was an extension of this monster, and just as he'd never voluntarily give up a limb, he'd never let me go. I *belonged* to him, as his arms and legs belonged to him, as he'd belonged to the nuns back in that nutso orphanage he'd been raised in. In contrast to his other limbs, that he'd branded with tattoos, he'd branded me with an entirely different kind of hurt. Every bruise, cut, and burn on me was part of his story. And my mother had run away and left me in that pain, *in his story.*

I curled up, helpless and shaking on the floor, closed my eyes and wrapped my arms around my head to protect myself. If I made myself real small and stayed real quiet, his anger might pass. He was like that. One minute a crazy psycho, the next a proud father. I waited for the blows, but this time they didn't come.

My mother finally spoke. I looked up. Dad had disappeared and I was alone with her. A door had appeared in one wall, and she stood within its frame, sunlight and blue sky behind her. She beckoned for me to join her. As I approached the door, she stood aside.

The door framed a life I hadn't had past the age of 6. I peered through the frame and saw a quaint rustic kitchen. Mama kneaded dough on a long wooden table. I sat on the floor by my *Easy Bake* oven, baking a mini-cake. We were happy and Mama sang a song about my "Auntie in France who loved to dance." I'd never met Auntie, as far as I could remember, but she sounded exciting.

Then I got that itch that I get when Dad's around, on the back of my neck, like the type you get when some weird tickle in the depths of your mind tries to warn you about an impending April fool's joke. I looked up in time to see him standing behind Mama with that cricket bat in his hand. It was the one he used on her when she'd disobeyed him, like if she brought home scotch instead of bourbon or if she'd talked to the milkman for too long.

I wanted to warn her, but I sat there on the floor, scared, lame and mute. She must've sensed my fear, because her singing slowed for a moment, and she reached for the rolling pin. It was a heavy one, made of marble. I knew her intention. In that moment, she decided that she wouldn't be hit again, and that scared me more than he did.

Six-year-old me crawled under the table and curled up, hands over ears and eyes shut tight.

With my eyes closed, my world went dark. But I couldn't escape the sounds. Shouting, banging, the glass in the front door breaking, my dad cursing my mom, then silence. The silence was the worst part. I could never predict what would come of it. Once I'd thought my mom was dead, and I'd had to lie to the ambulance guys about what had happened. This time, she was gone. Not dead, just gone. That was the day she disappeared from my life, the day she'd left me with *him*.

As present-day-me watched the scene unfold from within my prison-room, terror filled me. I leapt through the door frame, trying to warn little me to run, to follow Mama, and not to let her out of my sight. But the floor fell out from beneath me and the kitchen dissolved.

My mother stood in the door frame shouting to me as I fell. She grew smaller and smaller as I fell further and further down through clouds and blue sky, and she kept repeating the same sentence: "I didn't name you after Tigger!"

My dad reappeared, floating just out of reach as I fell past him through the sky. A giant-sized nun towered over him, arms crossed and displeased. He shouted, "Dirty whore! Child of sin!" He spat at me in disgust. Before he could say more, he and the nun evaporated.

Next in line was Vincent's girlfriend, Frankie. She grew taller as she raged, "Fuckin' slut! Boyfriend vampire! No one needs people like you!" Her face got redder and redder, and she grew bigger and bigger, until I thought she'd stomp on me and squish me like a cockroach. And, poof! She vanished.

Then came Gabe's turn. His was the worst. He scowled at me, utter disappointment in his eyes. No words, only disappointment. After a few seconds, he turned away and dissolved into thin air. Pain shot through my heart. I *was* a total disappointment. Gabe was right, and so was Frankie. Why was I such a terrible person? Why do I do the things I do?

Mama's voice became distant, and I tried to hang on to it. What did she mean? Tig *was* short for Tigger. She'd told me that when I was little, just before she'd run.

Another voice drifted up from far below. "Tig, Tig, Tig, Tig ..." Sam stood on a rock, in a vast sea, directly beneath me. Calm waters surrounded her, and her arms were outstretched, ready for a hug. Bewildered, I yelled down to her, "Move Sam! I'm coming in fast!" But she remained on her placid island, smiling naively, unaware of the danger about to break her.

I woke with a start. The sky I'd fallen through evaporated and was replaced with tubes and blankets and pastel walls.

Suddenly, it hit me. *Antigone.* My auntie's name. "Anti" to me, but to my mom she was "Tig." Mama would tell me stories about the Greek Princess Antigone, known for her unwavering passion, morals, and stubbornness. Fiercely loyal to those she deemed worthy, her lust for justice was stronger than for life itself. Not unlike my Anti in France who loves to dance.

Mama was in France.

CHAPTER TWENTY

No really, I'm fine

Early January — Sam

Tig lost consciousness as she was rushed into Emergency. Doctors and nurses appeared all around, and I was pushed out of reach. I stood still in the hallway, watching as Tig was carted off further and further away. I felt empty and sick. Why hadn't I seen it coming? If only I'd paid more attention. If only I'd listened more carefully. Was she going to die?

A nurse put her hands on my shoulders and looked at me intently. "Hey sweetie, she's on a rough ride, but she should pull through."

Did she say, '*should?*' I felt hot and dizzy.

The nurse sounded as if she were speaking through one of those homemade telephones from childhood, the ones made out of two cans with a wire between them. I could hear her but couldn't make out all the syllables. She asked me a question. Something about whether I was also high or drunk, like Tig. I shook my head for '*no*', hoping she'd be a gullible one. No, no, no to everything. I needed to get out of this hospital, away from the questions.

My vision began to blur and my legs became heavy. I wasn't going to be able to fake it for much longer. Something was happening in my stomach. This might not be pretty. I put my hand on the nurse's arm to steady myself and attempted a reassuring smile.

Then I threw up all over her shoes.

,

I woke up in a hospital room of my own.

Tig was in the room next-door, and she'd be fine, I'd been reassured. My stomach hurt from hours of dry heaving. That's what happens when you don't eat, get shit-faced, and have to rescue your friend from death in the midst of it all. I made a note to at least eat some peanut butter before the next party. But that was the least of my problems. I'd now involuntarily gained my own posse of curious doctors. The questions were no longer about Tig.

"Sam, I'd like to introduce you to Dr. Bisset. I'll leave you two to talk." The nurse smiled and exited the room.

"Hi Sam. How are you doing this morning?" Dr. Bisset studied me through wire-rimmed glasses. He seemed harmless enough, but I sensed he'd prove me wrong.

I nodded, tried for a smile, and shrugged my shoulders. What did he want me to reply? How was I? Things were actually quite shit presently. And I really didn't want to talk about it.

Dr. Bisset interpreted my silence as a cue for *'let's talk.'*

"Sam, I'm a specialist in eating disorders. Your doctor has called me in out of a concern for your health, both physically and mentally. Your weight is dangerously below average. I see this a lot in girls your age. You are not alone. And I am here to help you, as I have helped many others." He paused for effect.

I thought, *'Oh, god. I've got a 'saviour' on my hands.'*

"Now, Sam, although your blood and urine tests tell me a story about your physical health, I need to ask you some questions that will help me create an adequate therapy plan. Are you ready?"

Was this honestly a question? What was with adults anyway? Did they all miss the class where proper use of punctuation was addressed?

I stared at him blankly.

He continued, "OK then." He smiled warmly, like a supportive uncle might. "This shouldn't take long."

The following 45 minutes were hell, and the doc did most of the talking.

"Tell me about your diet. On a given day, what do you eat for breakfast?" Dr. Bisset plucked his pen from his shirt pocket and clicked it into writing mode.

"Dunno. Don't really like breakfast." I glanced out the window, then examined a loose thread on my blanket. This guy would never get it.

"And lunch?"

I fiddled with the thread. "Uh ... dunno. Depends, I guess. Carrots, bananas, and stuff. Some, uh, bread. You know, sandwiches." Thought I'd better add some grains, or he'd be all over me.

"Good. You're doing great, Sam. What about supper?"

I'm doing great? He actually said that as if he believed it.

"Supper? Uh … a bit of this and that, I guess. Veg. I eat lots of veg. I'm kinda vegetarian. Oh, and you know, rice, pasta." Veg was what I heaped on my plate to avoid having to eat other parts of the meal. It made my plate appear as if loaded with food. I had fooled everyone but my mom.

"I see. I'm also vegetarian. I'm particularly fond of stir-fried lentils, cashews, and potatoes with my veg. How about you? What's your favourite combination?"

Shit. I'd asked for that one. Thinking of stir-fried anything made me want to heave.

I shrugged. "Maybe rice. I guess."

Dr. Bisset smiled warmly and scribbled something on his pad. I didn't trust that smile of his.

"And what about your family. I hear you don't live at home. Tell me about that."

What? What did that have to do with anything? I shrugged again.

"Nothing much to tell. My mom had this dream and I'm not it. End of story." That truly was an accurate short version I thought. I made a mental note to use it again in future grilling sessions.

"I see. And what dream do you have for yourself? If you could create your ideal self, what would it be?"

My ideal self? Hmm ... well, I like the idea of a red cape and super-powers ...

"I dunno. Less messed up. Less frumpy, I guess. More like Madonna. Strong. Independent. With, like, control over my own, you know, stuff. And I'd like her talent too. Yeah ... I think I want to be Madonna when I grow up." I said, half joking, and smiled. If I had Madonna's looks, voice, and control, I'd be perfect. Some of her bitchiness could help too.

"What do you mean by *frumpy*?"

I rolled my eyes. "Me! That's what I fuckin' mean!" I regretted adding the 'frumpy' bit. It had more to do with a feeling than a look. It wasn't something I wanted to dissect.

"OK, Sam. I understand that my questions may seem a little invasive. Let's switch gears." He paused thoughtfully and clicked his pen twice. Was it nerves? Or was he trying to remind me just how much power that pen gave him.

"Tell me about your favourite home-cooked meal."

It occurred to me that if I didn't start talking, I'd never see the end of this guy. I'd need to come up with a plan to stop the questioning.

Meanwhile, I feigned nausea, ran to the bathroom holding my stomach, and shut the door behind me.

❡

Dave was next in line. But unlike Dr. Bisset, Dave had nothing to smile about. I shrank and pulled the covers up to counter his chill.

"Talk."

JANE POWELL

That's all he said. Then silence. He sure had a way with words. The pressure that followed his silence cracked me within a minute.

I told him everything.

Well ... everything that didn't have to do with me. I told him all about Tig and her troubles with her dad and her absent mom. I told him about the old abandoned house and the time her dad showed up, leaving out incriminating details of course. I told him about how her dad beat her so badly that she'd run away again, and we'd found her a place to stay. And I may also have mentioned Tig's new coke habit and blamed her just a tiny bit for my own curiosity.

Dave listened in silence, his owl eyes weighing my words.

He had this way of using silence to keep me talking. I pinched my leg hard to shut myself up.

"So, what do you suggest? How do we keep you from being shipped back to Manny Cottage?"

His glare was tinged with love, I told myself.

Dave went on, "Ms. Cohen is no miracle worker. She has rules to follow. There's a system, Sam. And our system is based on consequences for actions. You abide by the rules and you're rewarded with trust. You break them and you're punished with Manny Cottage. You get it?"

What the fuck? Manny Cottage? Was my offence that bad? I gawked at him, dumbfounded. I'd never seen Dave so angry. His words began to sink in.

"Yes, Sam. Manny Cottage. Where did you think your escapade was going to get you?"

I thought, *'Uh, duh? Nowhere! Wasn't planning on having to save a friend and getting punished for the effort'*, but responded with a shrug instead.

"You better pray Ms. Cohen has a favour she can call in, because I fear that'll be your only hope."

Dave suddenly deflated. The angry wrinkles on his forehead dissipated and I saw worry in his eyes.

"You've been on such a positive path, Sam. I don't know why you've slipped. I just want you back on track, OK? You're one of the ones that *is* going to make it. Please don't screw this up. I'll do everything I can to keep you in Charles A. But you have to promise me you're going to put the effort in. Because if we can keep you, this'll be it— your last get-out-of-jail-for-free card. Are you willing to put in the work Sam?" His expression demanded honesty.

My eye began to twitch. Damn, I really had fucked up. My nose started to run. I chewed on my lip in an attempt to control my emotions. What could I say? I nodded and muttered, "Yes. Yes. I'm sorry, Dave."

"OK. I'll see what I can do." Dave held my hands in his and said his goodbyes.

,

Ms. Cohen knocked and stepped into the room shortly after Dave left. She gazed at me with that motherly *'it's fucked up but going to be OK'* look of hers. My eyes welled-up.

"Hi Sam." She approached my bed and swept my hair from my eyes. She had this way of reaching me that my own mother had never managed. If Ms. Cohen ever had kids of her own, they'd be lucky to have her.

"Dave filled me in on what happened. I can't promise anything, but there are some strings I'm willing to pull. I'll do everything I can to keep you at the group home."

I blubbered "thank you" through my tears and snot, and motioned for a Kleenex. There was nothing classy about tearful regret.

When I could talk clearly again, I asked about Tig.

"She's not awake yet, but her prognosis is positive. Unless there are any surprises, she should make a full recovery. I've been appointed to her case. Now, Sam, the doctors don't have her full name. We need to contact her parents. Do you have that information?"

I pictured Tig waking up to her dad towering over her with his belt in his hand. A cold sweat spread through me.

"Dave said that you mentioned an abusive home environment. I assure you, if that's the case we won't be releasing her to her father."

I couldn't bring myself to speak. I had full faith in Ms. Cohen. But the system had a life of its own.

I studied my blanket as if it might advise me. "You need to find her mother." I gave Ms. Cohen Tig's last name and hoped it wouldn't mean she'd have to involve Tig's dad. "Not sure what name her mom's going by though. Her dad's first name is George."

When I glanced back up, the colour had drained from Ms. Cohen's face. She stared at me silently. She was the epitome of stunned.

"Are you OK?"

Ms. Cohen didn't respond. Was she breathing? I thought she was going to be sick and I handed her one of the disposable throw-up trays from the stack on my bedside table. You know, the ones shaped like crescent moons and not at all deep enough.

She waved the tray away, put her hand to her chest, and breathed deeply. "Sorry. Uh. Sorry, Sam. Not sure what came over me. Must be a migraine coming on. I ... Uh ... I will try to find Tig's mother."

"Her dad almost killed her. Once, it happened right in front of me. That's what'll happen if you send her back. She'll die." I said this with absolute resolve.

"I've fought for you, Sam. Rest assured, my armour is on and I'm ready for Tig's fight too." The colour began to return in her cheeks. I was curious but decided it was a mystery for another day. Something to guess about with Gabe.

Ms. Cohen smiled, then hugged me. I hadn't had a hug for quite some time. I melted into her arms and my sobs returned uncontrolled. What the hell was wrong with me today?

⁹

Breakfast was horrendous and lunch even worse. The word got around that I was under weight and I'd been assigned my own meal surveillance crew. The only thing I managed to avoid eating was the muffin I'd hidden during a nurse's sneeze. What was wrong with these people? No one ate this much! I felt disgusting, like a blob being force-fed more blob. I had to get out of this place.

As my noon meal ordeal came to an end, a doctor came by to say that Tig was asking for me. She'd finally awoken.

CHAPTER TWENTY-ONE

Ms. Cohen

Dearest Éloïse,

I was visited by a ghost from our past today. Do you remember George Macklin? The kid who tried to save you from transfer to Cité de St-Jean-de-Dieu? He was so sweet on you. The nuns saw through his ruse pretty quick though. Poor kid was put on morgue duty not long after. He didn't fare so well. Sadly, I learned today that he has turned into the monster he once feared, and his daughter is suffering for it. To be haunted by such evil. Remember the shock therapy? George went through a lot of that. I was a lucky one. There were some icy baths and beatings, but no electroshock or anything worse. Guess the nuns and doctors didn't deem me possessed enough. Apparently, I didn't need an exorcism (tongue in cheek), a good whipping was sufficient. Or maybe I escaped before my time. A reporter caught wind of the whole thing lately. They're calling us the 'Duplessis Orphans'.

There's been talk of digging you up, for proof of the experiments. This may be the last time I visit you here. Remember the cherry jujubes Sister Annabel would smuggle in for us? I found the exact same ones in a shop today. I brought some with me. She tried to pick up where you left off, you know. I guessed it was her giving you the books and paper. Sister Annabel was impressed at how much you'd taught me. But then, one day, she was gone. I think she was transferred. No one would tell me. Sister Judith whipped me for those books. That's when the beatings got worse. I was so lonely without you and Sister Annabel. But I have nothing worthy of complaint. When I ran away and old Mrs. Cohen took me in, my life changed completely. I am eternally grateful to her, God rest her soul.

My dear Éloïse, I want to thank you for your gifts of reading and writing. I come here often to chat about the goings-on in my life and seek your advice. Your voice and wisdom live on in my imagination. I stood in this same spot, in this field of wild grasses, bones and memories, many years ago and made a promise that I would fight for today's orphans, just like you fought for me. Know that I am doing just that.

I love you.

Abi xxx

I pulled the matchbook out of my pocket then lit the corner of my letter. Holding it carefully, I watched as the flame made its way across to the opposite corner. Just before it reached my fingertips, I let the letter go. The breeze carried it for a few feet, until it settled in a patch of frozen wildflowers.

I looked at the ashy corner and smiled. "Like we used to do with my lessons. Into the wood oven and gone, but far from forgotten."

The frost-covered wild grasses sparkled in the sunshine. I could hear Éloïse whisper, *"I love you too."* To most, the field appeared to be just another weed-filled empty lot in the suburbs. But this particular field was filled with unmarked graves. Amongst the orphans, it was known as the place the unlucky ones were buried. Murder and suicide were hidden in this field. Children abandoned by love. Scapegoats. Science experiments. *Éloïse.*

I took the scissors out of my bag, knelt down, and cut off a handful of the beautiful wild grasses that hid the misery below them. The frozen grass smelled sweet and fresh, like a new beginning. I tied them together with a red ribbon, the colour of those jujubes. I'd hang my bouquet up to dry at home. Then I said goodbye to my dear friend.

It was time to fight for Tig. My first stop would be the archives at the courthouse.

9

I gathered my confidence as I stood in front of Judge Beaulieu's door. She wasn't the judge that had been assigned to Tig's case. It was her influence that I needed. She'd been fair with Sam, I hoped she'd be open to helping me with Tig.

I knocked.

"Entrer." French was her *langue maternelle,* her mother tongue, and she always started with it.

Judge Beaulieu's voice had an edge that reminded me of the nuns. It made me feel like I had to pee, as I had felt every time a nun got angry with me.

I entered her office and gave a little nod, seeking approval to speak.

"Ms. Cohen. What can I help you with?" The edge softened and I relaxed a bit.

As the judge didn't signal for me to sit, I remained standing.

"I have a case that needs some special attention. The, uh, Heather—aka 'Tig'—Macklin case." I offered the judge the file I was holding.

Judge Beaulieu didn't take the file. "I don't remember this case. Is it one of mine?"

"No. But ..."

"I have enough cases to deal with Ms. Cohen. Why would I want an extra?"

"Well ... It's about serious abuse. I want to avoid a child being sent back to a highly abusive single father."

The judge looked at me with that stern nun-look, and I hesitated.

"And?"

"The case has been assigned to Judge Parizeau."

"Oh. I see. And you don't think you'll get a fair ruling."

An inkling of understanding entered Judge Beaulieu's eyes. I could work with that.

"I'm hoping you might have some influence. Judge Parizeau has been known to rule almost unilaterally in favour of fathers, no matter the situation. In fact, he has sent Tig back to her father already once, an event that resulted in severe abuse. It's the reason we're back in court."

"And the mother?"

I took a report out of the file I held and handed it to the judge. This time she accepted it.

"I believe Mrs. Macklin may have sought refuge with her sister in France."

The judge nodded. "OK. Why did she leave her daughter with an abusive man?"

"She lost a custody battle. She had been staying in a women's shelter after Mr. Macklin had threatened her life. Mr. Macklin claimed she was a neglectful mother who had abandoned her daughter and was now homeless with no means to support a child. The judge agreed and granted him full custody."

Judge Beaulieu scanned the report. "According to this, Mrs. Macklin hasn't been seen since that day in court. It does look like she abandoned her child."

"Yes. It does. However, as the report shows, she tried to leave several times. The previous times she took her daughter with her. There are medical records that show the severity of the beatings she endured at the hands of Mr. Macklin. I can imagine how helpless and afraid she felt." I paused and studied the judge's expression.

Judge Beaulieu was impossible to read.

"And what evidence is there that suggests the mother would be a better parent than the father?"

I wondered briefly how the judge had gained so many facial wrinkles without ever displaying any emotion. I caught myself and re-focussed.

"Well, really, it's about *lack* of evidence. There is no evidence whatsoever of abuse by the mother towards the child. Our records show that she tried several times to remove the child from her abusive spouse and the system failed her and her child each time. She left because her life was at risk and the system would not protect her."

Judge Beaulieu looked thoughtful. "Have you located Mrs. Macklin?"

"Not yet, Judge. The court date is set for tomorrow. This hasn't given us much time. I'm requesting that Mr. Macklin's custody over Tig be revoked and that she be placed in youth protection until we can reunite her with her mother."

"Do you know that Mrs. Macklin still lives?"

I chose my words carefully. "I have not been able to find proof of death, and her French driver's license has not been cancelled." I left out the part about the address on the license not being accurate. My gut said she was alive. She had to be alive.

The judge nodded. "OK. Judge Parizeau owes me a favour. I'll see if he's up for a case swap."

I smiled, "Thank you, Judge Beaulieu."

She waved me out of the room impatiently.

9

I sat at my desk and looked at the name and number in front of me. *Antigone Marchand tel. (33) 4 67 39 46 39.* It was the last one on my list. I crossed my fingers and dialled.

"Àllo? Tig ici. C'est qui?" *Hello. Tig here. Who is it?* Said a bubbly voice on the other end.

"Bonjour. Est'ce que je parles avec Madam Marchand, la soeur de Isabelle Macklin?" *Am I speaking with Madam Marchand, Isabelle Macklin's sister?*

There was a pause on the line.

"Oui ... c'est qui?" *Yes, who is it?*

I breathed a sigh of relief.

"My name is Abi Cohen. I have information concerning her daughter, Heather Macklin. Can I speak with Isabelle please?"

Another pause, this one long.

"Est-tu là?" *Are you there?*

"Oui. Oui. I'm afraid Isabelle commit' suicide two years ago."

Now it was my turn to hesitate. This couldn't be right. All signs had pointed to her being alive. Her death had not been recorded in any documents I'd found, neither Canadian nor French. Her French driver's license was still active. She couldn't be dead! Dead. Oh, no. Darn. This was horrible.

"Is Heat'er wit' you?" Madam Marchand sounded concerned.

"Um, no. No. But she's OK. She's in the custody of youth protection. Living at home with her father was not safe. In fact, she is in the hospital right now. She's had a bit of a break down. She's doing better. I was hoping to bring her mother back into the picture."

"Oh, non. I come. She come 'ome wit' me. We talk when I get t'ere." She said decidedly, as if there could be no other solution.

Glad for her immediate willingness to help, I responded, "That is exactly what Tig needs. Merci, Madam Marchand."

"Tig?"

"Yes, her mother nicknamed her after you."

"Oh! Lovely. Oh, my 'eart fills wit' joy. I found Isabelle's little girl. T'ank you, Madam Cohen, t'ank you. I book flight now."

Madam Marchand called me back a few minutes later with her booking details, and I arranged to pick her up at the airport. She'd be arriving the following day.

That evening I wrote another letter to Éloïse, as I did every time I had something big to share.

CHAPTER TWENTY-TWO

Strange Love

January

The woman in the green dress stood in the doorway and smiled at Tig. Concern creased her brow, but a deep sense of relief shone in her eyes. She understood Tig on a level that Tig knew nothing about. She loved this kid as she'd loved her sister. And she had a terrible truth to convey that filled her with dread. If facial expressions could speak, this woman would win the fluency championships. She should really be careful with that talent.

I squeezed Tig's hand, and she held on tight.

"It's OK. I'll be back later." I tried to make my escape. Things were about to get awkward and I didn't do awkward well.

"You said you'd stay." Tig shot me a stern glare. "Please. Stay."

"OK … I'll just …" I motioned to the chair in the corner of the room. Tig let go of my hand and I took up my corner post, hoping to disappear in the shadows.

It had been a week since Tig was admitted to hospital. I'd been discharged back to the group home but spent my afternoons meeting with Dr. Bisset and visiting Tig. Dr. Bisset was one of my 'consequences'. Him and the newspaper. If I kept on track with both, I'd avoid Manny Cottage. It hadn't been a hard sell. As for mom, she'd stopped speaking to me. That wasn't so bad either.

"Oh, *mon dieu*. Tig. It is so nice to be 'ere wit' you." Tig's aunt, Antigone, stretched her arms towards Tig as if asking permission to hug her.

Antigone was a funny name I thought. Sort of like Penelope. She pronounced it An-tig-oh-nee. Tig called her Anti. She had a classy French accent. Real French people made Franco-Quebecers sound like swearing hillbillies. I supposed it was the same for High Tea English accents and Anglo-Quebecers. I caught my line of thought and cringed. *Oh blimey, I sound like my father!*

Tig smiled cautiously. "Yeah, uh … you too."

"Anti. You call me *Anti*, jus' like befor'. Last time we met … so long ago … maybe you were t'ree or four. *Et bien* … so long, so long. " Anti approached Tig, no longer waiting for permission, and hugged her tightly. "Tig, I am so sorry about your mot'er. She was so sad. She loved you so much."

Tig's mom had struggled with depression for years before eventually ending it all. Tig would never be meeting her mom again.

Tig didn't return Anti's hug. She squeezed her eyes shut as if trying to keep her emotions locked up safely behind them. Forgiveness would take time.

A smudge on the wall became particularly fascinating. I stared at it intently. Was it a squashed mosquito? Splatter of blood? Perhaps a touch of spaghetti sauce vomit?

Anti released Tig and cupped Tig's face with her hands. "Oh, *ma p'tite chouette*, I know t'is is 'ard for you. You 'ave 'ad a 'oribble time. T'ere are no words to say 'ow sorry I am about t'is. But I am 'ere now, for anyt'ing you need. You will never 'ave to go back to t'at *diable incarné.* W'atever you need, Tig. You will never be alone again."

Tig opened her eyes and looked directly at Anti for the first time since she'd entered the room. Tig wrapped her arms around Anti's waist and buried her face in her dress. She'd become a little girl again. Last time I'd seen Tig crumble like this was at that bus stop, after her dad had attacked her at our abandoned house.

"I hate you! But I'm glad you're here." Tig sobbed. Love had finally found Tig, and she'd be holding on tight.

As touching as this all was, I took the opportunity to sneak out of the room and back into emotionless oblivion.

9

Gabe waited by the Tupper Street exit. One hand stuck in his pocket, the other holding a smoke, his shoulders hunched over and jacket unzipped. He was cold, but cool.

"Eh man, you should really go in and say hi for yourself." I motioned for him to pass me a cigarette.

"Whatever." Gabe glanced away as he handed me his pack.

"Chicken shit." I lit my smoke, inhaled deeply, and exhaled ringlets. Blowing rings relaxed me. Nothing else mattered in those moments. The world was reduced to rings of smoke.

"Fuck off." Gabe was annoyed. But honestly, if anyone should be annoyed it was Tig.

I smiled, teasingly.

He retorted, "Eh, you look like crap. You feeling OK?"

"Screw off." I shoved him playfully. But, truthfully, I had been feeling like crap over the past few days.

"No, seriously. You're super pale."

I shrugged.

We crossed the street and headed for the Dawson College campus.

"Gini show up this morning?" Gini hadn't returned after the holidays and no one would tell us anything. Gabe paused in thought, then shook his head for 'no.'

I was worried about Gini. She could be a real bitch, but she was still system kin. When kids ran away everyone knew about it. Silence often pointed to a bad scenario. And I hadn't exactly shown her much empathy at the skating rink. Not like she had ever earned any ... but, yeah.

Gabe spoke again as we entered the campus, "'Kay. Yeah. You're right, OK? But ... what would I say? Maybe Tig doesn't even want to see me. Does she honestly care anyway?"

We climbed stone steps to arched wooden doors and entered into warmth. The building had an interesting history. If I'd been a tourist looking at it from the outside, I'd have thought it was a cathedral. Once a nunnery and place of religious contemplation, now filled with students from all walks of life studying all sorts of subjects, one of which was journalism. Secretly, I hoped to be a student here one day.

The library was my favourite part. I stood in the entrance and gazed up at the intricate architecture. It had been built inside the chapel. There were huge lancet windows, an impressive arched ceiling, and timber beams holding it all up. The original pipe organ remained intact, as did the altar. Stained glass windows framed the altar. Bookshelves, desks and study corners were spread out on the main floor and on upper balconies. I wasn't religious, but this place could inspire a sense of awe in the Devil himself.

Gabe pulled me towards the stairs, and we headed for the microfilms.

I paused halfway up the stairs. "Shit. Gotta go to the ... I'll ... I'll ..." I couldn't continue. I turned and quickly backtracked down the stairs to the bathroom that was thankfully very close. I emptied my stomach into the toilet. *Damn.* I sat on the floor next to the toilet for a few minutes. I hoped this wasn't what I feared. The nausea passed. I made my way back up to where Gabe was sorting through microfilms.

"You OK?" Gabe eyed me, worried.

"Yeah, yeah. Just got some bug. Probably due to that slop we were fed for supper last night."

"Uh-huh." Gabe didn't look convinced. He turned his attention back to the microfilms.

The theme for our next issue of *The Montreal System Rat* would be *strange love*. Normally that would be flat out lame, but Valentine's Day was coming up and "strange love" was better than only "love." Also, Gabe was totally geek over Depeche Mode and their new song *Stangelove*, so ... there was *that*.

I inserted a microfilm into the reader and began to browse through old Gazette articles on the topic of "love."

"*NFB Film a Stark Descent into Porno's Lurid World*[10]... Oh man, gotta see this one Gabe—*Not a Love Story*—strippers, sex shows, naked guys and chicks all over each other. Full on porn, man. Looks like it's available through the National Film Board. Probably got it here in the library." I smiled thoughtfully. "D'ya think the library chick would let us watch 'em if we said it was for research?"

Gabe smiled, "Probably. In our dreams." He continued to scan articles, looking for something we could use. "Here's one, *Scientists Struggle to Define and Measure Love*[11]. Says here that they used electroshock therapy to try to figure it all out. Weird. Apparently, the secret to confidence is falling in love. Unless of course you're the jealous type, then it's all fear and depression and downfall and the end. Man, love sucks." He seemed genuinely discouraged, almost sad.

I searched through microfilm after microfilm. There wasn't much about love, besides the sleazy stuff in the *Classifieds* section. Then I found something way more intriguing. As I read, it got more and more interesting.

"Hey, check this out—an article about the crazy shit that goes on in youth detention centres. Look!"

Gabe came over to my machine and read the article over my shoulder.

"I saw some of this shit. Like the isolation stuff? There was this girl that was sent to isolation for like three days just 'cause she couldn't stop coughing. Man, she had a fuckin' cold! And this other girl, who'd been saving her smokes and selling them, got five days! She was a fuckin' zombie when she came out. Just lay on her bed and only got up when staff made her. I was isolated too when I arrived, but in a different kind of room, with books and shit—the luxury isolation suite, I guess. And even then, it made me feel crazy. That place is so messed up."

My eye began to twitch annoyingly as I reminisced.

"Man, Gabe, if they ever try to send me back, I'm totally bolting." I checked the date on the article. "This was written in 1975. There must be others. Scan through the 80s."

I motioned for Gabe to pass me another microfilm, so I could start searching for similar articles.

We spent a few minutes scanning newspaper issues from the 80s.

"What was the reporter's name?" Gabe wasn't finding anything.

I scrolled back to the original article, "Gillian Cosgrove[12]. I'm not finding anything past 1976. It's like the story broke, rich people got mad, then they had lunch and moved on. My mom and her friends do shit like that all the time. Hot topic, fuming mad, someone's gotta do something, someone's gonna pay, then pass the wine darlin' and it's on to the next hot topic. Man, if I ever act like my mom, whack some sense into me."

I suddenly felt exhausted, like everything was hopeless, like I might as well just curl up in bed and sleep forever.

"Hmm ... what about this one?" Gabe motioned for me to take a look.

I read through the more recent book review on Gabe's machine. "*Hey, Malarek!* ... I've heard of this guy—Victor Malarek[13]. He does pretty cool investigative reporting. Didn't know he'd been a system kid. Weredale Home for Boys ... That's that old orphanage that Dave was telling us about. Rough place. Ass whippings and other bad shit."

"The book's about the 50s though. Check it out." Gabe pointed to a section in the article. "Weredale Home for Boys was closed years ago. It was in the Youth Horizon's building."

"Shit. I'd been wondering about the bad vibes in that place."

I went back to my machine and resumed my search through the 80s.

"Nothing. Man, these guys are Teflon. Looks like the press just gave up. Scandal after scandal, and they're still fuckin' with kids."

"Anyway, we gotta go. Do we have enough about *love*?"

I glanced at Gabe and shrugged, "Guess so." I closed my notebook and shoved it into my bag.

"Maybe Dave knows where to find more info on the detention centre stuff." Gabe, always the optimist.

Me, not so much ..."Maybe ... not like much has changed. The same old crap's goin' on, so ..."

Gabe teased, "Guess we're just a bunch of low life delinquents with a sad story no one cares about." He winked at me.

"Oh man, that is way too close to the truth. I'm telling you Gabe, that is exactly what people like my mom think!" I laughed, but my sense of despair remained.

We arrived early for our bus at Guy metro station. I handed Gabe my empty McDonald's cup and stuffed my expensive bomber into my bag. Gabe put his own jacket on the floor, just inside the doors. We sat on his jacket and placed the cup on the floor in front of us. This was a trick we'd learned from Tig. When people see two scrawny looking kids wearing ripped jeans and no jackets in the winter, sitting on a dirty metro floor with a cup out front, they naturally assume they're homeless.

By the time our bus showed up a half hour later, we'd made enough cash for two packs of smokes. Of which we'd desperately need, as blowing smoke rings with Gabe is what got me through the coming storm.

CHAPTER TWENTY-THREE

Gini

January

This time, I'm the one who didn't make it.

Don't get me wrong.

I'm not dead.

Someone else is.

And he fuckin' deserved it.

It all happened on Christmas Eve, a few hours after I'd left Sam and Gabe at the rink.

❞

"Gini darling?"

Mum lay in her usual spot on the pullout bed in the decrepit room she'd rented on St-Laurent Street. It was in one of the seedy hotels. The hallways smelled like beer, cigarettes, and something sour that I couldn't quite place.

I could only imagine what she was exchanging for the room. She was only a couple of dimebags away from a park bench.

"What's up, mum?"

My mum's hands were shaking like they do when she's jonesing. She'd still managed her makeup and hair though. Always the beauty queen. But makeup didn't hide all. Sunken eyes, skin bruised, skinny as skinny gets. I wondered if she'd lost johns because of it. Maybe that's why she couldn't afford the last place any longer.

I put some incense in the wooden holder I'd given her for Christmas, lit the incense, and placed the holder on the upturned milk crate that passed as a bedside table.

"I need you to do something for me." Mum gazed at me with that pleading look I dreaded.

"I can't help you like that, Mum. Damn! If my social worker knew you'd been kicked out and was back on crap, I wouldn't be here. Y' know that, eh? Jeez, what happened, Mum? You were doing OK. Why d'ya go all backwards on me?" I was more exasperated than sad. I was done with fuckin' sad.

As far as my SW knew, Mum was running her own spa business, giving massages and facials to rich Westmount ladies. What she didn't know was that most of Mum's clients were men, and they weren't there for facials.

"Gini, please. I know I'm fucked up. I fucked up. But if you don't help me, I'm not gonna make it through the night. I just need a little. Y' know, just to get by, to stop the shakes. Then we can have a talk, 'kay? About how I'm gonna get sober again. I have a plan. Gini, you know I can do it. I've done it before, yeah?"

"Yeah. You've done it before." Talking to my mum was useless.

I felt drained and I'd only been in the room for a few minutes. I studied the peeling wallpaper, covered in green vines with pink flowers. It had yellowed due to age and smoke, but at one time had possibly made the room bright and beautiful.

"What d'ya need, Mum?"

"Aw, such a darlin'! I knew you'd come through." She pulled back the sheet on the bed and searched the mattress for the discreet hole she'd made to stash her money in. She pulled out a crumpled $10 dollar bill and handed it to me.

"Give this to my guy. Tell him it's for me, he'll know what I want."

"Same guy? The one on Berri?"

Mum nodded. Her eyes were full of need and greed. A starving pet. I'd pitied her before, but this time was different. It was more than pity I felt. Embarrassment. But now I was embarrassed *for* her, rather than because of her. I pushed my anger, that had started to bubble back up, down deep into its box, and locked it up tight.

❦

The dealer's place wasn't that different from the room my mother had rented. The main difference was that the dealer lived in a seedy apartment, rather than a seedy hotel room. This meant, the dealer's place had a lobby with buzzers, and there was no shady guy with greasy hair and wandering eyes at a desk upon entrance. The shady guy was contained behind a locked door instead, and you had to put in a special request to see him.

I pressed the buzzer with the name "Mad Max" scribbled above it.

"Yeah?" The voice that came through was that of a heavy smoker. Gruff, in a disgusting phlegm-filled kind of way.

"Shirley." No need to say more than Mum's name. That was the way.

The door buzzed, and I entered the building. Glad for my long winter coat, I pulled the zipper up as high as it would go under my chin. At times, this guy could be a perv.

The stairwell, dark and creepy as usual, stunk of mildew. I walked up past a little kid, no doubt waiting for his mother. He sat on the top step playing with one of those tiny yo-yos you get in vending machines. I briefly considered grabbing him and running, aimlessly, somewhere, saving him from all this pain. Mothers sucked. My anger was getting harder to contain.

I knocked on #23 and waited.

There were heavy footsteps on the other side of the door, then it swung open.

"Com' in." Mad Max turned without really looking at me and walked back through the living room and into the kitchen. Something was off. I sensed another presence in the place, and I hesitated in the doorway.

"Com' in!" He yelled from the kitchen.

I thought, *'what the hell, I don't give a fuck anymore'*, closed the door behind me and followed him in.

Mad Max sat in an old wicker chair next to a window that exited onto a fire escape. He was tall, lanky, and just as greasy as always. A well-kept younger looking guy occupied the other wicker chair. He didn't belong at all. He made me think of that segment on Sesame Street, the one with the song that goes, *"one of these things is not like the others, one of these things just doesn't belong ..."* That was this guy. He didn't belong next to Mad Max, or in this apartment, or on this street. He looked more like a john from Westmount.

"You don't *look* like Shirley." Westmount-john said this as if he expected an explanation.

"No. Uh ... So? I'm pickin' somethin' up. What's it to you?"

"Shirley knows what's it to me. Where is she?" This guy's vibes were all-in asshole.

This guy deserved my best scowl and I complied.

"Fuck off. I'm just here to pick up."

I peered at Mad Max, hoping for back-up, but he turned away, and suddenly became very interested with what a pigeon was up to on the fire escape. I thought, *'Well, so much for "Mad Max".'*

"Listen carefully. One of you is going to bring me to Shirley. I'm not *asking*." Westmount-john pulled a gun from his belt and rested the weapon on his leg to prove he meant business.

I tried not to acknowledge the gun. "She's broke anyway. What d'ya wanna see her for? Yer not gonna get zilch out of her. She's a fuckin' waste case."

I hoped he'd be discouraged, but he just sat there, calmly observing me, with that death-tool in his lap.

"Unzip your coat." Again, not a question.

Yeah right, dude. There was no way in hell I'd be unzipping. I stood my ground, firm and unshakable, and returned his ominous gaze.

Westmount-john smiled, amused. "Sorry. Did you mistake that for a question?" He lifted the gun and pointed it casually in my direction. He held the weapon with confidence, as if he'd been born to threaten people.

Before my brain could respond stubbornly, my hands took control, and my coat was unzipped.

Westmount-john leant forward and nudged my coat open with the barrel of his gun to get a better look.

"I can't see shit. Take it off." He said this almost flirtatiously. Like a spider coaxing a fly into its web.

I began to run through escape strategies in my head. The only ways out were through the door or the window. But first I'd have to deal with this gun. A sense of despair gripped me. I knew where this story was heading. This would be my end. I was going to be just like Mum.

I let my coat fall to the floor.

"Nice. Yeah, very nice. Tell you what, you come work for me—you know, just a couple of jobs—and Shirley can live. She's your mom, right?"

I couldn't find my voice. I shook my head. *Nope, no way, I would never work for you or any other fuckin' sleaze bag. Never, never, never, never!*

Mad Max shifted uncomfortably in his chair. He'd turned his attention back to Westmount-john, considering the situation.

Westmount-john got up from his chair. He was big. Quite big, not tall, but muscular. He put his hand on my chest, just under my neck, then glided it upwards, around my throat, until his fingers touched my ears.

"Again. *Not* a question."

From there, everything happened real fast.

Mad Max leapt up and attacked Westmount-john from behind, wrapping his arm around his neck and squeezing hard. Westmount-john tried to shake Mad Max off, but Mad Max stayed strong. Westmount-john kept shaking, trying to throw him off. Mad Max's face and neck turned bright red with his effort, but he was no match for this body builder. Westmount-john flipped Mad Max over his shoulder onto the floor in front me.

Terror had never felt so absolute. I was about to die and that was that. *No, no, no, I didn't want to die!*

I jumped up onto the counter to avoid the fight, then headed towards my closest getaway route—the fire escape window. I fiddled with the latch on the window, then struggled to heave it open. The damn thing was one of those heavy wooden windows that had to be pushed up to get open. There was ice around the edges and, judging from the piece of 2x4 on the windowsill, the window probably needed to be propped open too. My panic wasn't helping. The window kept getting stuck. These windows needed patience, and I didn't have the time for that.

Mad Max had way more stamina than I'd given him credit for. He grabbed Westmount-john's leg, tripping him up, and Westmount-john fell backwards to the floor. The gun went flying across the kitchen floor and settled under the table below me.

Westmount-john shot across the floor after the gun. Mad Max dove for it but was too late. Westmount-john seized the gun and trained it on Mad Max, point-blank, aiming at his head. But Mad Max wouldn't give in and tried to knock the gun from Westmount-john's grip.

Westmount-john pulled the trigger. "Wrong move, asshole!" He stared at what he'd just done. "Fuck!" He panted, catching his breath, leaning over Max Mad.

I froze in terror on the counter.

Mad Max was bleeding from his skull. Sprawled on the floor, unmoving. Just lying there, bleeding.

Before Westmount-john could get up and turn the gun on me, I snatched the steak knife off the counter, jumped onto his back, and stabbed him over and over and over, until something inside me got really tired and just couldn't anymore.

I sat back for a moment, in shock, my whole body shaking. I didn't feel like me. I had blood all over my hands, my clothes. Blood was everywhere. I had to get the blood off me.

In full panic, I stripped off my clothes, washed my hands and face, and put on an over-sized t-shirt and a pair of jogging pants I'd found on the floor in the bathroom. My coat looked fine, no blood, so I put that on too. Unsure anymore of why it mattered, I searched the kitchen drawers for Mad Max's stash, then realised what I was doing and stopped. Mum had become the least of my problems. Adrenaline pumped and I refocused. I heaved open the fire escape window as far as it would go, took off my jacket again, and squeezed through, out of the crime scene.

And exited right into the arms of four cops.

As luck would have it, the police had been hanging out hassling hookers right below Mad Max's apartment when everything went down.

9

I lay on my bed, staring into nothingness, in Manny Cottage's Bethel unit. I hadn't been able to sleep since that night. The guy was a fuck, but it was still murder. And I wasn't a murderer. Or at least I hadn't thought myself to be one. Somehow, I'd managed to turn out even worse than Mum.

I touched the bumpy bruise on the side of my face. It had a grate pattern, like the fire escape. I didn't put up a fight, but the cops weren't into taking chances. I smiled. Four huge cops against little me. They must've considered me some kind of super villain. As if I was going to fight my way out of that.

The girl I was sharing a room with wasn't sleeping either. The word had got around that I was a killer. I didn't care anymore. I turned over to face the wall, away from her terrified glances. If she didn't stop that shit soon, I'd be having some fun with her.

Yeah. *So?* This is me. The one who didn't make it. *Now, fuck off.*

CHAPTER TWENTY-FOUR

A Butterfly Flaps its Wings...

Late January — Sam

Dave caught me as I was heading up to hide in my room after supper. "Eh Sam, hold up! I need to speak to you for a mo'."

We'd just learned of Gini's fate, although we didn't know the whole story. She'd been shipped off to Manny Cottage and wouldn't be back, that's all we'd been told. From Dave's tone, something horrible had happened to her during the holidays. I couldn't stop thinking about how she'd come to me and shared stuff, which wasn't like her at all. Maybe I should've given her a chance. But man, could she be a jerk. Argh, guilt was a crappy feeling.

Dave motioned for me to join him in his office. I entered and sat in the chair by his desk.

"So, Sam, all good with you?" Dave started the conversation with his typical intro.

I nodded.

"Great. There'll be a couple of changes around here and, as they might affect *The Montreal System Rat*, I thought I'd share them with you first. That way we can discuss how to keep the paper going and share our thoughts with everyone else during our group meeting tonight."

I nodded.

"I'll be taking some time off, probably a few months. My wife's not well. I need to be home with my family for a while."

I nodded. *Hmm ... that doesn't sound good.* Dave's strained eyes and tired dark circles began to make sense. "Uh, sorry, um, about your wife."

Dave nodded back, and sighed. "Also, Ms. Cohen has been taken off your case. She has a very full case load, and beyond that I don't have an explanation for you, Sam. I know you are quite fond of her. I'm sorry. I would change things if I could, but it's out of my hands." Dave scratched at some imaginary stain on his desk and attempted a comforting smiled.

So, I was being passed on to some stranger, because ... *just because?* Nice.

"Why didn't Ms. Cohen tell me this herself?" I felt abandoned. Was I really that disposable?

"Well, she can't make your meeting this week, so she wanted me to fill you in. Her replacement will be coming instead. Ms. Cohen wanted you to hear it from me. But she will be by next week, to meet with Tig. She'll check in with you then." Dave sank in his chair, even more drawn and tired than when I'd first entered his office.

"OK. So ... what about *The Montreal System Rat*? How are we gonna print it without you?" I couldn't lose three important things in the same meeting. This day fuckin' sucked.

"I've set things up so you can have direct contact with my friend, Roy Church, in publishing. He works at The Gazette. When your spring issue is ready to go, call me. I'll drop by to approve it. After which, you can drop it off at The Gazette with Roy's name on the front of the envelope. I've left details for Cindy, my replacement, so there shouldn't be any problem. And I'll make sure all the part-time support workers are up to date on what's going on. Roy will drop off copies for you to distribute when they've been printed. Sound OK?"

"I guess." I lied. This sucked big time.

Life in this place was going to turn to shit without Dave. And good social workers were hard to come by. Most kids in this place hardly ever got visits from their SW. Gini said she couldn't even remember what hers looked like. I'd been lucky with Ms. Cohen. Now I'll be just like the rest, fending for myself.

"OK, then." Dave mustered up another comforting smile. "Eh, I'm proud of you Sam. I loved the last issue of *The Montreal System Rat*. I'm sure this issue'll be super fab!"

Dave was trying hard to sound happy and positive, but his eyes couldn't manage it. I wondered what kind of illness his wife had.

I got up from my chair, walked around the desk to where he sat, and gave him a hug. "I'm going to miss you, Dave."

He tapped my back awkwardly, "Yeah, me too. Thanks, Sam. Now go get busy with that paper of yours!"

9

Cindy was not a Dave.

She sat at one end of the long dining-room table and supervised our eating habits. She was only about five feet tall, but she ruled the room like a wolf in a sheep pen. Our survival was at her disposal. She flicked her long blond braid back over her shoulder. She wasn't eating with us, only supervising. And she had a code: no swearing, no fake swearing, no speaking loudly, no disagreements, no gossiping, no, no, no, no.

No one spoke. It was the quietest supper table I'd ever sat at.

Tema tested the waters. "Anyone see that new Def Leppard video? Uh, *Pour Some Sugar on Me*?"

Gabe looked up, startled by the daring interruption of Cindy's silent table. He stuttered, "Uh, yeah, it's, uh, cool. Love the garb."

That was pretty much it for the supper table convo.

I pushed my food around my dish to make it look like I'd eaten more than I had. Lately, I'd been eating more to avoid getting in trouble. It was impossible to fool Dr. Bissett. He was a little odd, but far from an idiot. Cindy made my stomach turn. I couldn't eat with her in the room. It was like having my mom at the table.

"Nice try, Sam. Eat up. No one leaves the table until everyone's dish is empty. Kids are starving in Africa.

Get with it." She glared at me to make sure I hadn't misunderstood her for soft.

I glanced at the empty plates around the table. It was all on me. I studied the food on my plate, shut my eyes for a moment, and thought of something happy. That time Tig and I screwed with those boys with the Ouija board always made me smile. Then Tig's dad popped into my mind and my stomach clenched again.

Damn. I tried another thought.

Concentrating hard, I thought of the time Frankie and I had written all those porn letters and sold them to the boys at school. The thought made me smile. I shovelled some mashed potatoes onto my fork, into my mouth, and began to chew. What was great about mashed stuff is that it went down quickly, without too much mouth time.

I began to miss Frankie. Boy had I fucked things up.

My second spoonful of mashed potatoes stuck to the top of my mouth, and I had trouble swallowing. I couldn't do it. The potatoes sat in my mouth like a life threat.

Gabe's glass suddenly flew across the table in Cindy's direction, spilling Orange Tang all over the place. Cindy jumped up to avoid the splash. Carl, the new kid, switched my plate with his and calmly ate my leftovers while Cindy busied herself scolding Gabe and ordering people to go grab cloths and a mop.

One of the part-timers tried to help, but Cindy wouldn't have it. "Please dear, this is on them, not you. Go finish those reports."

Cindy hovered over the cleaning crew, inspecting their work. "Eh, you're spreading stickiness all over the floor.

You need to soak, then mop. Didn't anyone ever teach you guys to clean?" Cindy grabbed the mop from Gabe and motioned for Tig to start soaking up the mess with a cloth.

Tema clicked her tongue and glared at Cindy. Lucky for Tema, Cindy was too preoccupied to notice.

I thought, *'man, this is gonna be a fuckin' long few months'* and said a silent prayer to the almighty God-of-Good-Luck for Dave's wife to recover quickly.

⁹

I woke up at sunrise feeling awful again. This had become a common occurrence of late. That mouthful of potato swam in my stomach. How could so little potato cause such misery? I'd never forgive Cindy for this. I felt dizzy. Then I felt sick. Then I was going to be sick.

I ran to the bathroom, threw open the toilet, and lost my few bites of supper into it. Shit. Maybe Cindy was poisoning our meals. She did have an Evil Queen essence about her.

I cradled the toilet bowl and thought about my day's plans.

I'd started at an alternate school before the holidays. Classes were small, days short, subjects quite basic, as long as I showed up, I'd pass my courses. I hated schools, but this place was OK. I did want to graduate. No way would I be working at McDonald's my whole life. And my teachers seemed to like me. Not at all like the stupid private school I'd been at the previous year.

I began to perk up.

Staying home sick with Cindy sounded like a miserable idea. Unless I was passed out burning up with fever, I'd be going to school. I wondered what Cindy would think if she knew she was my main motivation for going to school today. She'd probably brag to others about it.

I cleaned my face and brushed my teeth. My mouth tasted better. That was a plus.

Tig was waiting for the bathroom when I exited.

"Were you sick? You OK?" Her hair was wild, and she had sleep-sand in the corners of her eyes.

"Nah, it's fine. Just feeling a bit weird. Couldn't sleep."

Tig nodded sleepily and headed past me into the bathroom. I leant against the wall in the hallway for a moment to steady myself. I was still a bit dizzy.

My schoolbag was packed and ready to go. When I was dressed, I headed downstairs, grabbed a banana from the kitchen, put on my warm bomber jacket, and headed out. It was one of those mornings. The less conversation the better.

Cindy called after me as the front door closed behind me. "Is that all you're going to eat today?"

Her voice was like a pipe wrench clamped around my head, squeezing life out of my brain. I kept walking.

⁹

Gabe met me at the bus stop after school. "Cindy's out doing errands. Just part-timers at home. Wanna smoke a spliff?"

I nodded and smiled, "Uh, yeah. Bring it on, man." It was a mild winter day and the sun shone strong. I'd been getting much more fresh air since Cindy had started.

We headed down to the park along the canal and sat on a low branch belonging to our favourite gnarled, old oak. Gabe rummaged through his schoolbag and took out his pouch of Drum tobacco, some red rolling papers, and a pea-sized piece of hash wrapped in tinfoil.

"Strawberry rolling paper? Are you fuckin' serious?" I laughed.

"Eh man, don't diss' it before ya' try it. Anyway, just trying to get some fruit into you." He smiled teasingly.

I shoved him playfully, and lay back against the tree, gazing up at its twisted snowy branches. The snow sparkled under a winter sun, and the branches appeared as if painted onto a blue-sky canvas. The moment felt magical, peaceful. I closed my eyes.

Gabe finished rolling the joint, lit it, and took a long toke. He nudged me. I opened my eyes and returned to reality. I took the joint, put it between my lips, and inhaled deeply.

We passed the joint back and forth a couple of times in silence.

Gabe lay back on his branch. "If only life could be this sweet, this *euphonious,* all the time." He emphasized the word "euphonious" as if testing its power.

"What the fuck, 'euphonious'?" I laughed and took the joint from Gabe.

"Harmony! Pure unrelenting harmony." He smiled, pleased that he'd hit on a word that surprised me. "And my English teacher's word-of-the-week.'"

I exhaled, passed the joint, and asked, "Eh, Gabe? D'ya think there's, like, *true love* out there? Y' know, the real kind, like in the movies?"

"Movie love isn't real, dummy." Gabe laughed, "You gotta be in the movies to find that kinda love. And it's not real, eh ... did I say that?" He scratched his head and laughed some more.

"Tema told me, y' know for our Valentine's issue, she wants to write a story about a serial lover."

Gabe coughed, "Like a serial killer lover?" He passed the joint back to me.

I chuckled, "Dunno, didn't ask. Probably. She just like came into my room and announced that that was what she'd be giving us, told me '*I'd better not be fuckin' editin' nothin'*', then left. I suggested she tone it down, y' know, if she wants Dave to approve it. Like maybe substitute people for cats or birds or somethin' that's not, y' know, people."

I took one last puff, inhaled deeply, squashed the butt on the tree, and blew out rings.

"Guess it's gonna be a surprise then. As long as she's not thinkin' of doin' any field research, I can live with that!" Gabe chortled.

"She's almost 18. Gonna be leaving us a few days after the paper's published. If she doesn't like my editing, I'll hide under my bed 'til she's gone." I laughed.

"That's so fucked. I mean, aging-out. It must be weird. I mean, for kids without family. She doesn't even have a job. Where's she gonna go? Where am *I* gonna go?"

"Ha! No way Dave's gonna send you out into the world like a wandering duckling on Ste-Catherine's Street. You'll be fine, Gabe. As for me, I'm never going back to my parents. I don't care if I have to live on the street, luggin' a fuckin' milk crate."

I took another long drag on the joint. "Think Dave would take me in too?" I laughed.

We sat in silence again for a few minutes, staring across the icy canal, enjoying our high. It was surprisingly warm for a day in January. Must've not been much below zero.

"Eh Gabe?"

"Yeah, babe?"

"I think I'm pregnant."

"What the fuck?!" Gabe sat up straight, in shock. "What do you mean? Like, pregnant with happiness?"

"No, man. Like pregnant, pregnant." I looked away, a bit ashamed now.

"Shit, Sam."

"Yeah. Shit."

"Vincent?"

"Uh-huh."

"What d'ya gonna do?"

"Dunno. Get a test I guess."

"I'll go with you. Let's go now."

"Gabe, man. Chill. I need morning pee. I'll go before school tomorrow."

We sat in silence again for a bit, and then packed up and headed home. What a buzz breaker. I should've waited to say something.

,

I stared at the pharmacist like a moron unable to comprehend what she was telling me. I'd never been in this situation. How was I supposed to react? What was I expected to do? I'd given her my morning pee, she'd tested it, and I'd got the result I'd expected. Now, what was I supposed to do?

"Mademoiselle? Ça va? You OK? Did you 'ear what I zed?"

I nodded, but kept staring.

"Eh? You need zome 'elp?"

"Uh ... No ... Nope ... I'm, uh, just fine." I snapped back into the moment, paid the lady, and left.

Pregnant. I was pregnant. That thought lingered like a disoriented alien in my head. It didn't belong and didn't know where to go from here.

A baby? In me?

I imagined the fetus growing inside me, from kidney bean to baby. First the heart would start beating, next little arms and little legs would appear, and the head would take shape, and all of a sudden it would turn into a little human.

There was a pain in my chest, and I began to feel dizzy. I reminded myself to breathe.

The only thing I could decide on was to not decide on anything. I headed for school and continued my day as if nothing had changed, nothing at all. I was just the same as yesterday.

*

Gabe was at the bus stop again when I got off.

"So?" He peered at me intently, waiting for my secret.

"So, *what*?"

"Fuck, Sam. Are you?"

"Uh-huh." I looked at my feet and chewed on my lip.

"Wow. That's ..." His voice trailed off.

"Yeah. Exactly."

We walked back to the group home in silence, and I stopped on the steps.

"Eh, Gabe. Don't tell anyone, 'kay? Not even Tig."

"Yeah, yeah." Gabe's speechlessness was getting a bit annoying.

I entered the building and paused by Cindy's office door. Might as well get this over with. Didn't know who my new SW was yet. Cindy it would have to be.

I knocked on her door.

"Wait."

I waited. A few minutes inched by. I sat on the floor with my back against the wall outside her office.

"Enter."

I opened the door and sat in the same chair I'd sat in last time, when Dave told me he'd be leaving us.

Cindy finished filing away whatever she'd been working on.

"Yes, Sam. What can I help you with?" Cindy wasn't one for pleasantries.

Might as well get to the point. "I'm pregnant and I need a doctor's appointment."

Cindy sat back in her chair and studied me for a moment.

"You know you can't live here with a baby, eh? What's your plan?" She said this frankly, as if I'd told her I'd adopted a kitten without permission.

"Uh ... to make a doctor's appointment."

Cindy shook her head and picked up the phone. She dialed the number for the local gynecologist's office and made me an appointment for the next afternoon.

"Thanks, uh ..." I said, expectantly. I wasn't sure what I was expecting, but it seemed like there should be more coming.

"OK. Off with you. Go do your homework."

I picked up my schoolbag and headed out of her office. As I was leaving, I heard Cindy mumble, "Jesus, babies having babies."

,

The waiting room was small and suffocating. Someone had managed to squeeze six chairs in, and they were all occupied, one of them by me. The big lady next to me huffed as she was forced to sit up straight to avoid our bodies touching. I was the only kid. I grabbed a prenatal magazine from the rack on the wall and began to flip through it.

I flipped through ads for baby stuff—diapers, toys, bottles, breast pumps—and ideas for decorating Baby's room, until I came to a double page spread that displayed in full colour the miracle of pregnancy. There was a diagram illustrating the evolvement of the fetus from week to week during the first trimester, and from month to month during trimester 2 and 3.

It was quite something for such a tiny combination of cells to turn into something so significant in only nine months. At month 3 it began to look quite human, like one of those tiny Barbie babies. The changes were astonishing and terrifying. I wanted to close the magazine, but I couldn't take my eyes off that diagram.

"Samara Long?" A secretary shouted from her station outside the waiting room.

I looked up from the magazine to see one of the ladies staring at me, surely wondering about the relationship between my reading material and my presence in that waiting room.

I got up, returned the magazine to its place on the rack, and acknowledged the secretary's question. I thought, *'Yup, that's me, Samara Long, the pregnant teen in the waiting room.'*

She pointed to a door on the right.

The doctor's office was as stuffy as the waiting room. There was a desk, chair, examining table, and just enough room leftover for me and the doctor.

"So, Sam. Just here for a check-up?" The doctor was short, bald, and male.

"Uh. No. Uh ... I thought ..." I was sure Cindy had mentioned the reason for my appointment when she'd called. I clearly remembered her saying, *'Cindy ... yup, from Charles A. Group Home. Got another one ... yup, could be pregnant. Test done and positive. Need an appointment asap.'*

The doctor checked my file. His eyes widened, and then he regained his composure. "Oh, I see. Says here that you think you're pregnant. Is this correct?"

I nodded.

"OK. Well, tests can be faulty. To be sure, we'll need to do a blood test. That'll be our first step. When was your last pap smear?"

"Oh, uh, September." I'd had one while in Manny Cottage.

"OK. So, we'll do a blood test today. We can leave the exam for when we get your result in. It should take a few days. The nurse will be in to take your blood in a few minutes." He smiled awkwardly, nodded goodbye, and left the room.

,

On Saturday, Gabe and I sat on the floor in my room, sifting through all the material we'd received for our upcoming edition of *The Montreal System Rat*. We'd received three love poems, a bunch of drawings of roses and broken hearts and skulls n' crossbones, a corny pick-up line crossword, Tig's recipes, Gabe's love advice column, a couple of short stories, and my editor's column in which my topic was youth detention centres. I'd got the idea from the articles in The Gazette. I'd called it *What Has Love Got To Do With It?*, like that Tina Turner song.

To our surprise, Gini sent us a short story called *Strange love: a letter from the hole.*

She wrote us a note too. Said she'd thought up her story while in solitary confinement. Said it'd kept her sane for a while. She ended her note with *"Now, fuck off and publish this shit."* At least she hadn't been broken.

Tema had remained true to her word. She'd produced quite an impressive short story about a guy who was a serial bird lover. He had a mental disease that made him entrap hurt birds out of love and leave them to die. She'd wanted to make it a serial love-killer story set in Bethel unit, but I reminded her Dave wouldn't go for that, you know, 'cause of the setting and the prisoners being human and all, so she compromised and replaced humans with birds as I'd suggested. She called her story *'Mr. Kill Love.'* She's got some imagination, she should write novels.

"Valentine's Day makes people so fuckin' stupid. Oh my god, check this question out."

Gabe cleared his throat and read it with a dramatic flare.

"Dear LoveLots [that's me], *my guy is such a douche. I'm sure he's not gonna get nothin' for me. He loves me an' all. But he's gonna fuck Valentine's Day up for sure. How do I stop him from fuckin' it all up?"* Gabe rolled his eyes. "Man, I wish I didn't have to be fuckin' polite."

"Yup, glad I'm not responding to those. But that column was *your* suggestion, so deal." I smiled.

"Guess so. Eh, so, what did you write?"

"Not done yet. I find it weird that all these scandals keep happening, eh? Like the shit that was going on at Weredale Home for Boys? The one that Malarek reporter dude wrote about? And then, there's the one in the news now, about those orphans in the asylums in the 50s. And also, the one about that detention centre, the one The Gazette was all over in the 70s? That centre's still open, man. Crazy. And Bethel too. I mean, the same shit's going on. It's like no one honestly cares. The Newspapers only care as long as their pockets are lined. We are ghosts, Gabe. To the outside world, we are fuckin' ghosts, and every time we spook the gov by making it into the news, y' know, with a scandal threat, politicians or some other big cheeses call the Ghost Busters on us. Fuck. That must be what's happening."

"Bit dramatic, no?" Gabe laughed. "Can't be *that* bad. Press is a free entity, man. They pride themselves on it."

"Gabe. Did you read Cosgrove's story? It's fuckin' that bad. Why would the news just drop scandals about places fucking with kids like that? It's still going on. Read Gini's story!" I lay Gini's '*Letter from the Hole*' out in front of Gabe. "Businesses get their money from somewhere. Newspapers are no exception. That's why scandals die and nothing changes."

Gabe nodded, but his doubtful expression remained.

He changed topic. "Eh, check out Kate's poem, all about loving trees. How sweet!"

My eyeroll would've put Molly Ringwald's to shame. Kate was new. She was super hot, and boys' brains went to mush around her. And she was *so* 'sweet', like dripping with sweetness. If she was any sweeter, she'd keel over from sugar shock. She drove me nuts.

"Hmm ... think I'm gonna respond to that other chick that she should drop her loveless boyfriend and pick up loving trees. Think she'd take it well?"

I laughed, "Ha, yeah! I mean, no! But go ahead, it suits our *strange love* theme!"

"Yes! Thank god, I was dying here." Gabe grinned mischievously.

I looked at Gabe curiously and wondered whether I'd given the devil permission to come out and play.

"Gabe?"

"Uh-huh?"

"D'ya think I'd make a good mom?"

Gabe paused, and became preoccupied with his hands. "Dunno. I mean, yeah, why not? But, like, where would you live? Back at your parents' place?"

"Oh hell, no. That wouldn't work ... Maybe I could live on my own?"

"OK. So, like, work and have a baby too. What about school and stuff ... like, I dunno, your journalism dreams?"

"Yeah. School, dreams. Maybe this is my dream." Trying to keep my mood light, I smiled and sang, "I just *got this lovin' feeling*, y' know, for a baby?" I touched my stomach. "Weird that there's this little kid growing in me."

"You're talking about a pea-sized bean thing. It's not a little fuckin' kid. It's just a few fuckin' cells doing what cells do." Gabe sounded annoyed.

"What's your problem, man?"

"Sam! This whole baby thing is so stupid. You're not usually stupid. Wake the fuck up!" Gabe got up and stormed out of the room.

I lay on the floor, with my hand on my abdomen. I wanted to cry. I knew what I needed to do. But the idea of having a baby, someone who loved me so unconditionally, and who I could love back just the same, was an alluring fantasy.

I squeezed my eyes shut, holding my tears in. I would not cry. I'd fucked up and now I was going to make it right. I knew what I had to do. I'd known all along. Just some cells.

,

Cindy's office door was open, and I marched in without knocking.

"I want an abortion[14]. I need an appointment."

"Whoa, there. What happened to knocking? Back up, try again."

I glared at her incredulously, backed up, and knocked.

"OK, let's start again. What can I help you with, Sam?"

"An abortion."

"OK. Well, for that you're going to have to speak with your social worker. She cancelled her appointment again this week, and she has rescheduled for … let me see … " Cindy checked her notes. "Two weeks time. You can talk to her then." She waited for confirmation that I'd understood.

"Cancelled her ...? Two f ... weeks? No. I need to speak with her *now*."

"Well, dear, that's not possible. She's very busy. It's impossible to get her on the phone. Social workers never sit still, you know. She has many cases, Sam, that are just as important as yours. Two weeks it has to be."

"No! I won't wait two fuckin' weeks!"

"Eh! Language! Sam, you need to *cool down*."

"I won't fuckin' cool down. I want a fuckin' abortion fuckin' NOW, OK?!" I had begun to yell, and I could sense people begin to gather in the hall, listening.

"Sam. Calm down. You don't want this to end up with another trip to Manny Cottage, right?"

"Then call my fuckin' social worker!" My voice kept getting louder and Cindy's face got darker.

I grabbed the phone from the desk and threw it at her. "CALL!! FUCKING CALL!!" I'd lost it. I'd begun to shake with anger.

"That's enough! Rod?! Anne?!" Cindy called out for the two part-timers, and they produced themselves within a second.

"Sam is out of control. Escort her up to her room. She can come down and talk to me when she has gained control over her temper."

Rod and Anne stared from Cindy to me, and back to Cindy. I felt hot and furious and now I was crying too. They seemed unsure of how to proceed.

Anne took the lead, "Hey, Sam, why don't me and you go talk somewhere else."

"I don't want to fuckin' talk! I want a fuckin' abortion! This bitch won't let me call my social worker. Fuck! I don't even know who my fuckin' social worker is! Can someone just fuckin' call?!" I was fuming and not quite recognizing myself anymore.

Rod cut in, "Sam, I'm going to walk you out of the office. This is not a choice. You need to calm down and come with us. If you threaten us further, I will call the police."

"Not on your fuckin' life, asshole!" I screamed and went limp as he tried to grab me. I fell to the floor. They'd have to drag me out. They could call the fuckin' pigs for all I cared.

Rod grabbed my thumb and twisted my arm backwards in an attempt to restrain me. He pushed me down face first onto the floor, jamming my hand into my back.

I was now yelling gibberish, my words no longer discernible. I squirmed, trying to wriggle lose, but every time I moved, he tightened his grip and pain shot through my arm.

"Stop!" Anne shouted. I looked up to see she wasn't yelling at me. "Everyone out of the office! Leave me with Sam. I can fix this."

Rod shot Anne a *'what the fuck'* expression, but she held firm.

"Rod, Sam is not dangerous. There is no need for restraint. She has never been dangerous. I'm familiar with her file. Let her go."

Cindy seemed doubtful, but nodded at Rod, giving her approval.

To my surprise, Cindy and Rod obliged with Anne's request for control, and I was abruptly alone in the office with Anne.

Anne closed the door to keep the random listeners out too. She took a deep breath and regained her composer.

"OK. It's going to be OK. You are safe now, Sam. No one is coming through that door without my permission. We are going to solve this together. She helped me up off the floor and into the chair. I was shaking uncontrollably and couldn't speak through my sobbing. She brought her chair over next to mine and put her hands on mine.

"It's OK. Oh, my. Let me do the talking. I heard the gist of your conversation with Cindy. Sam, do you want me to make you an appointment for an abortion?"

I nodded vigorously, still unable to speak and having a hard time catching my breath.

"OK, I'll do that right now. We don't need to go through your social worker quite yet. We can make the appointment. All she needs to do is sign some papers. That can be done later."

Anne wrapped her arms around me, calming me with her warmth, with her support. My shaking slowed, and I could breathe again.

After Anne made the call, she sat in the office with me until I felt ready to face the hallway crowd. When I was finally ready, she opened the door. The hallway was empty. Cindy and Rod must've cleared it. I nodded at Anne, thanking her silently.

As I made my way up the stairs to my room, I heard Cindy return to her office. She said to Anne, "Well then, that's it for today's drama. Back to work team!"

I had rarely felt such hate for anyone as I did for Cindy at that moment. I almost lost it again. Tema came to my rescue.

Tema met me on the stairs, took my hand in hers, and whispered, "She ain't worth Bethel. Com'on Sam."

Tema followed me into my room. I collapsed on my bed, trying to keep my emotions in check. There was no way I'd be crying in front of Tema.

"Eh man, just wanna be alone, 'kay?"

"Yeah. Well. For what it's worth ... I'm sorry for the shit at Bethel. You're OK, Sam. I shouldn't have fucked with you like that. And ... I've been through the pregnancy shit, so ... y' know ... if you wanna talk ... sometime."

I nodded and motioned for her to close the door on her way out.

I lay on my bed staring at the ceiling. What the fuck was the sense in it all? Life was more battle than peace. I felt empty. I wasn't up to the battle anymore. Would anything ever change? People sucked. And the ones that didn't, never stuck around. I was exhausted. This battle was fucking exhausting. I glanced at my stupid butterfly tattoo, like a "fuck you" branded on my wrist forever more. If I killed myself, I'd do it by carving up that tat.

I fell asleep reminiscing on the way things used to be, before the butterfly tattoo, with Frankie. Did she have similar dreams? Was she as obsessed with her own butterfly tattoo? Had she tried to scratch it off? Would she forgive me? I thought back to the secret letters we used to hide for each other between pews in the McGill chapel, after my mom had banned her from my life.

Sleep took over.

CHAPTER TWENTY-FIVE

No, I swear, I'm fine!

February

Gabe and I dropped off the Valentine's issue of *The Montreal System Rat* the following Wednesday, right before my appointment at the Children's Hospital. Dave's friend, Roy Church, happened to be at The Gazette's front desk, chatting with the secretary over a smoke when we arrived.

Roy saw the name on the envelope and smiled at us. "Eh, you must be Sam and Gabe! So nice to finally meet you."

Tall and burly, if it weren't for the pencil stuck in Roy's curly hair, he'd have looked more like a shipwrecked sailor than a reporter.

Intrigued, we smiled and said hi.

Roy returned a jovial smile and continued, "I've heard so much. Dave raves about you. And I just loved your first issues of *The Montreal System Rat*." Roy paused for a second, thinking. "Actually, now that I have you here ... Sam, might you be interested in a Summer job? It's not much, you know, mail and copy stuff, but it is a step in." He didn't wait for a reply, "Yes, absolutely, you will fit in well here. Sound good?"

I nodded, thoroughly delighted. Wow. This was a day I wouldn't be forgetting, full of life-changers. I agreed to get in touch in May. We said our goodbyes.

Gabe gave me a high five as we left the building. "Holy fuck, Sam! A job at The Gazette! Fuckin' A, girl!"

"It's only mail and copy stuff he said." I tried to downplay the opportunity, but Gabe wouldn't let me.

"Are you fuckin' joking? That's how all these guys got started. I've got a feeling Sam. *You*, babe, are gonna be big some day!" He laughed with glee and I couldn't help but to follow suit.

We headed to the Children's Hospital. What a weird day.

⁹

My new social worker hadn't introduced herself yet. According to the papers I held, her name was Susan Field. I gave the papers to the woman at the abortion clinic's desk, along with my medicare card.

"Thanks, dear. The waiting room's the one on the left. Just take a seat and a nurse will call you in a few minutes."

I entered the waiting room and ran head on into Frankie. She was crying, hiding her face with her hands, and she didn't notice me. Her uncle stood beside her, comforting her, telling her it was OK, that he was on board with whatever decision she made. Frankie mumbled, "I can't do this. I can't do this. This isn't what I want." And they left.

Suddenly, I desperately wanted to consult with Frankie on this thing I was about to do. Maybe it wasn't what I wanted either. I held my stomach and sat down on the chair closest to the exit.

"Eh, what's up? You went pale." Gabe studied me, concerned.

"Nothing. It's fine. Just feeling sick."

We sat in silence.

"This is just a bleep, Sam. A bleep in time, y' know? You've got tons of happy shit coming your way. Like growing old with me, eh?" Gabe joked, trying to lighten my mood.

"Fuck that, I'm not growing old."

Gabe furrowed his eyebrows, a question in the making, but didn't get the chance to ask it.

The nurse called my name. I got up. This was something I was sure about.

"Do you want me there, Sam?" Gabe asked.

The nurse motioned for Gabe to stay sitting. "Sorry, kid. You'll have to wait here. I'll call you when she's ready to see you."

I followed the nurse into a room with one examining table and a lot of medical equipment. She gave me a gown and told me to put it on, then she left.

I put the gown on and got up onto the examining table, then I took in the room. Pasty green and white, everything profoundly sterile. Besides the stirrups and the barf tray, I didn't recognize much of the other equipment.

A doctor and two nurses came in. The doctor introduced herself as, Dr. Lou, and began busying herself with equipment.

"Sam, you can lie down now and put your feet in the stirrups." The nurse's eyes were kind and encouraging.

My anxiety must've shown through, because she took my hand in hers and said, "Everything will be just fine, Sam. You don't need to worry about a thing. Dr. Lou is one of our best. She will be very gentle."

I relaxed and obeyed orders. This is what I wanted. I breathed deeply. Someday, if I got out of this fuckin' hole I was trapped in, I'd create someone who I could share unconditional love with, but now wasn't my time. I nodded at the doctor and she began.

9

Gabe came into the recovery room after it was done, and Tig followed close behind.

Tig presented me with a Pink Panther teddy. She'd dressed it up with a tie-dyed scarf and Lennon glasses, and she'd made a little hole in its mouth and stuck a smoke in.

"Eh, Sam. " Tig sat Pink Panther on the edge of the bed, and wrapped her arms around me.

I had no words to share. Gabe joined in on the hug. None of us had words to share, but our hug spoke volumes.

A nurse came in, interrupting our silent moment. "You can stay for a half hour, but we need the bed after that. Take these every four hours, today and tomorrow, and these three times a day for the next seven days." She handed me two bottles of pills, then she left again.

"Man, I gotta get outa here." I flipped the covers off and attempted to sit up.

"Whoa, there. We can stay for a bit. We've got half an hour. Aren't you in pain?" Typical Gabe. Always watching out for me.

"Are you kidding? I'm on like 4 Tylenol. All's well. Trust me." I swung my feet off the bed and stood up. The pain was fierce, the worst ever period cramps, I tried to keep a straight face.

Tig eyed me, doubtfully. "Are you sure you're not in pain?"

"Yup. All's hunky-dory. Just fuckin' fine." I lied. "Let me get dressed." All I wanted in that moment was to be somewhere else, far away from the procedure I'd just gone through.

Gabe and Tig shared an uncertain glance, but left me alone to get dressed.

In the midst of this day's shit, the Pink Panther teddy made me smile. We'd spent a whole shrooms trip back in the abandoned house, tripping on Tig's Pink Panther t-shirt. He'd come alive and joined our trip.

I got dressed, grabbed Pink Panther and the pills, and joined Tig and Gabe in the lobby.

We caught the bus back to Charles A.

§

I stood in the shower and washed the day off me. What a mixed bag—job offer at The Gazette in the morning and abortion in the afternoon. Who else could claim that they'd had such a day?

I rinsed the conditioner from my hair. The warm water soothed me, and my worries fell away. Running my hands through my hair felt nice. This innocuous moment in the shower was what I needed. It grounded me. The abortion had been weird, but I was more relieved than sad. Relief felt nice.

I turned off the shower. The water ran down the drain, then it began to gather at my feet. Something was blocking the drain. I looked down to see what it could be.

A fleshy piece of something lay in the drain. My brain froze. *Shit, shit, shit! What the fuck?!*

I jumped out of the bathtub. I couldn't breathe. *Oh my god, oh my god, what the fuck, oh my god!* The squirrel in my brain went nuts. I started to scream, "Fuck! Tig! Fuck! Tig!!"

Tig banged on the door, "Sam! Open up! What's wrong?"

Now crouched on the floor in full panic mode, I couldn't speak. I unlocked the door and let her in, then pointed at the bathtub.

Tig took a look. "Oh. OK, I'll go get someone. It's uh ... OK, Sam."

Her weak re-assurance didn't do much for me. I tried to breathe.

"Eh! Not Cindy!" I blurted as Tig turned to find help. The thought of dealing with Cindy at this moment made my heart beat faster than a Lars Ulrich drum solo.

"OK! No Cindy! I'll find Anne!" Tig disappeared down the hallway.

Anne came in a few seconds later. I was relieved it wasn't Cindy.

She wrapped my towel around me, peered into the bathtub, and relaxed.

"Oh, Sam. It's OK. Just a bit that was missed during the abortion. Nothing to do with, uh, anything else." She put her hands on my arms and looked into my eyes. "This is natural, Sam. Nothing at all to worry about, OK?"

Nothing to fuckin' worry about! Holy fuck! Part of me just fell out into the bathtub 'cause the doc missed something! What the fuck?! I held my head in my hands and tried to breathe.

Anne's touch warmed me, calmed me. My breathing began to steady.

"Sam? Why don't you go back to your room. I'll join you in a few minutes."

I nodded, then I got up on wobbly legs and distanced myself from the scene in the bathtub.

Tig followed me to my room. She sat silently on my bed while I put my PJs on.

Anne came in a couple of minutes later. "I'm sure everything's fine, Sam. But, do you want me to make you a doctor's appointment?"

I shook my head. *Fuck that. I never want to see a doctor again.*

"OK. Well, I've been transferred. My last day at Charles A. is tomorrow. I'll put this in your file. Your social worker ... what's her name?"

I shrugged. I couldn't remember.

"OK, I'll figure it out. Anyway, I'll put this in your file. You can talk to her if you change your mind about a doctor's appointment, OK?"

I nodded. *Yeah, right. Whenever she shows up, I'll talk to her. Uh-huh.*

Anne hugged me. Then she left me with Tig.

Tig lay next to me on my bed through the 'lights out' call. We could hear Cindy making her rounds, making sure everyone's lights were out.

"Fuck Cindy. I'm staying here with you. She's gonna have to drag me out by my fuckin' curlies." Tig hugged me tightly.

Cindy usually poked her nose into each room to check on us, but tonight she just tapped on doors to remind us of her presence.

I fell asleep in Tig's arms to mixed thoughts, feelings, and dreams.

⁹

The next week was a blur. Wake, school, eat, sleep, dream. I was a zombie following prescribed habits. Sleep was my safe space, so that's what I did. Every chance I got, I slept. And this afternoon was no different.

I threw my schoolbag on the floor, curled up on my bed, Pink Panther against my chest, forced reality out of my head, and fell asleep. If only I had more control over my dreams.

Tig lay on the floor in Vincent's flat. She was on her side, dressed in a glimmering party dress I'd never seen before. She lay still, her crazy curls all over her face. No one else was in the room, but I could hear the band playing. Aerosmith's *Rag Doll* blasted from an empty stage. Where was everyone? The place felt eerie. I called out to Tig, but she remained silent, unmoving on the floor.

Instantly, the room came alive with multi-coloured disco lights. Tig's dress sparkled under the flickering lights. She was the only one I could see now. Everything else was dark. Just Tig, highlighted by the flickering lights. The music began to quicken. My heart began to quicken. Something was wrong, terribly wrong. I didn't want to know. I wanted to leave. I tried to turn, but something held me in place.

I glanced over my shoulder, towards the door behind me, but saw only darkness. I was surrounded by nothingness. There was only one direction to go, and that led to whatever truth awaited me under those twinkling disco lights

I turned and stared at Tig, still lying in her spotlight, sparkling. I took a step closer and the music sped up some more. Sweat beaded on my forehead. I forced myself forward. Might as well get this over with.

I knelt over Tig, heart pounding and hair now soaked with sweat. My whole body was wet. My pulse thumped in my chest, head, legs, arms, fingertips.

I touched Tig's shoulder. She didn't move. I called out to her, "Tig?", and her name echoed off the walls and disappeared into the music. I moved her hair from her face and then screamed.

She was blue, like glacier blue. She was ice. Frozen. A winter sculpture. My heart stopped, just for a moment, then she moved, and it started to race again. I jumped back.

Tig turned towards me as she sat up. She was cradling something. As she turned, she extended her arms, offering me the frozen newborn within them.

I woke with a start. My sheets were damp. I was swimming in sweat and sobbing.

I couldn't take this anymore. It had been weeks since Tig's suicide attempt and days since my abortion. When would my nightmares quit? Maybe Tig was right. Maybe life was senseless. Maybe there was no way out. We were voiceless, invisible, hidden, ghosts with uncomfortable secrets. When you were a system ghost, maybe you stayed a ghost forever. Maybe the only way out was to kill the ghost.

I reached into my bedside table and took out the two bottles of pills that I'd been given after the abortion. I emptied the bottle onto my bed and stared at the pills. Why had I saved them? I rarely took pills, and these were never going to be the exception. But I'd kept them anyway.

I picked the pills up one by one, gathering them in the palm of my hand.

Then I opened my mouth and shoved them all in, before I could change my mind.

I held them in my mouth, but I couldn't swallow. Something inside me wouldn't allow it. I tried to convince myself but the something just wouldn't have it. Then the bitterness set in. Fuck, they were bitter! I spat them back out all over my sheets.

I ran to the bathroom and rinsed my mouth.

No. I held my head in my hands. I didn't want to die. There had to be something else. There had to be light.

I curled up on the bathroom floor, and kept my tears in check. Light. Somewhere down the line, I could feel it, there'd be light.

CHAPTER TWENTY-SIX

The Montreal System Rat

February 14th

Roy Church dropped off copies of the Valentine's Day issue on the morning of February 14th. He'd wrapped the bundle in red paper and included a bouquet of red roses with those tiny white baby's breath flowers.

I picked up the note and read, "Congratulations on another successful issue of *The Montreal System Rat*. Great work kids! Best wishes from The Gazette."

"Thanks, Roy!" I gave him a huge happy smile. This was the good news I needed.

"Eh, you deserve it. This is excellent work. Sorry my delivery was a bit late. Dave gave me a list of the group homes that ordered copies. I have some time this morning. I'll drop 'em off—to be sure everyone gets them for Valentine's Day."

Roy said his goodbyes. I put the flowers, with the note displayed, on the kitchen table and hoped Cindy would read it too. We'd accomplished quite a feat, and I had no qualms about rubbing it in her face. Then I grabbed the wrapped bundle of papers and brought it up to my room for safekeeping. We'd open it when we were all together after school.

9

Our subdued suppertime came and went without a hitch. Even with our big news, Cindy wouldn't tolerate any emotion at the table. We ate as quickly and silently as possible, so as not to give her any excuse to hold us up after supper.

When all the dishes were washed, Cindy gave us her grim nod of approval and retreated to her office, while everyone else gathered around the table. I rushed upstairs, returned with the parcel, and placed it in front of Gabe.

Gabe carefully unwrapped the red paper from the bundle, and picked up the top copy.

"So, as Dave is not here, I've prepared a few words." He put on his best Dave impression, hummed and hawed for a few seconds, and everyone rolled their eyes. "You kids have come a long way. I must say ... when I was your age, we didn't have such opportunities. Hell, we didn't even have a typewriter! Only stories we made up were the ones told around the supper table ... and, of course, the tales to get us out of trouble ... and into." Gabe flashed his practiced Dave-wink. "Let me tell you a story ..."

Tema grabbed the paper from Gabe and said playfully, "Shut it, freak!" She opened the copy and lay it on the table for all to see.

Cindy yelled from the office, "Eh! Noise! Language!"

We ignored her.

Everyone crowded around the issue to get a glimpse, then each in turn took a copy from the bundle, sat back down and the room turned quiet as everyone read.

I opened my copy and smiled. Yup, this was my thing. I was going to love my summer job.

THE MONTREAL SYSTEM RAT

What Has Love Got To Do With It?
By Sam, Editor in Chief

So, you're looking for love, eh? That tingly feeling at the bottom of your gut ... that addictive pounding in your heart? We all want love, we need love, whether we admit it or not. And, wowzer! Is the pressure ever on at this time of year! Will you get her flowers? Or chocolates? Will you write him a love letter? Maybe offer a first kiss, and a second, maybe third base?

In the midst of all this Valentine's Day pressure to 'love' someone, have you ever stopped to ask yourself what the frignibbles does love really got to do with it?

Let's think on love for a moment ...

The Miriam-Webster dictionary defines love as an "unselfish loyal and benevolent concern for the good of another." That's the kind of love we need. Words and actions that tell us we mean something, that our happiness matters, that our life matters, that we are loved through thick and thin, no matter what.

So, on this Valentine's Day, reach the frig out, not only to the guy who's giving you flowers (or who doesn't), but also to the friends and roomies roughing it by your side. Because we all know that the only way we're going to get through the system's twisted version of 'love' is hand in hand, together.

Mr. Kill Love
By Tema

Mr. Kill Love picked up the skeleton key and opened the cages one-by-one. The robin eyed him curiously. She'd been trapped in this cage since before she could fly, when the bird watcher had found her starving and alone. There were others too, and he made his way from cage to cage, unlocking each in turn. He cried as he did this. Each bird looked at him, not sure of how to proceed. The door was open, but where would it lead?

"Today I set you free, my precious ones." Mr. Kill Love snivelled. "I've loved and protected you for as long as I could, but now I must move on to new adventures. Fly away birdies, fly away!"

The birds glanced at each other. A few had broken wings, others damaged beaks, and then there was the one who'd been pushed out of its nest by a mother who didn't want it. All of them wanted to be free. Being trapped in a cage was not what any of them had hoped for or expected. But how would they survive without help from their rescuer, without being able to fly or eat or find food all by themselves, alone in the world?

Mr. Kill Love looked at them in wonder. "Oh, what an honour! I see you will miss me. You don't want to go. I have cared for you so deeply, kept you safe from the dangers outside. Your lack of song I thought was because you didn't respect me and all I do for you. But now I see that I was wrong. You did not stop singing because of me. It must be because of something else, something wrong with your head, something out of my control. Please understand, my little birdies, I do not release you out of lack of love but because I have no choice." The bird watcher shrugged, as if stressing 'c'est la vie', live with it.

The blue jay hopped to the door of its cage and dared to fly away. The bird would figure out how to eat on its own with its broken beak, it hoped.

Feeling confident after seeing the blue jay take off, the sparrow hopped to the door of its cage. But looking out, it had second thoughts. Would its broken wing hold up? Seeing the sparrow's hesitation, Mr. Kill Love nudged the bird with his hand, pushing it off the edge of the cage, forcing the sparrow to take flight whether it wanted to or not. The bird struggled to fly, falling towards the ground, then swooped sideways, almost hitting a tree, until it finally managed to land uncomfortably in a thorny rose bush.

A little yellow bird flapped its wings within its cage, testing its own broken wing. It jumped up and down, trying to flutter upwards, but couldn't do it. It paused on its perch, panting, heart beating fast, a terrified look in its eye, thinking of the predators in the outside world. Its heart began to race like crazy, until it finally dropped dead from fear.

When the yellow bird dropped dead, the other birds panicked. Would they also not be able to fly and feed themselves on their own? They hadn't learned to survive in these cages, only to depend.

Mr. Kill Love quickly made the bird's body disappear and swore to the other birds that they'd been imagining things, they were safe, that the yellow bird was obviously disturbed.

Now the other birds feared for their lives. Whether they stayed or left, they were in terrible danger.

The bird watcher got impatient. He had places to go, his new adventure awaited. He unlatched the bottoms of the cages and then shook each one until every bird was out.

The birds, no longer his responsibility, hopped and fluttered away, off to some unknown fate.

Mr. Kill Love packed his bag and left, never to be seen by the birds again.

Corny Pick-up Line Crossword
By Jen

Down

1. Cute _____. Can I talk you out of it?

3. Hey, you look exactly like my next _____!

5. Yowzer! Sweet as pie! You must be made of _____.

7. Did it hurt? When you fell from _____?

9. You better know _____ baby, 'cause you take my breath away.

Across

2. _____ called. Says your heart's lookin' for me.

4. Hey, thief. Give me back my _____.

6. Hey baby, you got a _____? I keep getting lost in your eyes.

8. Look no more baby. Welcome to my one stop _____ shop.

10. You know what you get when you re-arrange the _____? U and I together.

11. Excuse me, I lost my phone _____. Can I borrow yours?

Poems

A Tree's Heartbeat, by Kate

Roses are red
but
love is more
than
what is said.

To feel
to speak
to do
it's in the lore,
like
a wise old tree.

Solid
Honest
Heart
Beat.

Cherry Pie, by Ron

All I want is
cherry pie
so I can throw
it in your eye

You'd say "no!"
and I'd say
"I love you so!"

Or maybe I'd lie
and keep throwing pie.

No Escape, by Joy

No love here
inside
this place so dark
you call me dear
beside

you lay your mark
never to escape
this place so dark

Ask LoveLots
By Gabe, Assistant Editor in Chief

Hi there LoveLots,

I think I'm in love with my hot new SW. Can't stop thinking about her, like, down and dirty thinking, eh? Even dreaming about her. She's like super hot, man. Hard not to stare at her boobs, get what I'm saying? I can't even hear her when she speaks. Too taken away with, you know. Is this love or am I possessed?

Boobs

Dear Boobs,

Glad you asked. Yes, you are possessed by hormonal moron demons. But it should pass soon as, statistically, your SW will unlikely be visiting you again before your next transfer. Happy dreaming!

LL

Hi LoveLots,

my guy is such a douche. I'm sure he's not gonna get nothin' for me. He loves me an' all. But he's gonna fuck Valentine's Day up for sure. How do I stop him from fuckin' it all up?

All the best,
V-day

Dear V-day,

You sound like an interesting girl that has found herself a bad match. My advice is to look inside your heart. What is it telling you? Yes, it's telling you to be like a tree. Trust your heart. Good luck. P.s. you should read Kate's poem.

LL

Eh LoveLots,

Me and my boyfriend have been dating for 2 months. I'm not sure if we're going steady. Should I ask him or wait?

Sincerely,
Confused Love

Dear Confused Love,

If the stars are aligned on Valentine's Day, then yes. If they aren't, then no.

LL

Hi LoveLots,

My girlfriend's in Bethel and I'm in Pine. We write, but I have my needs, eh? What should I do?

Sincerely,
Wish Man

Dear Wish Man,

What options do you really have in there? J**k-off. We all do it. You're welcome :-)

LL

LoveLots,

I have such a selfish boyfriend, I'm telling you. Never does shit for me. I'm always thinking of him, but I bet you he's going to go out of his way to forget me on Valentine's Day. Man, the things I do. I don't want to be sitting there empty-handed as other guys give their girls lovey-dovey stuff. Tell me LL, what can I do to make him see the light?

Yours truly,
Love Me

Dear Love Me,

███████████████████████████████
███████████████████████████████
████████████████████

[Response was inadmissible. See response to V-day and also Kate's poem]

LL

Strange Love: A Letter From The Hole
By Gini

My dearest anonymous,

Yes, you, the social worker in the pretty dress dining by candle-light with your husband in a restaurant in Old Montreal. Is it good? That tasty tourtière? That glass of fine French wine? How about your conversation? Did you finally finish fixing-up that playroom? Are your kids happy? Have they raked in all the right awards? Vacation booked, summer planned? Is it all you can talk about? Those kids of yours really hit the jackpot. Good for them. Pat yourself on the back, you deserve it.

Me, I'm also loved. A ward of the court, placed in special protection, you know, to keep me safe, out of love. All children have the right to be safe and cared for, right? So, here I am, trapped in an empty room, by myself, being taken special care of, you know, for my own good. F-ed up kids like me never learn. We need the extra tough kind of love. It's for the best, eh? At some point I'll trade in this cage for another, bigger one, with people in the room, but still no one listening.

My life is like that princess story, the one of the chick with super long hair who's trapped in the tower? A prince eventually comes to her rescue—her saviour, so noble and full of good will. Without a word, he whisks her away, from her tower prison to his guarded palace. I mean, she didn't have anywhere else to go, right? I've always wondered, did she really escape, or did she just trade one sad story for another?

I'm a danger. I killed a guy, some dealer of my mum's. It was me or him. I decided it should be him. It's true, I can be a jerk. What can I say, I didn't hit the good-life jackpot and I'm a little pissed off. But never thought I'd be a killer. Yet here we go, I'm a killer, locked in a cage all alone for my protection they tell me. Lucky me, to have such noble saviours.

How's your meal going? Are your kids safe, at home with the babysitter, playing in their danger-proofed playroom, the one they've always wanted? Perfect. I'm glad they are loved. I'm glad they are safe. I'm glad you don't have to worry about them being trapped in an empty padded room with bars on the window, screaming for help with no one listening.

Say hi to my social worker—uh, what's her name?—haven't heard from her in weeks.

Yours truly,
I. Matter

Tig's Kitchen Love

Cheesy Love Grilled Cheese

Cheddar cheese
Ham
Sliced tomato
or paper-thin slices of apple
2 slices bread
Oregano

Black pepper
Butter or margarine

Layer top three ingredients onto a slice of bread, with top and bottom layer being cheese. Sprinkle with oregano and pepper. Slap the other piece of bread on top. Melt lots of margarine in a pan. Add sandwich to the pan. Butter the upside of the sandwich too. Flip when downside turns golden and cheese begins to melt. Fry until done.

Lonely Day Coffee

1 tsp instant coffee
3 tsp Carnation hot chocolate mix
¼ cup milk
¾ water
Whipped cream (if you have)

Heat water and milk with tender loving care. Add instant coffee and carnation hot chocolate mix. For extra love, add whipped cream on top.

Fast Love Fudge

1 tsp cocoa powder
3 tsp icing sugar (or normal sugar)
Enough hot water to make a paste
1 extra huge tbsp crunchy peanut butter

In a cup, mix cocoa and icing sugar to form a thin paste. Add peanut butter and mix well. Can add tiny bits of water if too thick. Done! Eat up!

❦

Cindy stood in the dining room doorway like a giant wasp come to crash the party. "OK, tick-tock. Time for quiet hour. Tidy it up, folks."

People started to get up, then Tema motioned for them to stay seated.

"As far as I can see, we've got another 12 minutes. That's 11 ½ minutes if we take clean up time off it. Rules are rules, right?" Tema glared at Cindy defiantly. She only had a few days left before aging-out of the system, so I guess she'd decided to make the best of it.

"Are *you* challenging my authority?" Cindy practically spat the word "you" at Tema.

Gabe and I glanced at each other. The rest of us would have to live with Cindy for a while more.

"Just pointing out the rules is all." Tema said quite matter-of-factly.

"That may be the rule, but I'm the rule enforcer. When I say it's time to clean up and go to your room, I expect obedience. Disobedience never gets anyone anywhere they want to be. I trust, *you* know that better than anyone here. Now, back down and pack up." Cindy had emphasized that "you" again.

We all sat, frozen to the spot, wanting to stand for our rights but also terrified of the consequences. For some of us, including me, Manny Cottage was high on the list of possible punishments.

"I SAID, PACK-IT-UP! NOW!!" Cindy bellowed at us all.

The room emptied as our gut-reaction kicked in.

Gabe stopped me on the stairs. "Eh, this shouldn't go down without witnesses. I've had it with Cindy's crap."

"What are we gonna do? Tell on her?" I shrugged my shoulders.

I was so tired with workers like Cindy and, really, there was no one to tell. As far as I knew, telling could mean a sentence right out of this place and back to the Queen Bee psychos in Bethel.

"Well, no. But, y' know, for Tema. Think we should keep an eye on things, or at least listen, in case stuff goes sideways."

"Honestly Gabe, I don't want to be anywhere near stuff going sideways."

Gabe sighed, then sat down on the stairs, just outside the dining room.

"Ah! Fine." I sat down beside him.

We couldn't see anything but could hear them both clearly.

Tema's voice was cool and level. "I'll be here for another 10 minutes."

Paper shuffled.

Cindy huffed in anger. "You put that ridiculous newspaper down and get up to your room! Now! Don't make me call in back-up!"

More shuffling of paper. Tema must've turned the page.

Then there was action. Cindy's huffing increased. Paper was ripping. A chair fell over.

Gabe and I moved closer, so we could see what was going on.

Tema and Cindy were face to face, inches apart. Tema's chair lay on the floor behind her. They both gripped parts of the same paper. Cindy had obviously tried to grab it, but Tema had held on tight.

Tema, being a few inches taller than Cindy, scowled down at her. "I—am—not—going—anywhere." She said this slowly, to be sure Cindy understood that this was not negotiable.

Gabe and I were transfixed. This was going nowhere good.

"Maybe we should get Rod. Where is he anyway?" Gabe was talking about the other childcare worker.

I shook my head, "No, no, that'll just go badly for Tema. Rod's a total jock, all about restraint. He's probably in his office with his headphones on, listening to a cassette on how to be an effective asshole." Rod deserved a personalized eyeroll. The *Rod-roll*: hand to forehead, sigh, eyes to the sky, and tie it all together with "fuckwad!"

Considering our bare-bones options, I offered, "Maybe we could create a distraction? It works for MacGyver, right?" I laughed nervously.

Cindy stood under Tema's nose, glaring up at her. For onlookers, it was actually quite comical. But what Cindy said next made my blood boil.

"Girls like you never learn, you know that? I feel sorry for you, truly do. Wasn't like the apple fell far from the tree. Not something that's your fault, just the way it is. Well, in a couple of days, you can go back to your street corner. In the meantime, my house, my rules. Get it?!" Cindy sneered. "Now, back off or I'll call for Rod."

For a moment, Tema appeared as if she'd been punched in the gut. Then she lost it.

"You fuckin' dwarf bitch!" Tema grabbed Cindy's braid and pulled her to the floor. She sat on top of Cindy, pinning her head to the ground as she gripped her braid tightly. And Tema began to scream.

At first her scream was incoherent. It came from a place so deep and in pain that words could not describe it. I knew that scream. Every kid who'd been fucked with knew that scream. My gut ached and my heart skipped a beat.

As the scream got weaker, Tema's words became clearer, and the scream became a wail. "It's ... it's ... people like *me*?" She leered at Cindy and waited for a reply.

But Cindy had none. She lay on the floor under Tema, surrendered, terrified, and no doubt wondering where the hell Rod was.

"You know where I'm going when I age-out on Monday?" Tema didn't wait for a reply this time. "No, I guess not. Me neither. Someone'll drive me to the Metro, I guess. Or maybe I'll take the bus, eh, if my social worker gets busy and doesn't show. There's a motel I've heard of, near Berri. Some other aged-out kids start there. Maybe I'll go there. I've heard that they waive the first month's rent for a few favours, so I should have time to get a job, y' know, to pay my way from there. Maybe I'll work at the Dunkin' Donuts by the Metro, eh? Probably never make manager though, with no high school degree. Gotta be smart to work kiss-ass jobs." Her sobbing had slowed, and she grinned at Cindy. "You should know all about that, eh? Being an educated kiss-ass and all." Cindy looked around for Rod, wild-eyed.

Tema breathed out an exhausted sigh and relaxed her shoulders. She let go of Cindy's braid. "Don't worry, I'm not gonna hur ..." And she was suddenly tackled my Rod.

As Rod stormed into the room, Gabe let out a desperate, "Ah! Rod!!" But it was too late, Tema was torn off Cindy and shoved down onto the floor, front first. Rod sat on her back, jamming one of her arms behind her and pushing her head into the floor with his other hand. "Don't fuckin' move! Cops are on their way!"

Tema began to yell again. "Get off me you dumb fuck!"

"Oh yeah? You think I'm a dumb fuck?" Rod squeezed Tema's face and she momentarily stopped screaming, then she bit his finger.

Rod yanked his hand away, "You little cunt!"

Gabe jumped up from the stairs and ran into the dining room. "Eh! She was coming down! She's gonna be fine! Just ... get off her!"

"Back up! Now! Out!" Rod's face burned with anger.

I got up and yelled at them all, "Stop! Stop! Just stop!! Oh my god! Gabe, come here!"

Gabe backed up and we stood together in the doorway. We wouldn't be leaving Tema on her own with these two.

I looked at Cindy, who was now leaning on the wall, catching her breath, getting her voice back. "We are not leaving." I said decisively.

Cindy glanced at Rod. "Hold her still, Rod. Cops'll deal with her."

Tema's low sobs painfully penetrated our silence as we waited.

The cops finally showed up, and Tema was taken away in handcuffs. She kept her eyes down, avoiding our gaze, as she was escorted out, flanked by an armed cop on either side.

And then she was gone.

CHAPTER TWENTY-SEVEN

New Beginnings

June

I stood in line with Tig in front of the Air France check-in counter at Mirabel Airport.

At this time tomorrow, Tig would be in a beautiful French countryside, enjoying grapes off the vine, freshly baked bread, and coq au vin with her Aunt Antigone, or so I imagined. France was *'le pays de l'amour éternel et de la bonne cuisine'*—the land of eternal love and great food—and that is precisely what was in store for Tig.

My heart exploded with happiness for Tig, while simultaneously imploding with grief for the distance that was about to come between us.

Tig couldn't stop talking, as she did when nervous. Her whole world was about to change. She'd found unconditional love. Antigone had written to her weekly since they became reacquainted in the hospital. She was the genuine thing, that aunt of hers. Would Tig ever return? She spoke and spoke, but I wasn't listening.

Tig looked at me, waiting for a reply to a question I hadn't heard.

"Sorry ... uh, what?"

"Sam! Weren't you listening? My aunt, she asked when you'll be coming to visit. So?"

"Oh, yeah, for sure. I dunno, soon I hope. Not really in control of my finances. But I'll save up this summer." I paused, "Tig?"

Standing before me, uncharacteristically quiet, Tig gave me the floor.

I searched for words. "I'm gonna miss you." Those were my feelings in a nutshell. I couldn't think of any other words that would make my feelings clearer.

Tig's eyes grew sad. She was so beautiful, in a wild-child kind of way, with her freckle-specked cheeks and crazy fire-red curls springy out all over the place. She wrapped her arms around me, and we hugged in silence.

"Pen pals, right?" I said, unsure of what else to say.

Tig smiled, "Of course! And I'll send some French recipes for *The Montreal System Rat*, 'kay?"

I nodded, then glanced away. Time to go. This was just going to get harder.

I hugged her again. "Bye, Tig."

"*À la prochaine*, Sam." Tig kissed each of my cheeks, like we'd practiced—the '*faire la bise*' French kiss. She made an exaggerated '*mu-aah*' sound each time, and I couldn't help but laugh.

Ms. Cohen took over from there and saw Tig off through security.

We drove back to Charles A. in silence.

"Sam?" Ms. Cohen sounded hesitant, like she wasn't sure how to proceed with her next sentence, so she'd started with something simple.

"Yeah?" We were almost back at the group home. If she thought I was up to a heart-to-heart after she'd left me in the ditch without an explanation, she should think again.

I gazed out the passenger-side window—cement, street signs, shops, diners, people buzzing around everywhere.

"I want you to know how proud I am of you. You've done a fantastic job with *The Montreal System Rat*. You're going somewhere, Sam. This job is your ticket to freedom. You've done really great."

I nodded in acknowledgement. Why should I give a shit what she thought? She abandoned me. If she truly cared, she wouldn't have left me alone when I needed her most. I still hadn't met my new SW, *Mrs. Field*. Calling her 'new' was a stretch. She'd phoned once though, you know, to confirm I still lived I guess.

"I also want to apologize. The way I left, it wasn't right." Ms. Cohen pulled over and parked. She looked at me, waiting for an acknowledgement.

I glanced at her, then away again. Social workers all sucked. I'd thought she was an exception, but she'd proved me wrong. There was nothing she could say to make it right again. No one fuckin' cared. We were ghosts.

"Sam?"

I turned and glared at her. "I have nightmares, eh?! Of fuckin' Tig dying, of fetuses falling out of me, of my mother suffocating me in my sleep, of being raped and just lying there like a fuckin' hopeless invalid, unable to fight for fuckin' anything, not even to save my fuckin' self! And no one else is around to save me either, 'cause no one fuckin' gives a shit! A while back, I didn't kill myself 'cause I wanted to say bye to Tig. I have no idea what tonight's gonna bring. And you're fuckin' *sorry*?!"

I was fuming. I had to get away from her. I got out of the car, slammed the door, ran up the steps to the group home, entered, and slammed the door again behind me.

Ms. Cohen persisted though. I heard her come into the group home as I made my way up the stairs to my room.

"Sam! Please, we need to talk." I turned to see her looking up at me, pleading with me.

"I wasn't finished, and I think you weren't either."

I sat down on the stairs. "OK, go."

Ms. Cohen came up the stairs and sat down beside me. "I made a mistake, Sam. I won't make excuses. I made a big mistake that affected you badly. It caused you to be neglected. There were some things going on that were out of both our control. But I should've fought to keep your case. I should've fought harder for you, Sam." She put one hand on my shoulder, encouraging me to look at her.

"But you can't fix it. There's no one here for me. Cindy is *not* Dave. If I were to O.D., she'd wait until she finished her filing before calling 911. She's horrible! And you're sorry?!" There was really nothing else to say about it. Ms.

Cohen had left me to fend for myself in a broken system where very few took the time to give a fuck.

"Sam. Will you take me back? If you want me, I have a space open again. I talked with Mrs. Field. She's overwhelmed with cases. She's agreed to hand over yours, if you agree to it. This is highly irregular, as social workers normally have little say in case distribution, but I had a card to play and I thought you were worth it. So, what do you say? Will you give me another chance?"

My anger dissolved immediately. I threw my arms around Ms. Cohen and sobbed, "Fuck, yeah."

,

Gabe was sprawled on my bed when I entered my room. He'd just returned from work and was still wearing his *The Main* shirt and name tag.

"Man, Gabe, take your smoked meat smelling ass off my bed. For fuck's sake, you stink!" I grabbed my pillow from under him, letting his head drop hard against my mattress. My pillow smelled like it had been used as a serving tray. I hit him with it, then hit him again and again.

Gabe laughed, "OK! OK! Stop!" He paused, then continued jokingly, "Shit, Sam. They've got the best smoked meat in town. Quit complaining. They should sell their smell, they'd make a killing."

"Yeah, well not with me they wouldn't. Now, get off!"

"Fine." Gabe rolled off my mattress and onto the floor. He sat with his back against my bed.

"All of you off!"

Gabe laughed. "Well, aren't you Miss Bossypants." He moved away from my bed and sat in the middle of the room, being dramatically 'careful' not to touch anything.

I collapsed onto my bed and sighed.

"So, first day tomorrow. You nervous?" He smiled.

"I don't get nervous."

"Uh, yeah. Right." His smile grew.

"Fuck off, Gabe."

"What? I ask because I care. You've been all weird lately. I'm guessing it's 'cause you're nervous, that's all."

"Or maybe it's 'cause we just lost Tig?" I threw my pillow at him.

"Maybe. But it's also 'cause your nervous."

I rolled my eyes, exasperated. "OK, fine. I'm nervous! Get over yourself. Not like you never get nervous."

Gabe lay back on the floor, placing my pillow under his head. We both stared at the stars on the ceiling.

"Hey, Sam?"

"Uh-huh?"

"I'm pretty sure I'm bi … like … as in, bisexual."

I rolled towards him, eyebrows raised, and replied frankly. "No kidding, Sherlock."

Gabe regarded me with comical shock.

"Gabe. First off, I don't care. Secondly, I don't care. Thirdly, no kidding Sherlock." I rolled onto my back again, letting him absorb my response.

Gabe thought about it for a few seconds then replied, "'Kay ... good then. That's good. So ... Cindy's out at meetings 'til 8. Wanna go smoke a joint?"

I smiled, "Damn straight, Sherlock."

Gabe shot me a crooked smile, obviously wondering whether I'd intended the pun. My expression said it all. He laughed and threw the pillow at me. Then we headed out towards carefree pot-bliss, to be had in the grace of our gnarly oak tree by the canal.

9

Roy Church met me in the lobby at 8:30 sharp on my first day. He stood at the front desk, chatting with a secretary as I walked through the doors. She motioned in my direction and he looked over.

"Eh, Sam! Nice to see you again. Seems like we keep meeting in the same place."

The secretary smiled. I thought she may have even giggled.

"Uh, yeah. Hi. I start today. Am I late?" My nerves were threatening to betray me.

"Nope, right on time. I'll get you set up. Follow me." He winked at the secretary, pulled a cigarette from his shirt pocket, and led me past the staff room, towards the elevator.

Roy searched his pants pockets for his lighter. "Damn. You don't have a lighter by chance?"

I produced a lighter, flicked it on, and he lit his smoke.

The chatter from inside the staff room got louder as we waited for the elevator. A heated debated went on about whether it was ethical for news agencies to be owned by aristocrats with ties to politicians who might encourage the covering up of certain scandals. I slowed my pace so I could hear more. Someone was talking about those orphans, the ones in the asylums in the 50s and 60s.

A man with a deep voice said, "No way, man. It's all about stories that create fame and money. Profit and fame is all, press is free. We go after politicians all the time. If they had a hand in the pot, we'd never be able to touch 'em. The Duplessis scandal is wavering 'cause readers just aren't that interested. It sucks, but *c'est comme ça.*"

Another man, with a slight French accent, let out an exasperated huff. "*Tabarnac.* Seriously? We're a business, man. And just like any other, there've gotta be higher influences that affect which stories make it to press and which are squashed. Sure, I agree, it's about profit and success, but politics play a role, man. It's why we're more liberal than conservative. It's why we'd never publish a pro Quebec separation piece. The government was up to its elbows in what happened in those asylums, to those kids. Some of those politicians are still around, eh? Some helped cover it up for years before the press got wind. It's not exactly a scandal that's good for any of 'em. I doubt they're just sitting around, hoping it'll go away by itself. Bet they're calling in all sorts of favours."

Deep voice replied, "I dunno, man. Seems like a stretch to me. I certainly haven't felt pressured."

Roy noticed me listening. "Eh, uh, over here Sam." He motioned towards the elevators. One was opening and he rushed me over to it. "Don't want to be late on your first day!"

I stood next to him in the elevator, thinking through what I'd just heard. Was there something to my suspicions?

I looked up at Roy, "Is that why nothing's being done about system kids?"

Roy considered how to respond. "Uh ... what do you mean?"

"Well, the politicians. Do they get in the way?" I was being very blunt for my first day, but bluntness was expected from wayward system kids, so I reckoned I'd be OK.

"Hmm ... what can I say? Politicians do have their agendas ... and some of them hold a lot of sway too. It takes a bit of creative thinking at times, you know, to manoeuvre around them."

Nope, I didn't know. Creative thinking? Wasn't it black and white? I mean, lives were at stake.

"So ... you're saying that kids are still suffering in the system, in solitary confinement and stuff, because someone lacked creative thinking?"

Roy glanced desperately at the elevator buttons as they each lit up in turn on the way up to our floor.

"Gee! Tough questions on your first day. To be honest with you, Sam, if you want to create significant change, you've got to go into politics. That much I can say. But journalism is definitely a good place to start, as we hold all the juicy secrets." Roy winked at me. Then he sighed in relief as we reached our floor and the doors finally opened.

"Sam, I'd like you to meet Joe. He'll show you the ropes." Roy then paused and studied me thoughtfully. "You're going to make a fine reporter, or politician, whichever you choose. Best of luck, Sam. See you in the halls, eh!" And then Roy was off, onto some creative mission somewhere else.

Joe was older, short and slim, with thick black-rimmed glasses. He smiled warmly, completely unawares.

"So, Joe, what's your take on political influence in the press?"

Joe's smile faltered, he looked at me dumbfounded. "Uh ... let's just, uh, focus on the photocopier for now, OK?"

I had a feeling the best part of this Summer job would be the breaks in the staff room.

Politics. Me?

Well, why not?

But first I'd stay for the secrets.

Meet the Author

Jane Powell grew up in Quebec on a small island on Rivière des Prairies and came of age in Montreal's youth protection system. Jane has been a passionate writer, storyteller, and defender of human rights since high school. Her passion is rooted in her personal experience with assault, discrimination, and bullying. The tools she uses to help fight for human rights include creative writing, opinion pieces and blog posts. Storytelling is Jane's favourite mode of communication as it allows her to express concerns about social issues in a way that readers can relate to.

Jane chose to write her first two novels, *Butterflies in the System* and *Sky-bound Misfit*, as fiction because she wanted to tell the broader story, rather than just her own.

Both are about issues that are very dear to her, and both are based on real events experienced by herself and her peers. Fiction allows one to tell the story, and get a point across, while also honouring the anonymity of the people represented within it.

Butterflies in the System was inspired by Jane's experience during the time she spent under the care of *Ville-Marie Social Services* and *Youth Horizons*—now known as *Batshaw Youth and Family Centres*—in 1990-91. Events within the story are based on interviews with people who were under the care of youth protection in Quebec between the late 1950s and early 1990s, as well as youth counsellors, childcare workers, Erika Tafel (author of *Slave to the Farm*), and the journalists Gillian Cosgrove (who covered the scandal at Maison Notre Dame de Laval in the 70s) and Victor Malarek (who wrote a book, *Eh, Malarek!*, about his own experience in youth protection in Montreal in late 1950s and early 60s).

Every child enters the system carrying emotional baggage that is usually the catalyst for them being there. A few years prior to Jane's registration into the system, shortly before her 14th birthday, she became a victim of rape (of which she writes about in *Sky-bound Misfit*). Her relationship with her parents, teachers, and peers took a turn for the worst as she dealt with untreated PTSD, anxiety, and bullying associated with the assault. The lack of available resources led to rebellious behaviour and conflicts, ultimately landing her in youth protection at the age of 16.

Youth protection has the potential to be a valuable resource for struggling children and teens. However, the experiences of Jane and her peers varied tremendously, and depended on the level of empathy and training of each individual worker that they came into contact with. Furthermore, the youth protection system lacked resources and did not provide psychological help for trauma, in spite of the fact that every child in the system was there because of traumatic events in their past.

Another huge obstacle for children was the lack of an adequate plan to help them age-out of the system and become independent. Upon discharge at the age of 18, many kids had nowhere to go, no idea of how to live on their own, and no clue about how to find helpful resources. Some returned to abusive homes, some couch-surfed, and others took to the streets. All had to adopt methods to survive. This often meant stealing to feed themselves, selling drugs, or prostitution. Many re-entered the system within a few years because of criminal activity. Most of the people Jane came to know in the system continue to struggle emotionally and financially.

In the long run, Jane was one of the lucky ones. Although the system did not prepare her for independent living, and she struggled tremendously because of it—which included an attempted suicide a month before her discharge—Jane managed to turn her life around at age 19. Interestingly, it was when she became a young single mother that resources for independent living became more easily accessible.

Jane's path forward at this time wasn't easy. She had to abandon some unhealthy relationships (which meant she had few friends for a while) and rebuild her relationship with her parents. She put most of her time and energy into caring for her son and continuing with her education. She was no longer a victim, she was now *a survivor.* She'd figured out how to fight for herself, her son, and her dreams. Jane completed a diploma in Languages and Literature at Dawson College (Montreal), a BA in Anthropology and World Religions at McGill

University (Montreal), a diploma in From Mountain to Fjord: Geology and Ecology of Western Norway at Sogn og Fjordane University College (Norway), and a MA in Education at the University of Otago (New Zealand). She found love and had two more wonderful children, and has become very close with her parents, who have proactively supported her dreams throughout the years. Jane's story has a happy ending.

There have been some minor changes in the system since the 1980-90s. However, as is evident with the currently ongoing class action lawsuit on behalf of past and present system kids, it hasn't changed nearly enough.

With this book, Jane hopes to help bring more awareness to the public on what system kids deal with and the effects of both positive and negative care on their wellbeing and futures.

For more about Jane and her writing projects, be sure to check out Jane's website, https://www.janepowell.org, and blog, https://www.janepowell.org/blog.

Jane Powell (left) with Lyne Meilleur
(right), Snowden Shelter, 1990.

Acknowledgments

Writing a book is no small endeavor, neither is it a lonesome one. It is a team effort. *Butterflies in the System* would not have been possible without the awesome people on my team who helped bring it to fruition.

I am eternally grateful to my husband, children, parents, and siblings for their continuous unwavering support. Thank you, Ken, Devon, Zarya, Liam, Mum and Dad, Andrew and Brenda, Chris and Helen for always being there for me. Without your love, support, and encouragement my writing projects would not be possible.

To my proof-reading group I owe a huge thank you. Your feedback has been invaluable and helped make my story the best it could be. Janet Gallagher, Alicia Grills, Ross Hillenbrand, Lyne Meilleur, Bill Powell, Penny Powell, and Erika Tafel: thank you for your honesty, time, and all the effort you so kindly gifted me as you proof-read my book and helped me through the editing process.

This book was based on personal experience, as well as research and interviews. Everyone involved in my research process helped add candor and depth to this story. My interviewees were exceptionally engaged and influenced my storyline significantly.

I thank the following people profusely for caring about my book project and helping me build a strong foundation:

Lyne Meilleur, Youth Horizons and Shawbridge alumna (1989-92), was the first friend I made while in youth protection and has remained a dear friend since. Our chats are what encouraged me to write this story, and she has been my top confidante throughout my writing process. Thank you for your love and inspiration, Lyne.

Ross Hillenbrand and James Roberts, both proactive childcare workers in my first system placement, helped me understand the value in highlighting in my story the effects of positive and negative care in the system. Their proactive care is what made my own introduction into the system positive. The kids in your care were lucky to have you, Ross and James. Thank you.

Erika Tafel—author of *Slave to the Farm* and youth protection alumna (1983-86)—provided me with firsthand knowledge and advice concerning youth detention centres in Quebec, and our numerous chats have led to a budding friendship. The bond that has developed between us will no doubt continue. Thank you, Erika.

Journalists Victor Malarek and Gillian Cosgrove helped me form a clearer picture of the system through time.

Victor Malarek—investigative reporter, author of *Eh, Malarek!*, and youth protection alumnus—was so kind as to spend a couple of hours on the phone with me talking about the time he spent as a ward at Weredale House in the late 50s and early 60s. He also described his early career-start in journalism, and it is this that inspired me to include journalism in my story, as a tool made available by *Dave* and 'The Gazette', to help *Sam* and her peers give voice to their struggles and concerns. Thank you for the inspiration, Victor.

Gillian Cosgrove—who won an award with The Montreal Gazette for her news breaking undercover work and reporting of inhumane disciplinary techniques at a youth detention centre in the 1970s—was also very generous with her time. She discussed her undercover work and provided insight into the development of the current class action lawsuit launched to help compensate former wards of reception centres in Quebec. Thank you so much for your help and time, Gillian.

I would also like to thank Sarah Osadetz, who is a friend and local artist in Golden BC, for spicing up "The Montreal System Rat" (Ch. 26) with her contribution of the heart and skull diagram. Thank you, Sarah—it's perfect!

Finally, a big thanks to my friends for their emotional support—via chats over bike rides, ski trips, hikes and more—and steadfast understanding during the times I disappeared into my computer for weeks. Without your friendship, I would not be whole. Thank you for your love and patience.

Discussion Questions

1. Can you relate to some of the characters in this story? Which one do you relate to most and why?

2. How do the characters differ from each other? What influences these differences?

3. Sam is from an upper-middle class family. Why is she in youth protection? How might it have been avoided?

4. Discuss the control tactics—isolation, restraint, shame, lack of empathy, withholding resources— used by adults in this story. What effect do they have on Sam, Tema, and Gini?

5. What coping mechanisms does each youth character adopt in order to manage their challenges?

6. Discuss instances where the youth control their circumstances. What actions do Sam, Gabe, Tig, Tema, and Gini each take, at various points in the story, to influence a desirable outcome?

7. What kind of support do the youth in this story receive from the adults in their life? How does this support effect their opportunities and wellbeing?

8. How could have the adults more effectively supported teens' mental health? And, what effect did lack of mental health support have?

9. Compare Dave with Cindy. How do they differ? How does each effect the well-being and opportunities of the youth in their care?

10. Comment on how the following statement made in Quebec's Youth Protection Act relates to Sam, Gini, Tema, Tig, and Gabe's experience in the system: "Any intervention in respect of a child and child's parents under this Act, (a) must be designed to put an end to and prevent the recurrence of a situation in which the security or the development of the child is in danger; and (b) must, if the circumstances are appropriate, favour the means that allow the child and the child's parents to take an active part in making decisions and choosing measures that concern them." (Quebec Youth Protection Act, Chapter II: General Principles and Children's Rights, 2.3, 1984. Quebec Official Publisher, updated 2020, http://legisquebec.gouv. qc.ca/en/ShowDoc/cs/P-34.1)

11. In your opinion, why did the author call this book *Butterflies in the System*?

12. Which part of the story did you find most troubling? Why?

13. If you had the power to make changes in the youth protection system, what changes would you make?

Endnotes

1   Although Quebec's Youth Protection Act states that a child's participation in decisions concerning their situation, placement, and future should be encouraged, people included in the author's interview process emphasized that this was rarely the case. Read Quebec's Youth Protection Act here: http://legisquebec.gouv.qc.ca/en/ShowDoc/cs/P-34.1

2   AWOL is the term used by children in youth protection to describe leaving their place of residence without permission.

3   Although Gabe's mother came out as gay, generally gay people in the 80s and 90s were more secretive about their sexuality due to systemic discrimination. In 1985, the "Equality for All" report was released by The Parliamentary Committee on Equal Rights. The report emphasized that gay people in Canada suffered frequent discrimination and abuse, including physical and emotional violence, based on their sexual orientation. "Sexual orientation" was added to the Canadian Human Rights Act in 1996, when it was finally made legally possible to argue discrimination based on sexual orientation. See CBC *Timeline: Same Sex Rights in Canada* https://www.cbc.ca/news/canada/timeline-same-sex-rights-in-canada-1.1147516

4   The "3-day induction program" was one form of isolation used in youth detention centres to control behaviour. Other forms included complete isolation as a consequence for disobeying rules and displeasing staff, in which children were locked in a room for days, alone with only a mattress on the floor. The use of isolation practices seems to be in violation of The Quebec Youth Protection Act, (section 118.1), as it states that isolation should not be used as a disciplinary measure (see Quebec Youth Protection Act, Chapter II, 10. http://legisquebec.gouv.qc.ca/en/ShowDoc/cs/P-34.1), although the Act has been reviewed

over the years. Erika Tafel describes isolation practices in Shawbridge youth detention centre (Batshaw Youth and Family Centres) in the 1980s in her autobiography *Slave to the Farm*. Gillian Cosgrove describes them in the 1970s in her article for The Montreal Gazette, *Anguish in Girls Centre Verified* (see endnote #11).

5   Roch Thériault was the leader of a small religious cult in Quebec, called the Ant Hill Kids, between 1977 and 1989. He was accused of assault, sexual assault, torture, and murder. Thériault was found guilty in 1993 for brutally murdering Solange Boilard, who was one of his many wives. Tema's story about Roch Thériault and his family in *Butterflies in the System* is entirely made up. For more on Roch Thériault, see: https://globalnews.ca/news/5168566/dark-poutin e-podcast-recap-roch-theriault-ant-hill-kids/ or https:// omny.fm/shows/dark-poutine-true-crime-and-dark-his tory/069-roch-theriault-and-the-ant-hill-kids

6   Sam and Tig's plan to sell the "illusion of sex" to 15-year-old boys is implemented as a method to make money in order to survive. It is also a form of prostitution. In the 1980s, 70% of adult prostitutes in Canada started before their 18th birthday, as a way to survive on the streets. For more information on prostitution see: Government of Canada, Department of Justice, *Identifying Research Gaps in the Prostitution Literature* https://www.justice.gc.ca/ eng/rp-pr/csj-sjc/jsp-sjp/rr02_9/p1.html

7   Marion Davies quote copied from IMDB: https://m.imdb. com/name/nm0203836/quotes

8   The Boys Home of Montreal, often referred to by alumni as "Weredale," was founded in 1870 by philanthropist Charles Alexander, as a way to help orphaned boys become educated and employed. Over the years, there have been reports of neglect and abuse. Victor Malarek, Investigative Reporter and Weredale House alumnus, wrote a telling autobiography, *Eh, Malarek!*, describing his own experience. For history on The Boys Home of Montreal see: http://batshawcentreshistory.ca/pdf/ weredale-when_a_fella_needs_a_home.pdf

9   In the early 1990s, several news outlets picked up on horrific abuses towards orphans that had occurred in Quebec asylums during the 1950s and 60s, after many Catholic orphanages were converted into psychiatric hospitals and orphans declared to be patients. These orphans were nicknamed the "Duplessis Orphans," as Maurice Duplessis (Premier of Quebec, 1936-39 and 1944-59), along with the Catholic Church, played a significant role in the amalgamation of asylums and orphanages. For more on the Duplessis scandal, see CBC's Digital Archives: *The Duplessis Orphans* https://www.cbc.ca/archives/topic/the-duplessis-orphans, Canada's Human Rights History: Duplessis Orphans https://historyofrights.ca/encyclopaedia/main-events/duplessis-orphans/, Read about the mass grave site discovered near Montreal here: http://www.orphelinsdeduplessis.com/wp-content/uploads/2014/05/P-250-Mass-Graves-Of-Children-Found-Near-Montreal.pdf Watch an interview with a Duplessis orphan here: https://youtu.be/Gg3lZcUcVp8

10   The Montreal Gazette, 9 September 1981, *NFB Film a Stark Descent into Porno's Lurid World* by Bruce Bailey

11   The Montreal Gazette, 20 February 1978, *Scientists Struggle to Define and Measure Love* (author not listed)

12   Gillian Cosgrove was a reporter at The Montreal Gazette whose undercover work in 1974 revealed severe forms of discipline and neglect at Maison Notre Dame de Laval, a youth detention centre for girls. Her undercover work and subsequent article *Anguish in Girls Centre Verified* (The Montreal Gazette Jan. 3, 1975) won her and The Montreal Gazette a Governor General's Michener Award. More recently, she has been involved in organising a class action lawsuit for people who have suffered while in the care of Quebec's youth protection services. Many recent ex-clients claim that nothing has changed since the 70s. See CBC Fifth Estate: *The Forgotten: The Children of Marion Hall Speak* https://youtu.be/cT310zw-0Jk and CBC *Ex-Client's, Parents Caught up in Quebec's Youth Protection*

System Voice Pain, Frustration, that Nothing's Changed (Simon Nakonechny) https://www.cbc.ca/news/canada/ montreal/quebec-youth-protection-laurent-commissio n-english-hearing-1.5430278

13 Victor Malarek is a retired investigative reporter who has hosted documentaries and news programs on CBC Fifth Estate and CTV W5. He was also a resident at Weredale House (The Montreal Home for Boys) in the late 50s and early 60s. His autobiography, *Eh, Malarek!*, describes his experience under the care of youth protection. A movie, based on this book, was also made.

14 In 1988, the Supreme Court of Canada ruled it legal for women to have abortions without restrictions. In Montreal, abortion services became available and/or more easily accessible at several Hospitals (including The Montreal Children's Hospital) and community clinics (CLSCs). Although Quebec leans more towards pro-choice today, Quebec has a history of heated pro-life advocacy. For more about the history of abortion in Canada and Quebec, see *The Morgentaler Decision* http://www. morgentaler25years.ca

Printed in the USA
CPSIA information can be obtained
at www.ICGtesting.com
LVHW070623180923
758461LV00001B/98